COME *get* SOME

A NOVEL

ALSO BY NANE QUARTAY

The Badness

Take Two and Pass

COME get SOME

A NOVEL

NANE QUARTAY

STREBOR BOOKS

NEW YORK LONDON TORONTO SYDNEY

SBI

Strebor Books
P.O. Box 6505
Largo, MD 20792
http://www.streborbooks.com

ISBN 978-1-59309-192-7
ISBN 978-1-4165-7630-3 (e-book)
LCCN 2008920030

First Strebor Books trade paperback edition April 2008

Cover design: www.mariondesigns.com
Cover photograph: © Keith Saunders/Marion Designs

10 9 8 7 6 5 4 3 2 1

Manufactured in the United States of America

For information regarding special discounts for bulk purchases,
please contact Simon & Schuster Special Sales at 1-866-506-1949
or business@simonandschuster.com

The Simon & Schuster Speakers Bureau can bring authors to your
live event. For more information or to book an event, contact the
Simon & Schuster Speakers Bureau at 1-866-248-3049 or visit our
website at www.simonspeakers.com.

FOR TERESA STERRETT
No one has ever stood through the fire with me—
until you. Imagine the feeling when I discovered that
our heat was much stronger than the flame!
Love you, girl!

ACKNOWLEDGMENTS

I want to give much love to all those who supported me during the telling of this story. To each and every one, your support is invaluable and I want to take a moment to give thanks.

Shouts to the Taylor clan—My mother, Marion (Get well, Ma! For all of us 'cause we need you here and we Love You). My brothers and sisters, Cathy, Alonzo, Ricky. Dary, Tammy and John.

To my extended family; Jermaine, Chenica and Neltineca Farilien. Janese Taylor. Sheena White, Andrea Peterson, Rick and Lisa Watson, Eugene "The Governor" Burgess, JC and Beauty Watson, Jay Watson, and a heaven-sent shout-out to my late cousins Jeffrey Watson and Julia Watson. Barbara Watson and Julius Watson (Thought I forgot, huh?) The Tillmans—Margie, Retta, Tyrone, Famous, Freda, Paula and Rita.

My Aunt Matty Smith, Uncle Joe, and Uncle James.

To my boys—Brandon Johnson, Jason Ferebee, Chris Pickren, Jonathan Brown, Anthony Salazar, Marcus Glivings, Adryann Glenn, John Powell.

To other friends who hugged my neck when needed—Gerry Garner, Hannan Salah, Linda Jones, Beverly Williams, Yolanda Williams, Margie Rowe, Lori Denormandie, Tracy Rockbythewood, Ajeenah Miller.

Also gotta holla at Earnest Armstrong and William Sterrett (Teresa said, "Stop being hardheaded"), Doris Caloway and especially Marguerite Sterrett.

To my fellow writers—Tracey DeBrew (*Searching For Sula*)— Wishing you much success and the Strebor Crew—Tina Brooks McKinney, Allison Hobbs, D.V. Bernard, Rique Johnson, Jonathan Luckett, Michael Baptiste, J.L. Woodson, Naleighnai Kai, Che Parker, Rodney Lofton, Janet Stevens Cook, Dante Feenix, Suzetta Perkins, Lee Hayes.

Thanks to the many writers that have befriended me and helped me along this writer's path. To my dear friend JD Mason (*This Fire Down In My Soul*), Keith Lee Johnson (a brother who always has my back. Thanks, bruh-man!), Naija (*Spanish Flyy*), Michelle Janine Robinson, Teresa Rae Butler (*Don't Even Trip*), Peron F Long (*Pulpit Confessions*), Shannon Holmes and Carla Dean.

I'd also like to take a moment to thank some lifelong friends who gave of their time and extended a hand— Norma Chapman (thanks for the seasoning), Bernard Moseby (keep it moving), Cheryl King, Darlene Roberts, Pam Shepard, Jennifer Moak, Hugh Matson.

I'd also like to thank the Albany Public Writers Group,

Reston Community Writers Group and The Washington Area Novel Writers' Critique Group!

Dale and Kathleen Roseboro—Much love for keeping it real with a Dank Brotha!

To anyone that I've forgotten, please forgive the omission.

Finally, I'd like to thank the many readers who have supported my efforts at telling stories. The greatest accomplishment for me is making a connection with the reader and I want to send out my thanks to you all.

Peace!

Nane Quartay

"You talking!" Mugwump teased him. "Get it to him."

Whiteboy Paul rolled the ball and Willmon waited a second before he ran forward and kicked it. The ball arched lazily toward Whiteboy Paul but sailed over his head, just out of his reach. Mugwump raced forward and made a shoestring catch before the ball hit the ground. Willmon stopped halfway to the base and swore softly when he saw that he had made an out.

"Stop cussing," Mugwump said. "It was a good kick, Willmon." Willmon bowed his head and walked slowly back toward Truitt.

"We gonna get 'em, little man." Truitt rubbed his head encouragingly. "After I get on base, you're going to bring me home!"

Willmon's head snapped up and a slow smile spread across his face. His energy was infectious. He ran around like a cyclone, as if nothing in the world mattered but the path he chose to take. Little, curly naps dotted his head. They doubted if he had ever combed it, and he talked with a strange "but, though" whenever he felt like he had a point to make.

The alleyway behind Warren Street had become their personal playground; the backs of the houses presented interesting diversions that they explored with regularity. Truitt's house stood directly behind them. Truitt and his dad shared an apartment on the second floor of a three-story brick house that led out into the alleyway. The backyard stretched out toward the alley with spots of grass growing beneath the huge apple tree that grew right smack in the middle of the property. A woman named Gloria lived on the first floor, though they hardly ever saw her come outside. The few times that they had seen her had only been for a minute. Sometimes when she was putting garbage on her back porch, other times when she would stand there for a minute as if she were breathing new air, before disappearing back inside her house. Truitt didn't understand her but he secretly yearned to know more about her. Gloria was a dark, firm-looking woman with an intense stare that made Truitt's virgin imagination run wild. She always wore a pair of worn jean shorts that showcased a tight, well-made body and the prettiest legs he had ever seen. Once she had even popped out the door while Truitt was sitting on her porch. His voice seemed to have crawled back inside of him and a lump caught in his throat when she looked at him.

"Hi," was all that he barely managed to whisper.

She glanced at him, looked down at the porch floor searching for something, and mumbled a greeting in return. She spotted a bottle cap lying on the ground and reached down to scoop it up before turning back to Truitt with a smile on her face.

"Hi, Truitt." She brightened and quickly stepped back inside the house.

Truitt had carried that memory with him, his remembrance of her always a secret yearning that he had never shared with anyone.

A big garage stood directly across the alley from Truitt's yard. It was long enough to hold eight cars and while they had never seen the old, wooden doors open, they knew that there were some ancient-looking cars inside. They imagined the same cars that Eliot Ness drove on the old television show *The Untouchables* with the whitewall tires and the big, metal grills. They discovered the cars one day when they were playing two-hand touch football in the alley and Mugwump's errant pass landed on the roof of the garage. They stood there looking up at the building, waiting for the ball to come rolling back down like it would off the slanted roofs, but this one was flat. When it didn't come back down, they all turned and looked at Mugwump.

"You have to go get it," Whiteboy Paul said.

"With your non-throwing ass," Truitt said.

"You should have caught it," Mugwump said to Whiteboy Paul.

"Yeah. Sure. Maybe I'm thirteen feet tall!" Whiteboy Paul made a face at him.

"You scared!" Willmon shouted. "I ain't, though. I'll go get it." A small fence ran around the perimeter of the yard that was next to the garage and a crab apple tree stood by the side of the building. Willmon ran over to the fence and began to climb it but Mugwump grabbed him and pulled him back down. "I'm not scared," he said. "And you are way too small to get up on that roof." He paused to look up at the crab apple tree. "I'll go get it." He stepped over to the fence, climbed on top of it, and swung himself up into the tree. They watched from the ground as Mugwump scaled the tree and went up to the roof before disappearing from sight.

A long minute later, they heard Mugwump yell out. "Hey! Truitt! Check this out!"

"Check what out?"

Mugwump looked out over the ledge. "The ball went down a hole in the roof. It's an old car in there. One of them real old ones. Come up here, man!"

"For real?"

"One of them kind that they don't make anymore."

"What color is it?" Willmon yelled out.

"Black. But ya'll have to help me get the ball out of there."

"I'm coming up," Truitt said.

"Me too," Whiteboy Paul said.

"I can climb too," Willmon said.

"No." Truitt took hold of the fence and began to climb. Whiteboy Paul followed. "You're too small," he said to Willmon before he started to scale the fence.

Willmon crossed his arms and sat down hard on the ground with his lips poked out. When Truitt and Whiteboy Paul joined Mugwump on the roof, he was lying on his stomach and looking down into the garage through a ragged hole. When they joined him, they could see the old car, sitting long and sleek in the musty darkness.

"See," Mugwump said.

"Where's the ball at?" Truitt asked.

"On the side of the car. See it? Stuck between the door and the wall. Right there."

"Damn," Truitt said. "How we gonna get the ball outta there?"

"We can jump down on the roof of the car," Whiteboy Paul said.

"How we gonna get back up, though?" Truitt looked at him.

"One of us stays up here and pulls us back up," Whiteboy Paul said.

"That sounds right," Truitt said. "I'm going. Who gonna come with me?"

"Me," Whiteboy Paul said.

Mugwump readily agreed. "I'll wait and pull you back up."

Truitt walked over to the edge of the roof and looked over. "Hey, Willmon!" Truitt yelled out. "You right. Mugwump is scared."

Mugwump shot an ugly look at Truitt but said nothing.

"Come on," Truitt said to Whiteboy Paul. "Let's go."

They pulled at a few of the planks and the rotted wood easily gave way. When they made the opening wide enough for them to climb through without catching splinters, Truitt squeezed down into the hole feet first and landed on the car's roof with a solid thud. Whiteboy Paul followed. They quickly retrieved the football from the space between the passenger side door and the wall and tossed it up to Mugwump.

Truitt looked at Whiteboy Paul. "I wonder if the

door is unlocked. There's room on the driver's side. We can probably get inside."

Whiteboy Paul slid off the car to the floor and tried the handle. The door came open easily. "We're in!"

He stood with the door open and waited for Truitt to join him. They both climbed inside the car. Paul opened the glove compartment only to find it empty. Truitt pretended that he was driving, turning the wheel back and forth, pushing the stick for the windshield wiper and pressing the buttons on the old radio.

"I bet I could drive this car," Truitt said.

"It's a big car," Whiteboy Paul said. "It probably takes up too much of the road. That's why they don't make them anymore." He was rolling the window up and down with the handle, pausing to reach out and move the sideview mirror around.

"Get outta here!" Truitt said. "That ain't true."

"It is a big car, though," Whiteboy Paul said.

"What you doing down there?" A hint of worry tinged Mug-wump's voice.

"We driving!" Truitt said and Whiteboy Paul laughed. "The man left the keys in the car. We getting ready to back right through the back door."

"Stop lying!" Mugwump's voice cracked. "Come on, man! Come out of there."

"Come on," Truitt said to Whiteboy Paul. "We better get out of here before Wump pee in his pants." They got out of the car and stood on the roof, waiting for

Mugwump to pull them out. When they got back on the roof of the garage, Truitt looked back down at the car. "One day, I'm gonna get me one of those."

The alleyway held no secrets that they hadn't discovered and they had come to feel possessive of their small piece of the city. They kept the secrets they learned to themselves.

"All right now!" Truitt called out to Whiteboy Paul. "You ready?"

Whiteboy Paul nodded his head and went into his windup, preparing to roll the ball toward Truitt.

"Hold up!" Truitt raised his hand in the air. "Here come a car."

A dark-green 1976 Brougham D'Elegance with metal flecks in the paint rolled into the alley. The car had a shiny, gold grille and a butt-naked fairy posed as a hood ornament. "It's A Man's World" by James Brown was blaring out of the speakers when the front door swung open. Uncle Dope stepped out and stood there, doing his pimp primp as he looked around the alley. Uncle Dope was a fixture around town, one of those old school players who had never escaped from the era of his youth, the Sixties, and he swore—from the shine on his Gators to the smoothed-out brim that sat atop his graying Afro—that he would always remain a king in his pimpdom.

"What's going on, youngbloods?" Uncle Dope turned and started walking up through the yard toward Gloria's house. "Ya'll watch my ride and I'll hit you off when I get back." He glided up to Gloria's backdoor and went in without knocking.

Mugwump and Truitt leaned against his car while Whiteboy Paul and Willmon tossed the ball back and forth. "You know he *had* to park here, right?" Truitt said. "And you know once Uncle Dope get up in there running his mouth…"

"Yup," Mugwump agreed. "Uncle Dope be talkin' mad shit. All the time."

Mugwump was the kind of kid who went unnoticed. Usually he remained quiet, aloof, only coming out of his shell when he was with his friends, and at times he seemed to render himself invisible. It was this anonymity that often made him privy to grown folks' conversations because they would talk as if he weren't in the room. Mugwump loved to share the gossip with his friends; it often gave him a feeling of importance to tell them things that they didn't know. Uncle Dope and Mugwump's uncle, Big Daddy, were drinking buddies and they would often get loud and drunk in front of the television while watching the Yankees play.

"Uncle Dope always be over at Big Daddy's house getting drunk," Mugwump said. "He always be talking about all the women he be having."

"Oh, yeah." Truitt was disinterested.

Whiteboy Paul and Willmon gathered around Mugwump, their curiosity piqued.

"Does he talk about sex?" Whiteboy Paul asked.

"No, he probably talk about pussy," Willmon said and giggled.

"Sex and pussy are the same thing."

"No they not. That's what they said on TV! No they not!" Willmon shouted.

"Willmon," Truitt cut in, laughing. "You don't know one from the other anyway."

"Yeah," Mugwump joined in. "What you talkin' 'bout, Willmon?"

They all chuckled at the old joke but Willmon was stung by Truitt's remark, so he turned serious when he responded. "For real! 'Pussy' is a noun; 'sex' is a verb. They different."

Willmon loved to read, especially comics, and sometimes he would pull out words from his book knowledge to even the score when they ganged up on him. He smiled and waited.

"Truitt," Mugwump said. "Willmon is tripping again."

"Naw," Truitt replied. "Willmon is smart."

Willmon beamed and rubbed his hand over his nappy hair.

"Okay, then," Mugwump said carefully. "Uncle Dope was talking about how many nouns he was verbalizing with…That sound right, Mister Smart Guy?"

Willmon shrugged.

Mugwump continued. "But this one girl! Uncle Dope said that she gave him the claps."

"The claps!" the others replied in unison.

"Yeah. The claps. Uncle Dope said that green stuff

was leaking out of his ding-ding for days. Then he said that when he peed, it was like pissing razor blades."

A loud groan arose as each one of them clutched at their crotches.

"What did Uncle Dope do?" Truitt asked when he recovered.

"He had to go to the doctor and get his ding-ding fixed."

"I'll kill a bitch for doing that to me," Truitt said with conviction.

"Uncle Dope said that's what happens sometimes when you get all the womens," Mugwump said. "Matter of fact, he said that he was glad he didn't get nothing worse."

"I'll kill the bitch," Truitt insisted.

"And you'll go to jail for the rest of your life," Whiteboy Paul said.

"That's too bad," Truitt said. Willmon watched him intently. "I'll get me a gun and shoot that bitch. Better not give me nothing!" Truitt's voice rose as he spoke. "Don't never let nobody do you like that. I'm gonna be a man about mine!"

"Big Daddy told Uncle Dope that next time his dick was gonna fall off."

"Get outta here!" Whiteboy Paul tossed the ball in the air. "It's not going to fall off!" He tossed the ball lightly to Mugwump, who caught it and tried to spin it on his finger.

"So you saying that it ain't never happened before?"

"What? That someone's thing fell off? No, that hasn't happened."

"How you know?"

"Something like that would be on the news or something," Whiteboy Paul said. "If someone's thing fell off."

"Everything don't make the news, though." Mugwump gave up on trying to spin the ball on his finger and tossed it back to Whiteboy Paul. "My cousin was in church one time and this lady came in…they said that she was a church lady at one time but now she was a stripper… and they started praying for her and she disappeared into thin air."

"Get outta here!"

"And that joint wasn't on the news."

"That's because it didn't happen!"

"Yes, it did. How you know? You wasn't there."

"Whatever, Wump," Whiteboy Paul relented. "Whatever."

Truitt looked on, bemused. As the oldest, he sometimes felt the need to set them straight about things. Even though Mugwump and Whiteboy Paul were only a year younger than he was, Truitt felt that they were very naïve about the real world. "Listen," he said. "I know that if a woman gave me any kind of disease-type shit that messed up the mighty rod… Somebody is getting jacked up."

Willmon watched him, taking in every word that Truitt uttered. "For real?"

"For real," Truitt answered. "Somebody got to pay

for that." He paused to smile at Willmon. "But you ain't got to worry about nuthin' like that, right?" Willmon returned his grin. "'Cause I know you ain't fucking!" Mugwump and Truitt laughed.

"Mugwump ain't getting no ass either," Truitt said.

Mugwump stood with the ball in his hands. "That ain't funny, Truitt."

"Ain't no shame," Truitt continued. "You still shoulda seen some poontang by now, though. Some real, live, in person poontang."

This time Whiteboy Paul and Willmon laughed and exchanged high fives while Mugwump glowered. Truitt's words cut him; they always seemed to bother him more than anyone else's words could, and Mugwump was left feeling powerless.

"An empty can makes the most noise." The only weapon that Mugwump could use against Truitt was words. He had been saving that zinger for the right moment, and watching the grimace that flashed across Truitt's face, Mugwump felt a twinge of satisfaction.

"What the fuck does that mean?" Truitt said.

"What?"

"What you mean by that?"

"It means that you don't know what you're talking about."

"Like a virgin! Hey!" Truitt sang. Laughter erupted and Truitt raised his arms in victory and started screaming. "Sexual chocolate! Sexual chocolate!"

✪✪✪

When Uncle Dope walked through the door, Gloria was cooking horse in a spoon. After the white powder liquified, she carefully drew the clear liquid up through a hypodermic needle, slowly, until there was nothing left in the spoon, and leaned back in her chair, preparing to shoot up. Uncle Dope paused to watch her profile and counted himself lucky to be in love with her.

Gloria was life's big payback to him. Fate's retribution for all the dirty deeds that he had done had come back and cost him more than he could have ever imagined. At times, when he was being completely honest with himself, he realized that he had become that which he pitied the most: a sugar daddy. He was a weak man, a man who had lost his mojo. He was in love with a woman who loved heroin.

Gloria was a basic woman, the epitome of simplicity, and her home reflected the blandness of her life. Her home showed not a hint of a woman's touch. Her cupboard was bare, her furnishings stark and ragged. Uncle Dope hid a sigh as he took the seat across from her at a rickety kitchen table that she had thrown a threadbare kitchen tablecloth over. There were only two chairs left of the original four that came with the table and he was afraid that the bent and beaten metal legs would give way under his weight. The kitchen sink was piled high with dishes which, oddly enough, was unusual for Gloria because, despite her drug habit, she could throw down in the kitchen.

The first time that he met Gloria was when she had handed him a plate of food at his friend Kevin's cookout. Uncle Dope had plowed through a serious plate of barbequed beef ribs, collard greens, and macaroni and cheese with a square of cornbread on the side. The only thing that was missing for him was a glass of Kool-Aid. She had been watching him when he started splashing hot sauce on his collards and ribs as he prepared to devour the food stacked up on his plate. "Now that was some serious grub right there." Uncle Dope relaxed after he polished off his meal. "Somebody need to be on the cooking network up in this piece."

Gloria appeared next to him and took the empty plate. "Glad you liked it." Uncle Dope looked at her. She was young, in her late twenties he guessed, very pretty with slightly curly hair that cascaded down past her shoulders. When their eyes met, she held him with a haunting sexuality that intrigued him and, when she smiled, Uncle Dope heard far more than she could say. A thrill raced through his body as he returned her stare, but then he stopped a moment to take in the rest of her. She was skinny. Well, not skinny, he mused. She didn't have the full thickness that he usually required in his women. He quickly cast that thought aside; he could work with what she had. By the time the cookout was over, he had her name and number and knew that he would soon have her.

Their courtship had been intense. Uncle Dope fell into an emotional morass that defied his every instinct of self-preservation as he fought to bend her to his will, to mold her into the woman he wanted her to be, only to find himself being twisted and molded. He was well past the point of no return, trapped by a love that he had never thought possible before he realized that Gloria loved another.

She loved Heroin. White cricket. The chemical didn't care about Uncle Dope's dilemma while it callously claimed a part of Gloria that he could not touch because she loved the rush of the dope more than she cared for him.

❁❁❁

Truitt turned when he heard a door slam and then Uncle Dope came strolling toward them with that pimp stroll he had maintained from his younger days—he would always be old school. When he reached the car, they all looked up at him.

"Uncle Dope," Truitt said. "Can we ask you something?"

"What's that, young buck?"

"Do they got some diseases out there that will tear your dick up?"

"You got dick issues, youngun?"

"Naw, Uncle Dope," Truitt said. "Naw. Just askin,' is all."

"I know you be getting your dick wet, though, huh?" A big smile spread across Truitt's face. Uncle Dope paused to look at his watch. "Then time is definitely not on your side." Oblivious to the questioning stares of the teenagers, Uncle Dope got in his car and drove away.

Me and Miss Jones

Whiteboy Paul felt a chill. She had tangled her legs in the covers and twisted and pulled until he lay naked and exposed. The air conditioner was turned on full blast and the room felt as if the temperature had plunged drastically as they lay on her living room floor. He looked over at her. Even lying at the odd angles that her body was twisted into, he could marvel at the roundness of her hips, the smoothness of her thighs. He reached down and tugged at the covers, pulling them back between her tightly clamped legs but to no avail; there was no prying them loose without waking her up. It was getting late and he knew that he had to get up and go home. Paul didn't want to make any mistakes and ruin the good thing that he had going.

He was having fantastic sex with his English teacher. Miss Jones.

His father was cool. He knew what was going on and had given Paul his full blessing. But if his mother ever found out, Paul knew that there would be no stopping her, so it was best to keep his business on the discreet side. He sat up and gently moved away from her.

Nina Jones' voice was thick with sex and sleep as she turned over on her back, watching him. "You leaving already?"

"Yes. I need to get home."

"It's still early." She came fully awake and sat up, causing the covers to fall away from her body.

"Not for me, it's not," Paul said. "You know the rules. You've got more to lose than I do. Much more. Remember? You should count your blessings that I don't want to stay here and put my karate on you." That was what they called their clash of the sexes—karate. Miss Jones was good, though; she had plenty of fight in her, and was satisfied to sometimes lose a battle here and there but she had to win the war.

"You're a young buck," she said. "You've still got tons of fight in you. The exuberance of youth."

Paul liked it when Miss Jones talked like that—talked to him like he was an adult. It always gave him the chance to respond in kind and show her that he was mature beyond his sixteen years. "I think that I have an energized sex gene in my DNA," Paul said. *And you know you like it!* He was convinced that Miss Jones liked him because he was young and hard but he sensed an emotional flaw in her, a need, a desire that was slanted, maybe tainted, but he reasoned that all women were like that so there was nothing for him to worry about. Miss Jones was like the girls in his English class in a lot of ways, but she was his English teacher…and that made the sex even better.

"You remember what we talked about?" Miss Jones reached over and rubbed his shoulder.

Paul snorted derisively. "Yeah. I remember."

"You have to understand," she said. "I have to be sure, okay? Okay?" She waited for Paul to nod his head in understanding before she continued. "I trust you. I do. You're already a man…you're just waiting for the years to catch up. I know. But I ask more for my benefit. Peace of mind is a beautiful concept. And I need that."

"Yes," Paul replied. "I know." He turned fully toward her. "You like sex a lot, don't you?" He understood the urge—he felt like he was in constant heat, but she was crazy at times. Her sex was so demanding that she left him confused by her wants and desires.

Miss Jones didn't answer.

"We've got to be extra careful," she finally said.

Paul turned his back to her, a sly smile playing across his face. "I did tell somebody." Miss Jones became instantly alarmed. "You know how hard it is to keep this thing to myself? Everybody thinks that I'm still a virgin. And they are all out there having sex."

"Who?" Miss Jones voice was loud. "Who did you tell? Why would you do that?"

"I only told two people." Paul could feel the tension coming from Miss Jones. "Damn!"

"Okay." Miss Jones blew out a deep breath as she tried to calm herself. "Okay. Obviously you trust them.

Who?" She was speaking calmly, but Paul could hear the anger in her voice.

"Relax," he told her. "I only told my cousin Naomi and her friend Tracy. They won't say anything." Naomi and Tracy could instigate riots with their nonstop, know-it-all gossip. As far as they were concerned, everybody's business was their business and they were obligated, like CNN, to start spreading the news as soon as they heard it. Miss Jones folded her arms and clenched her jaws as she glared at him for a moment.

"No, you didn't," she finally said. "You've got much too many brains for that." Paul felt the tension slowly draining from the room. "You know that you play around a little too much, Paul." He turned toward her with a self-deprecating smile on his face. Her full, round breasts were balanced above the bed sheet and he felt a stirring as his manhood responded to the visual stimulation. There were a few girls at school with breasts like Miss Jones, but none of those girls were easy. They wanted to do everything under the sun: go to movies, go out to eat, hang out with their friends; everything except for getting naked and bumping uglies, but Miss Jones cut straight to the chase.

"I'm bad, right?" Paul said. "I mean, I like to do bad things." He reached out to her protruding breasts and twisted the nipples like he was tuning into a radio station. "I like to play with your—"

She slapped his hands away. "Stop it, Paul."

"Why?"

"Because some things you can't joke about! Okay? And that is one thing that you can't joke about." She moved closer to him. "Listen. I'm serious. We've talked about this before. Have you told anybody about what we do when we're alone?" She sat back and watched him, her hair hanging raggedly around her soft shoulders. Her eyes were clear and penetrating but Paul knew that she was nervous. She had no reason to be. Paul planned on riding the gravy train of easy and passionate sex until he graduated from high school. He wouldn't say a word to anyone about Miss Jones.

He moved closer to her until their faces were inches apart and then he took Miss Jones' hand. Looking deeply into her eyes as a smile spread across his face, he guided her hand down to the stiffness between his legs. "Sex with you is too good to mess up." He pressed his lips to hers; driving his tongue into her mouth the way that he knew she liked it. She gently began sucking his tongue like she was giving him head. "Way too good," Paul managed to say when he broke away. Rising from the floor he reached down for his pants and began to get dressed. "But I really need to get home."

Miss Jones smiled at him. "You know, you need to find a way to spend the night with me."

"That's like an impossible dream," Paul said. "I already thought about it from every angle and it can't happen." He looked down at her for a second. "Believe me! I've dreamed that impossible dream."

"You sure about that? Anything is possible."

"Look. I have to go." Paul finished dressing and quietly crossed the room to the back door. He took a long look out of the back window into the lush foliage that hid the back door of Miss Jones' house from the rest of the neighborhood. He remembered the first time that he was with Miss Jones. They had sex on the couch and he noticed that her living room was visible through the window near the back door. When he mentioned it to Miss Jones, she simply quieted him with a kiss and he hadn't mentioned it again. Later, when they had established a routine, he had come to understand why. Whenever they would meet, he would have to sneak around the back and look in through that window to make sure that there was no one there. Even then, he still had to knock twice, slip back into the trees for a minute and, after she appeared at the window, he would have to knock twice again before she would let him in. They had to be extra careful.

Paul gave the yard one last look before stepping outside. Miss Jones lived in a townhouse that stood behind a long tract of trees and foliage that separated her house from the row of townhouses on the next street. Paul walked down a slightly beaten path to where he had chained his bike to the thin trunk of a young tree. He emerged from the bushes nearly two blocks away near a huge, brown wooden house.

Paul jumped on his bike and started pedaling toward Promenade Park. The park sat next to the Fannie Mae building, its large, grassy manicured lawns interspersed with concrete walkways encircling the small, manmade lakes that were edged by multicolored flowers. Couples could often be seen in the middle of the fields, lying on their backs, looking up at the sun as they enjoyed its warmth. He was supposed to meet Truitt up by the Fannie Mae building, but now he was running late. He pedaled harder, hoping that Truitt would still be there.

His mind drifted back to Miss Jones. She was kind of crazy. Something about her was a little off. Paul couldn't quite put his finger on it, couldn't supply a name for her malfunction, but he knew it was there all the same. If word ever got out that she was having sex with a student, she would be labeled a sexual predator and her life would be ruined, yet she attacked him in bed like she was a lion that had been unleashed. A smile spread across Paul's face while the wind swept through his hair, his eyes glowing with the memory as the blocks sped past on his way to the park.

Sex.

Actually, Miss Jones was better than sex. She was better than he could ever have imagined sex could be, and sometimes he felt as if he could not contain his excitement. He was banging Miss Jones!

Paul stepped up his pace another gear as he approached Underhill, a steep, upward climb that always required great effort to reach the top. Steep hills created challenges for Paul whenever he was on his bike; especially if he happened upon a hill when Truitt and Mugwump were with him. They treated each hill like it was a personal challenge from the Man above that they had to meet and conquer, with a certain measure of pride and bragging rights going to the first one to make it to the top. The upside to their race to the top was the relaxing glide down the other side, with feet and legs dangling stress-free as the cool wind blew against their faces. Paul was panting when he topped Underhill and was still breathing hard as he glided downhill, turned on Union Street and coasted into the park. Truitt was sitting on a bench near the entrance with his bicycle lying on the ground near his feet. Paul coasted over, pulled up next to the bench and dropped his bike on the ground next to Truitt's, quickly taking a seat next to him.

"Whattup?" Truitt leaned back on his elbows while watching a group of kids playing a pickup football game.

"Shit," Paul said. "You want to get next?" He indicated the football game.

Truitt looked on as one of the boys came sweeping around the corner on an end run, striding in open spaces for a second, but that opening was quickly slammed closed and he was met with a vicious tackle that forced the ball from his hands. "Fumble!" The cry rang out, followed by a frenzy of bodies diving for the ball.

"Jermaine thinks that he's all that." Truitt spoke of the boy who had hit the ball carrier. "He ain't, though."

"Yes. I know," Paul said.

Jermaine stood over the pile of players who were battling with each other, trying to recover the fumble while he glared at Truitt with a daring smirk on his face. Truitt was Jermaine's only competition on the football field but Truitt had an edge on him.

"Jermaine takes it to heart too much," Truitt said. "He can't see me, though." Truitt returned Jermaine's stare before yelling out to him. "You cock strong, boy! You need some pussy in your life, kid. For real." The smile faded from Jermaine's face. "You too aggressive, man," Truitt continued. He and Jermaine had been through a few scuffles and had achieved a fighting peace. Now their battles were all talk.

"Why don't you come out here then?" Jermaine said.

"You need some ass, dude," Truitt said. "And I ain't talking about when your finger slips through the toilet paper either!" Paul broke out laughing. Jermaine stomped over to them. "What you laughing at, white boy?" he said.

"Why do I have to be white?" Paul said.

"'Cause you white, white boy." Jermaine looked at him for a moment, puzzled, when the other players called him back to the game.

"You know," Truitt said. "Sometimes you can be white as hell. You know what I mean?"

"Yep," Paul said. "But my father told me that one day it was gonna pay off for me."

"Your pops is a trip, too. But he ain't never lied."

They gave each other some dap and then sat back to watch the game for a few minutes. Jermaine took the ball and ran straight up the middle of the line, plowing through a few tacklers before being dragged to the ground. He spiked the ball and looked at Truitt.

"Truitt," Paul said. Truitt turned to him. "If I told you something, could you keep it to yourself? A secret. A *for real* secret! Never tell anyone?"

Truitt leaned back on an elbow and regarded Paul. "Probably. What kind of secret?"

"A serious one," Paul said. "Heavy. Matter of fact, I'm scared to tell you because you might not be able to hold it."

Truitt's chest puffed up. He had a few secrets of his own that he never planned to share, yet he resented Paul for thinking that he couldn't hold one. "Paul, you the one who can't hold water."

"Well, I'm holding this one. I need to know that I can trust you. That's all."

Truitt was silent. Paul looked at him with those bluish eyes glittering with an intent that Truitt had never seen before. His tone let Truitt know that this was very serious. "You my boy, Paul. What's up?" Paul paused for a moment and looked out at the football game. Jermaine was staring at Truitt again and he seemed to be much too close for comfort. "Let's go for a ride," he said. Minutes later, they were gliding past Underhill where they stopped by the lake and Paul told Truitt about him and Miss Jones.

Into Your Rhythm

Truitt fought the cold insecurities of his sexuality. His indecision stemmed from the dysfunctional relationship that he had with his father, Troy, a real man's man. His father had never provided any guidance for him, choosing to instead teach by example. He was a terrible instructor, so Truitt gleaned knowledge from any source he found credible. Books, television, schoolmates, the streets…those entities were his tutors but the lessons they taught were purely superficial, knowledge with no depth of meaning.

Perhaps his dad didn't possess the knowledge himself. His father was a lifeless man; the only spark of humanity that enabled him to function was the flame of bitterness borne of anger. Anger at the world for what one woman had done to him. His wife. Truitt's mother. She had left them when Truitt was barely two years old, so his memory of her was mostly sensory—a feel, a smell—and the rest was information gathered from others who would sometimes speak of her in hushed tones when Truitt's dad wasn't around. His father's pain was doubled by the fact that she had taken his daughter Anna, Truitt's older sister, with her and simply disappeared from their lives. Truitt sometimes glimpsed the haunted pain in his father's face though he tried to mask it with alcohol and the many women that he paraded through their home. It would be there, a darkness, a sadness that defied explanation and blunted any real feelings that may have simmered below the surface. Troy related to his son as if Truitt were a locker room buddy—joyously relating his experiences with women, his general disapproval of the opposite sex and the nasty ecstasy that they provided for him. Truitt knew that there was more to life than what his father said so he stopped listening to him.

"Your mother was a whore," Troy ranted. His speech was slurred as he sat slumped on the couch with a bottle of liquor in his hand. "She took my baby from me. My baby. Anna. She ain't never coming back." His head lolled to the side as Truitt pointedly watched the television. Bringing the bottle up to his mouth, his father took a long drink and then his voice exploded. "She better not bring her sluttish ass back up in here. I knew that's all she was good for when I met her." Truitt got up from his seat and went to his bedroom. He didn't remember his mother, but he refused to listen to Troy talk about her like that. He lay down on his bed and thought about how quickly another year could go by. He would be eighteen then, grown and able to leave his father's house. Freedom would be so sweet.

But what would he do with his freedom? College,

perhaps? Not if it depended on Troy providing any type of financial help. His money was always funny. College was probably a dream for Truitt, a far-off fantasy that would never happen. He often imagined the women that he would meet there, maybe a nice girl that he could hook up with whenever he called her. Yet he didn't want to be like his dad.

Truitt was at a crossroads, caught between the conflicting messages regarding sex and the willing female. On the one hand, there was the belief that women wanted to make an emotional connection as part of the sex; at least that was the conclusion that he had come to. On the other hand, there was the pure animal lust that waged a war inside of him. He had a million questions but there were no answers to be found.

Truitt thought that he had found the answer to this conflict one day when he went over to his friend Garrett's house. They were watching a talk show with Garrett's older brother Sam. One of the guests had written the show and asked if they could help him fulfill a dream that he had nurtured all of his life. It seemed that the man desperately wanted to star in a porn film with his favorite adult film actress.

"Well, guess what," the host said. "We are going to make your fantasy come true!" The man's face lit up when a movie producer and the favored starlet came onto the stage. The producer took the seat next to the man and held up a sheet of paper. "All you have to do is sign this contract and we will film a scene with you in our next movie, *Thirty-Year-Old-Virgin*!"

"Like bags of sand!" the man said.

"Like bags of sand," the producer agreed. The man leaned forward and looked past the producer at the porn star in the next seat. She wore a tight, white miniskirt that rode up her thighs and when she crossed her legs he got a hint of the sex underneath. The top that she wore barely contained the huge breasts that strained against the fabric and her nipples stood out with no shame, tall and proud. She was artificially beautiful with long blonde hair that hung down to her shoulders and features that were slutty sexy; just like he had dreamed. He snatched the pen and paper from the producer's hand.

"Now, hold on a minute," the talk show host said. "Before you sign that contract, we have one more guest. There is one more person that you have to talk to. One person who is strongly opposed to you making this dream of yours come true and she wants to talk to you before you make—what she thinks—will be the biggest mistake of your life." The host turned to the audience. "Please welcome to the show...your mother!"

His mother slowly made her way to the stage and took the seat next to him. She wore an ankle-length, one-piece, flowered dress that hung formlessly over her ample figure. The years hadn't been kind to her; her face, partially hidden behind horn-rimmed glasses, was lined with wrinkles, and her old lady wig completed the picture as she looked to the host with tears forming in her eyes.

The host spoke gently to her. "Ma'am, why don't you want your son to fulfill this dream of his? He says that this is something he has always wanted to do."

Her eyes seemed magnified through her thick glasses and, when she answered, the tears began to roll down her face. "Because..." She pulled out a few tissues and began dabbing at her teardrops. "This is going to ruin his life."

"Now that's some shit right there," Sam roared. He was sitting in a chair, facing the television with a forty-ounce of beer in his hand.

"How they gonna have his mother up there talking to him about fuck movies?" Garrett pitched in.

"They doing some shit on these talk shows," Sam said. They looked on as the mother cried and pleaded with her son not to go through with the movie. His only response to his mother was that this was his dream. "That shit is crazy," Sam said. "Moms is definitely going to lose that one."

"Why you say that?" Truitt looked at Sam.

"Ain't you never had no pussy before?" He cocked an eye at Truitt. Truitt didn't respond. "Ain't nobody," Sam said. "Not mother, father, sister or brother, ever gonna come between a man and his dick. Whatever dick want, dick gonna do."

The man stood on the darkened stage, highlighted by

a spotlight, pausing to look out at the audience. He paused as raised voices rang out, giving them one final glance before finally signing the contract with a flourish. He slammed down the pen on the desk and raced across the stage toward Mystic Ryder and had to be restrained by the show's security squad as he shouted that he wanted to start filming right away.

A few weeks later, Truitt lost his virginity to Jackie Thicke.

He had put in many hours of work with Jackie leading up to that moment. He would often go over to her house, looking for her nephew, Dasaan, whom Truitt sometimes hung out with, and then find himself alone in the house with Jackie. It was a secret ritual that they shared. Jackie would tell him that Dasaan was upstairs in his room and Truitt would go up there and wait, knowing that his friend wasn't there. If Dasaan had been home, Jackie would simply have yelled upstairs and let him know that Truitt was there. If Jackie sent him up the stairs, Truitt would wait and she would join him shortly.

Jackie was a year older than Truitt and she already had the thick, curvy body of a woman. At sixteen years of age, Truitt was the only virgin that he knew of, so his only sexual experience had been solitary ventures. His knowledge of sex consisted of discerning between the drunken wisdom of his father and the pages of the adult magazines that he had hidden in a box in his closet, buried beneath the many comic books that he also collected. So when Jackie came up the stairs, pushed him against the wall and slid her tongue into his mouth, Truitt was frightened and excited. Initially hesitant, his fingers traced the contours of Jackie's full breasts, his imagination exploding with the feel of their full softness. Emboldened, he ran his fingers down her back until he reached the fullness of her ass. He squeezed. A soft groan escaped from Jackie's lips and she pressed her hips firmly between his legs in the start of a slow grind. They would do this slow grind, dry hump whenever they could get away with it, and Truitt found their quick moments extremely satisfying. They shared a secret lust that made Truitt happy that a girl would be willing, and apparently was pleased, to let him go that far with her.

But this time was different.

When Truitt knocked on the door and Jackie let him in, she pulled him into the kitchen and pressed him against the wall before he even had a chance to ask for Dasaan. There were sparks in Jackie's tongue as it danced in his mouth, so Truitt responded in kind, throwing all caution to the wind. He massaged her breast and felt a hardened nipple accompanied by a sharp intake of breath. Jackie suddenly stepped away from him and looked Truitt in the eye. He smiled and reached for her, his body aching for the delicious contact that she had taken away, and then spun her around and pushed her against the wall. His need had quickly become urgent and so was the force of his hips as he moved between her legs, electrified by the connection of his throbbing erection directly contacting the swollen mound between her legs.

"Wait a minute." Jackie pulled her lips away and walked over to the stove to check the food that was cooking in the oven. Truitt studied the full roundness of her ass in her tight jeans as she bent over and found himself giving in to the temptation, reaching out to trace his hand over the inviting curves. Jackie glanced up at him with a sly smile and closed the oven door before walking through the kitchen to the back door. She pushed the screen door open and said, "Ma, I got the food in the oven."

"You watchin' it?" came the reply.

"Yeah."

"You bet' not let it burn 'cause I'm sitting out here wit' my drink and I ain't 'bout to get up."

"I'll watch it."

Jackie closed the screen door and motioned for Truitt to go up the stairs. For a flash of a second Truitt thought about Jackie's mother sitting outside on the back porch until Jackie turned toward him and he glimpsed her full breasts…and then all doubts were erased. He took the steps as quickly and quietly as he could and stopped at the top. Jackie came up behind him and turned to her bedroom. This was a new wrinkle; he had never been in her bedroom before. Truitt followed, grabbed Jackie by the waist and firmly pulled her body to him. She reached past him and pushed the door closed before returning his heat, tongues dancing while their bodies pressed together; the moment taking on more meaning than their usual encounters. Jackie reached down between their bodies and began to unbuckle his belt. Truitt was oblivious, lost in the sweet taste of her lips and tongue, until he felt his swollen erection spring from his pants and the soft flesh of her hand gripping it. He jumped away from her.

"Don't be scared," Jackie whispered. Truitt stepped back to her.

"Oooo-weeee!" Jackie said. "This thing is big!" Truitt waited to see what would happen next. "Come on!" Jackie began taking her clothes off.

Truitt dropped his pants and was naked before she was. He followed Jackie as she lay down on the bed. This was Truitt's first look at a real, live vagina and he couldn't move. Jackie had more hair between her legs than he did and he couldn't see the hole where his dick was supposed to go, but he knew that the answer to his lifelong question was in there somewhere.

Jackie took charge.

She grabbed his dick and guided it inside of her. Truitt took it from there. With one hard thrust, he felt himself tear into her dry flesh and her entire body stiffened. He looked at her face for a sign that he was in the right place and all he saw was a mask of pain. Right then, the contracting muscles of her sex gripped him and all conscious thought was banished. A wetness sprang up inside of her and she reached up to pull Truitt to her. Her lips were demanding but Truitt had the answer. He pounded his hardness inside of her, fast and fierce, and thirty seconds later it was all over. His very first sexual orgasm tore its way through him; an unstoppable and delicious ecstasy. The sounds of their high-pitched groans echoed throughout the room, seemingly intensified by the squeaking of the bed. Truitt grunted out loud when he made his final thrust deep inside of Jackie and he held himself there. Her pussy gripped him and pulsed around his shaft, pulling at him until every last drop of his seed was inside of her.

"Damn!" Truitt grunted before he collapsed on top of her.

They lay like that, him still inside of her while she held him against her soft body.

Jackie whispered in his ear. "You was a virgin, wasn't you?"

Truitt's body stiffened and he pushed himself up to look at her. He nodded his head, admitting it.

"That's all right, though," Jackie said. "It's big and it's still hard. All you gotta do is keep going."

"For real?"

"Yeah," Jackie said. She reached down and gripped his hips, holding him inside of her. "And this time you gonna last longer."

"Stop playin.'" Truitt began to move his hips again.

"Wait." Jackie reached over to the side of the bed for the remote control on the nightstand. "We were making too much noise last time. Hold on a minute. Wait!"

Truitt had started thrusting himself inside of her again. He was already looking forward to another orgasm. Jackie hit a button and the television flashed to life, bathing their bodies in a soft gray light. Jackie grasped Truitt by the back of his head and arched her body toward him, giving him a glimpse of the swell of her breasts that urged his motions to increase their intensity. Jackie dropped the remote and wrapped her legs around his back.

The television was tuned to a twenty-four-hour news channel. The newscaster's stern voice blared out:

A woman and her daughter were found dead in an apartment earlier today.

Truitt felt Jackie's lips fasten on his nipple. He pumped harder as a pleasant tingle shot through his body. Her tongue flicked out, back and forth across his nipple, and Truitt grunted. Dipping his head down, he sucked on her neck. Jackie leaned her head back and cried out. Truitt took that moment to fasten his lips on her nipple. His hardness throbbed, swelled up and got really, really swollen but he didn't feel her sex yet.

In a breaking story, two elderly women died of smoke inhalation when a fire broke out at their residence.

Jackie had him by the back of his head now, firmly forcing her breast into his mouth. Her breath was coming in short gasps now so Truitt figured that she must like what he was doing. Her body was thick and strong, qualities that mesmerized him, and her skin was a smooth, walnut color that seemed to pulsate with every stroke that he gave her. Truitt opened his mouth wider and tried to take in as much breast meat as he could. When he heard her breath catch again, her sex responded, again pulling at his thickness…and he fucked her with renewed strength. Now he felt her sex. He felt it!

A woman whose two children were drowned when her car plunged into a river today said that she saw a Black man fleeing the scene.

Jackie put both of her hands against Truitt's chest and pushed his body off of her. Truitt rose up and looked at her. Jackie lifted her legs and draped one over each of his shoulders. His penetration deepened.

Jackie looked him in his eyes. "Now fuck me," she said.

A sense of power flooded through his body, as if his dick was growing even bigger. He started stroking with all his might.

"Fuck…This…Pussy." Her voice was deep. "Fuck me!"

Truitt lost control. There was something in her voice! He leaned forward and threw all of his weight into each thrust, urgency building inside of him as he felt an orgasm come racing through him. The slapping of their flesh registered in the back of his mind, followed by a high-pitched squeal as Jackie's body tightened and trembled. His hips picked up even more speed as his body rushed to spit the come out of his shaft. Jackie let out a long, thin wail and Truitt emptied himself inside her again, pumping until he felt air emitting from his dick. He dropped her legs and fell on top of Jackie, laying there while gasping for air. After a few moments, he was conscious of the TV again.

And now, your local weather. Well folks, we're looking at heavy rain all day tomorrow, so make sure that you wear your rubbers! Or it is going to be nasty!

"Damn!" Truitt said. "Rain all day tomorrow. We had a game tomorrow."

Jackie smiled at him. "Yeah, rain. Get up. I gotta go check on the food in the oven."

Falling Apart

The delightful aroma of lasagna and garlic bread wafted up to Mugwump as soon as he closed the door behind him. A smile crossed his face because he knew his mother usually reserved lasagna and garlic bread for special occasions that warranted a full meal, followed by good company. Voices rose in good natured debate, emanating from the living room, and Mugwump stopped in his tracks to see if he could identify each person by voice.

"You know how we do, Teresa!" a voice boomed out. That was Roman. Roman was carefree and loud whenever he was feeling especially emphatic about something. He was a warm-hearted man whose exuberance drew people into his circle before they knew they were there. He liked to smile. And he liked to have a reason to smile. However, that same deep baritone could turn into a guttural warning when Roman found a reason not to smile. His bad side was not a good side to be on. "We have what is called urban style. Some brothers want to make it cutthroat, but it is style nonetheless.

Now, White people don't understand it sometimes but that's only right, too. *I* don't even understand Black folks my damn self!"

"You understand them enough," Janese said. She and Roman had been together for as long as Mugwump could remember. They were a couple that battled regularly but could never be without each other. "And love them, too," she finished.

"Well, I love you, too, baby, but I don't understand you for nothing."

"What's not to love?"

"You got that right," Roman said. "But that's because you understand me."

"You two have gone through some fire together," Teresa said. "That type of thing will bring out the truth."

"So where does that leave me?" Artis was a short man who carried himself with the presence of a big man. He was graying around the fringes of his balding head and wore a pair of wire-rimmed glasses that intensified his steely glare. "I've only known ya'll a little while. Remember that day down by the river? I thought that I was the angriest Black man in America that day. I thought that I was standing alone. Until Roman and Janese came and stood right with me." The room was silent for a moment as each of them played back the memory of their first meeting. "I could have easily killed me a White man that day."

"And we wouldn't have nothing to show for it but another dead Black man," Teresa said.

"Yeah." Artis' voice was solemn. "I know. And I don't know if I ever thank ya'll enough for saving me that day." Mugwump hardly ever heard them speak of the day, as if the memory itself would bring back some forbidden ghosts. "Hard times," Artis continued. "Hard days."

Mugwump walked into the living room.

"Here go my man!" Roman was sitting on the couch next to Janese.

"Julius, boy, you getting bigger every time I see you," she said.

"Sure is," Artis agreed.

Mugwump took a moment to return their greetings before going over to stand by Teresa. They started bombarding him with questions about school, his grades and his plans after he graduated from high school. Mugwump patiently answered their questions before arriving at the question he really wanted to ask.

"Ma," he said. "How did all of ya'll meet? You know, back in the day?"

The room turned silent.

"Nothing, son," Teresa said. "Not now."

"Was it really that bad?"

Teresa's laugh had little humor. "Many things were; back then. But we always had the idea of carrying ourselves with enough pride to go on living."

"Yeah," Artis said. "We always thought that, for our kids, the next day might be easier. Who could have known that there would be a generation of youngsters like there is out here today?"

"We're a new breed now, Artis." Mugwump had heard this argument from them many times before and he often found himself having to defend all teenagers for being teenagers.

Roman leaned forward on the couch. "Man, all I see of this new breed is the next round of Negroes! Mostly pants-sagging, gold teeth-wearing, drug-toting Negroes!"

"That's not true," Mugwump said. "Not true at all."

"Do you know what the future generations are going to see when they look back on this age of Black folks? They gonna see a race of people who like to sex each other or kill each other, with little in between."

"People always pay attention to the bad stuff. And the media makes up the rest." Mugwump warmed up to the subject. "I know you remember when they said that Martin Luther King was a communist. They said that Malcolm X was a pimp. That ain't who they were." Mugwump had done a paper on the Civil Rights Era and had surprised Mr. Shoodin, his social studies teacher, when he had included Malcolm X in the report. "Sometimes history can be wrong."

"One thing they had in common," Artis said. "They carried themselves with pride and dignity and that's what made them great."

Roman jumped in. "Now how much pride, how much dignity, and even more importantly, how much social impact do you think that they would have had if they went around calling themselves 'niggers'? Sounds downright insane, doesn't it? I'm a man! I'm human. I'm a nigger." A murmur of agreement accompanied this sentiment. "These kids today need to stop that mess."

"Sometimes I think that they really don't know any better," Janese said. "It's on television, and the music! Good Lord, the music! That one word can make a Black man a million dollars nowadays. The only thing that has changed is the amount of money it takes to sell out."

"And these kids are definitely selling." Teresa shook her head.

Mugwump had heard enough. "Now wait a minute! I think that ya'll are wrong on this one. Most definitely."

"How so?"

"I can't tell ya'll."

"Why not?"

"Yeah! Why not?"

"Ain't nothing to tell! That's why…"

"That's not it," Mugwump said. "See, if I tell you what I think, you are going to dismiss me like my words don't mean anything. And that's part of the problem."

"Alright," Teresa said. "I promise." She looked pointedly at everyone in the room. "We won't do that to you. We're going to show respect. That is, if your opinion makes sense." She motioned toward the room. "The floor is yours."

Mugwump took a step toward the center of the room before he spoke. "Okay. Here is a serious part of the problem: The older generation—that means you—has got to understand that we—and by 'we' I mean us young *adults*—cannot learn from your experience. Not in any real type way. You have to understand that 'nigger' doesn't mean the same thing to us that it meant to you. When we say 'nigger' there ain't no dogs biting us in the butt, there ain't no White man with a hose or a cracker in the woods with a rifle. It's only a word. We've even turned that negative word from your time into a term of endearment. And ain't that what you marched for? So that the word won't have any more power over us? Well, now it doesn't…and ya'll don't like the results." He paused to look around at each person as they watched him. "Our lives are different now…and so is the mindset."

Janese broke the silence that followed. "That boy is good, Teresa. He is not playing."

Artis waved a finger at Mugwump. "Julius, don't you see the damage of that word? Son, it goes way beyond experience. Black folks are the most socially commented upon people in the history of this country. And I'm not just talking about socially. I'm talking about spiritually. Words can define you. And in a very real type way! You can define the history of Blacks in America by name. Names that we were given, not anything that we chose! It went something like this: slave, nigger, colored, Negro, Black, African-American…and now you young bucks want to go back to 'nigger'! That's just a step above 'slave.'"

Mugwump thought for a moment. "I've got a question then. Is it possible that we had to go through all of those steps so that we can figure out what the real deal of equality is? Being Black is a lot of different stages, like you say. Stepping through a whole bunch of stuff."

"Only problem, Julius," Teresa said, "is that we've stayed in that 'nigger' state for so long that it seems like we're falling apart."

"Enough of this," Janese said. "When are we going to get some of that lasagna, Teresa? Don't you hear my stomach singing? *We are the world! We are the children!*" Agreeable laughter filled the room and Teresa rose to go set the table. She looked at Mugwump with a touch of pride in her eyes. He had presented his opinion in a well-thought out argument and, more importantly, had given her a few things to think about.

"You know something." Roman caught Mugwump with some dap. "I'm expecting great things from you, Julius. You talk like a man."

Show and Prove

"**D**on't never let nobody know where your goat is tied, Julius," Teresa told him. "Because then they can always get your goat." Mugwump was helping his mother with the cleanup after everyone had gone.

Teresa rose from the table and began clearing the dishes, giving him a questioning stare to see if he understood her meaning. She walked over to the sink with a slight limp which was barely perceptible, but it was there. She had been injured when she was much younger, before Mugwump was born, during a demonstration down South during the Civil Rights Movement. By all accounts she was too young to have been there, but she had explained to Mugwump that Black folks had needed all the help that they could get back then, both young and old.

His mother was a strong woman; he saw strength in her high cheekbones and her eyes, which could hold glimpses of wisdom and the darkness of intimidation. She held hard to her convictions—a stance that pained him sometimes and made him proud of her all of the time. She was an ardent believer in education.

"Black people won't ever find their true strength without finding their mind power." Teresa drummed that edict into Mugwump but he didn't need much urging. Mugwump had a natural thirst for knowledge. As soon as he had learned how to read, he spent hours with his face crammed between the pages of comic books and children's stories, devouring them until there was nothing left to read; and then he would read the same books again. Mugwump got to the point where he would sometimes rather read a book than go outside and play with his friends, but Teresa put a stop to that. She wanted her son to know that there was a world outside which held experiences that couldn't be found on a written page. She wanted him to have balance.

"And that gives them power." Teresa deposited the dishes in the sink and ran water over the dinner plates. The aroma of the Shrimp Alfredo and toasted garlic bread wafted in the air as Mugwump leaned back in his chair. He shared his mother's love of Italian food, which she cooked on many occasions because she knew that Mugwump would eat his fill. "That's what happens." She looked over at him. "People will draw conclusions about you by watching your reaction to different types of drama. Because your reaction to stress is your moral denominator."

Mugwump looked at her questioningly.

"'Moral denominator!' The place where you stand!"

She paused for a moment. "Like I'm going to find out where you stand if you don't get up and put the rest of them dishes in the sink. How many times I got to tell you?"

Mugwump quickly gathered up the rest of the dishes and put them in the sink. He did not want his mom to start on one of her lectures about cleanliness and godliness. His mother always seemed to connect the two and he still could not understand her reasoning.

"You have to live where you stand," she resumed, making her point. "The place you live will be clean, orderly and everything will make sense."

"I make sense, Ma."

She looked at her son with love in her eyes. "Yessir! Most of the time you do. And you know that I'm so proud of you. You know your history. And that's a good thing. I always wanted you to understand the struggle. The ups and downs of what Black folks have been through socially. Our history is so random, so up and down that most Black folks don't even know what to call themselves. We're unique in that way. We lack a basic grasp of where we are *at!*" Teresa paused and gave a short laugh. "Anyway, I know that you do good, Julius. But in these times…that ain't enough."

"I do damn good, Ma." He knew that his mother understood him. Knew that his words meant no disrespect to her but a greater respect of the truth. "And you know this."

Teresa walked over and stood in front of her son and

firmly grasped his shoulder. "I know. And I am proud of you. You do good in school…you use your brain! And I like that. You can do great things with that brain you got. You can be anything. Anything at all." She looked at him with a challenge in her eyes. "You know that you got that from your mama, right?"

Mugwump snorted. "Of course, Ma! Who else?"

"Certainly not your daddy."

"He ain't shit," Mugwump co-signed. There was no malice in his tone; his father lived a few miles away, but Mugwump simply thought nothing of a father who had absolutely no role in his life. Mugwump didn't even bother with the thought of his dad's existence. The few times that Mugwump had seen his father on the streets, he hadn't bothered speaking to him, passing him by as if he were a stranger. Once his father had tried to start a conversation with him and Mugwump had simply replied, "Why bother?" and walked away.

"I want you to do good," Teresa said. "I want you to be proud of yourself." She moved back over to the table and sat down. "Summer's coming and business is picking up. I'm about to start getting a lot of overtime hours." His mother worked two jobs. She had a customer service job during the weekdays and worked at the pillow factory on the weekends. The extra hours meant that they would see even less of each other in the coming months. "So I don't want you out in the streets; especially with that friend of yours. That boy Truitt is a bad piece of work there."

"My friends don't really matter," Mugwump said. "Do they?" The doorbell rang before she could answer. "I'm still me, Ma. You taught me that much."

"But that ain't everything, Julius. That's not everything at all. We are the sum total of our experiences. I've found that to be true. We become a product of what we go through. That boy, Truitt! He's now part of your experience, which means he's a part of you."

The doorbell rang again and Mugwump excused himself without responding to his mother's argument. When he opened the door, Truitt stood there with a bemused look on his face.

"Whattup, Wump?"

"Truitt."

"Come outside, man." Truitt motioned toward Paul, who was standing with his bike on the sidewalk. "We getting ready to trip you out, bruh! Hurry up! Chop! Chop!"

"Truitt," Mugwump said. "You know you can't come over here without speaking to my mother. Come in."

A look of consternation passed over Truitt's face as he followed Mugwump into the kitchen. "Hi, Mother Teresa," Truitt said.

"That's one smart-ass mouth you got there," Teresa said. "Does Julius talk like that when I'm not around?"

Truitt turned serious. "No, Ma'am."

"Oh. So it's 'ma'am' now, is it?" She regarded Truitt with a disapproving eye.

Truitt didn't answer. Teresa dismissed them with a

wave of her hand. When they were safely outside, Truitt turned to Mugwump. "Why your mother hate me?"

"Because you're evil." Mugwump tapped him on the arm. "What ya'll got to tell me?"

"I ain't evil!" Truitt said. "Do you think I'm evil?"

"You know that grown folks think that they know everything," Mugwump said. "Why do you care what my mother thinks anyway? Things ain't the same as when they were kids. We deal with real nasty stuff now."

"And I'm a nasty motherfucker!" Truitt said. They both laughed as they approached Paul who eyed them like he wanted in on the joke. "Now Paul," Truitt said. "Paul is probably the nastiest out of all of us."

A sly smile spread across Paul's face; a mischievous grin when accompanied by the glint in his eyes. "You going to get your bike?" Paul said.

Mugwump looked up at the cloudless sky that was starting to darken and said, "No. Let's walk."

They walked down the street in silence; the only sound heard was the flapping of the playing card as it drummed against the spokes of Paul's bike. Truitt was too cool to do that anymore.

"So you're not going to tell me?" Mugwump felt as if he had waited long enough. "What's up?"

Truitt and Paul exchanged glances.

"What?" Mugwump was getting impatient.

"You can't tell anybody," Paul said. "I really, really mean it, Wump. You can't even tell your mother. Especially not your mother."

"All right. I won't."

"Especially not your mother!"

"I said I won't tell!"

"Promise, though. I'm serious!"

"He's dead serious, Wump," Truitt said. "This gotta be between us. Nobody else."

Mugwump had never seen his friends so intense about anything before and now his curiosity was piqued. He hadn't seen Paul acting so anxious since the time they had watched Jean, his next door neighbor, get undressed through her bedroom window. They thought that she had been putting on a show for them because she would undress in front of the same window at the same time every night. But the exhibition came to a screeching halt when Vanessa and her husband Henry started coming over to visit. Suddenly, the blinds were shut.

Paul had gone ballistic. Jean was a voluptuous woman with thick full lips and gravy curled hips, deep brown and round ass for no reason at all. When Paul was deprived of the sight, he cussed up a storm. He swore with as much strength as Mugwump had ever seen him exhibit. The entire way from Jean's house, back up past the high-rise apartments, Paul had muttered and cursed about the demise of Vanessa and her husband. He said that if God was just, He would make the house fall down on top of them and then Jean would be able to undress in front of the window again. Yeah. Paul could get carried away sometimes.

They turned the corner onto South Street and headed toward the elementary school library.

"Go ahead," Truitt said. "Tell him, Paul."

Paul turned to Mugwump with a solemn look. "You have to swear to God that you won't tell. Swear!"

"Man, I swear! Damn! Now what the fuck!"

Paul visibly relaxed and his frown was replaced by a happy smile. "I'm having sex with Miss Jones." There was a stunned second of disbelief and Paul basked in it. "Miss Jones!"

"Ta-dow!" Truitt threw in. He was smiling, too. "I betcha that is some good rumble pie up in that joint! That shit look good, the way it walk. That ass got a wiggle in it."

"You and Miss Jones," Mugwump said.

"Me and Miss Jones."

"Get the fuck outta here!"

"*Me and Misses Jones*," Paul sang out. Mugwump and Truitt exchanged glances before they were overcome with laughter. Paul was singing. And way off key. "*We got a thing! Going wrong! Meeee aaannd Misses! Misses Jones! Misses Jones! Misses Jones!*"

"Boy, shut up! Shit!" Truitt said. "That shit is like that? Hoochie coochie! Hoochie coochie!"

"Truitt, won't you stop hyping Paul up like that. You know good and well he ain't hitting that. Please!"

"Why you hating?" Paul said.

Mugwump regarded him with a raised eyebrow. Paul

never used slang. That was one of the things that Mugwump really liked about him; he didn't try to talk like he was a Black kid. He was just Whiteboy Paul.

"Because you exaggerate sometimes," Mugwump said. "You get a little wild with the imagination, kid."

"Sounds like somebody been drinking haterade!" Paul said and Truitt burst out laughing and gave him a high-five.

"Whatever, Paul," Mugwump said. "So you trying to say that you took your penis and put it into her vagina? And took it out and put it in, and took it out and put it in?"

Paul laughed. "We had sex, Wump. No lie! And she likes giving it to me. She wants to give it to me more and more."

"So, you still getting it?"

"That's what I'm trying to tell you! Yes."

"Prove it then! I'll believe it when I see it; with my own two eyes."

"I don't think she wants anyone to know, Wump. Why do I have to prove it to you anyway? Why don't you believe me?"

It wasn't like he *didn't* believe Paul; he *couldn't* believe Paul! And though Paul was not the type to lie, for some reason, Mugwump wanted proof. "Listen," Mugwump said. "Leave some curtains open."

"What?"

"Leave the curtains open, like Jean used to do. So we can see with our own eyes."

"Hell yeah." Truitt was down with that plan. "We gonna see Paul in action. Get up in there and do the electric boogaloo, dude!"

"You guys are crazy," Paul said. "There's no way."

They walked up to the library, where Paul and Truitt chained their bikes to the bike rack, but instead of going inside they all took seats on the concrete steps at the entrance. Ornate, stone statues of lions sat on either side of the stairs at the entrance to the library. When they were younger, they used to sit on the lions' back and pretend that they were the kings of the jungle, riding them in the shade of the huge trees that stood in front of the building. They had tamed many a jungle terror atop the king of all beasts, but those days were gone. Now they had their feet planted firmly on the ground.

"Paul, you gotta stop being scared." Truitt jumped up and ran toward a low-hanging tree limb. He leaped and grabbed ahold of the sturdy branch and tried to do a pull up.

"Or you can stop lying," Mugwump said.

"I'm not lying!"

"Well, exaggerating then."

"I'm not exaggerating either."

"Yeah." Truitt grunted as he dropped to the ground. "Why do you think he's lying?"

"Exaggerating is not a whole lie," Mugwump said.

"Anyway," Paul said. "I'm not scared; she is. Miss Jones told me not to tell anyone because she would get in serious trouble."

"And if you ain't laying down no lumber…" Truitt leaped for the branch again. "Then she getting in trouble for nothing."

Paul was silent.

"Show and prove, Paul. Show and prove."

Truitt struggled to do one more pull-up, grunting with the effort as his body slowly rose and he touched his chin to the tree branch before dropping to the ground again.

Paul got to his feet. "Okay," he said. "I'll do it. We have to make sure that no one else will find out."

Willmon Angel

Willmon Angel had a pen in his hand. For the past two weeks he had been writing, trying to catch the rhythm of his life to capture his world in word pictures and colorful beats…and he couldn't stop. Nothing could escape his poetic vision. No aspect of life was safe from the imagination that pulsed inside his brain.

But the pulsations ached sometimes. His head pounded, thumped in a dizzying rage whenever "The Fits" overtook him. That was what his mother called the episodes that plagued him since the bike crash. His mother seemed to enjoy reliving the accident that had led to his condition.

"I remember," his mother told the tale. "I remember that time." She would rock back and forth, hugging herself as she warmed to whoever her audience might be at the moment. "Him and that White boy, Loomis, they went and built some ramps at the bottom of the hill behind the house back there. They hardheaded. Told 'em 'bout jumping them bikes over them ramps back there. I saw 'em before. Told his hardheaded ass to stay from back there, too." She stopped to flash a narrow stare at him. Sometimes she scared him with her venom. Sometimes he could feel her hate. "Boys can be so stupid," his mother spoke to the three women who were sitting in the living room. Fanny Mae and Pearl sat on the couch and Sissy leaned back in the recliner as his mother entertained them with the story of how Willmon's head got cracked on the ground. Willmon sat at his mother's feet, his gaze fixed straight ahead, his mind twisting through imaginary stories that he longed to write. She made him sit at her feet because she wanted to keep her eye on him after she caught him writing on the wall. His head hurt so much. But now was not the time…his mother was telling a story.

"They was jumping them bicycles way up in the air. You shoulda seen them." His mother was getting to the good part. This part of the story was always weird to him because he had no memory of what happened. It was as if a black curtain descended over that part of his memory and he couldn't lift it. So Willmon was forced to relive the incident through his mother's eyes…and she seemed to fill in more detail with each telling. "They used to rig it up, too! Him and Loomis. They would lay down some bricks. Sometimes they would use them sawhorses; anything they could stack up six foot or so high. Then they would lay down some two-by-fours and then lay a flat board on top of that…and they done made themselves a ramp. They would build that thing at the bottom of that hill back there. I heard Willmon say that they would hit maximum speed and get a maximum jump. That's what he said, *max-a-mum*, if they put the ramp at the bottom of the hill. Remember that?" His mother was talking to him but Willmon didn't answer. His fingers were twitching. *I need to write!* When he didn't reply, his mother continued, "Didn't I tell you that boys is so stupid?" She turned back to her audience. "Now, they was out there jumping up in the air like they was Evel Knievel and carrying on. Now Loomis, he a White boy and you can kinda expect that from them. They do shit like that. Like they find the meaning of life in damn near killing they self. But Willmon! He got White people's kinda sense sometimes. That's what got his head rung."

Damn! She does not know how to tell a damn story! I wish Sissy would come over here and slap her lips off and make her get to the point.

"So I was checking on 'em. You know how hyper Willmon could be. That boy was always into something. Loomis, too. Both of them is some bad-asses. Him and Loomis. But then I saw little Arto sitting out there with them. He sat there and watched Willmon and Loomis jump the ramp a few times and then he decides that he wants to be part of the show. You shoulda heard 'em…"

❂❂❂

"I can jump farther than that," Arto said.

Willmon got mad. "No, you can't. You lying bitch!"

"Your mama's lying," Arto screamed.

"Your mama got doo-doo wrap in her hair."

"Doo-doo wrap? No she don't."

"And hoop-a-stank up in her butt!"

Loomis started laughing and Arto's eyes narrowed. They were still laughing when Arto jumped back on his bike and glared at them.

"You the bitch, though," he barked at Willmon. "'Cause I'm gonna jump way more far than you did. Just watch!"

Arto pushed his bike to the top of the hill and paused to look down at them before taking off. His front tire hit the ramp and then Arto was airborne. He soared up into the air with his weight shifted over the front tires and when he landed he was nearly thrown over the handlebars, which bent downward from catching the brunt of his weight. Arto fought the bike until he brought it back under control and he rode back to the spot where he had landed. He stopped and glared triumphantly at Willmon as he stood nearly two feet beyond the best jump.

Willmon walked back and pushed his bike up the hill. He called his bike "The International" because it had parts from all over the neighborhood. He found the frame in the Second Street alley in the overgrown grass of the lot that let out onto State Street. The handlebars were taken from another rusted frame behind the Sanchez house down by the river. He took the seat off of a bike that someone had left in the parking lot at Murphy's Bar and he bought the chain at Steiner's Sports Store. After sanding the frame down to the metal and spray-painting it a deep maroon that matched the seat with the gunmetal piping, his bicycle had that two-wheeling, motorcycle look. Willmon thought his bike had flavor.

He stood at the top of the hill and looked down at the ramp. He looked up and saw Arto waiting at the spot where he had landed. "Hey, Loomis," he called out. Loomis looked at him. "How far you think I can jump?" Loomis shrugged. "Go mark a spot for me." A huge smile spread across Loomis' face and he ran to a spot that was easily five feet beyond Arto's mark. "Move out the way, Arto!"

Willmon studied the distance for a moment and then he began to back the bicycle down the runway—he was going to need more speed. He stopped to study the distance one last time and he backed up a few more feet before pushing his feet down on the pedals. He built up as much speed as his little legs could muster and when he crested the hill, the ground flashed past his tires. His bicycle hit the ramp and Willmon shot skyward like a daredevil, flying higher than he ever had before. At the top of the arc, the bicycle flew away from beneath him and Willmon found himself flailing in mid-air. As the ground rushed toward him, he closed his eyes slightly before his shoulder and head struck the pavement with a loud crack.

✪✪✪

"Lawd! You shoulda seen his little ass come running in this house then," his mother continued with the story. "He laid his ass down then! He slept for damn near twenty-four straight hours. I was getting ready to take him up to the hospital…and you know ain't nobody got no money to be going to no hospital…but I was gonna take his little bad ass to the hospital, but then he woke up." She stopped to scratch her arm and adjust her bra. "We didn't know his brain got damaged, though. We thought he was alright, but he got damage to his brain."

The women turned and looked at Willmon sitting at his mother's feet. Sissy and Fanny Mae wore sad smiles on their faces. Sissy spoke up first. "He's so different now. I remember Willmon was a bundle of energy a few weeks ago. You couldn't have paid him to sit still for even this long."

"Now all he wants to do is stay in the house and write on my walls and everywhere," his mother said.

"Girl, I don't know what you talking about," Fanny Mae said. "That boy is better than the rest of them." His mother started to object but Fanny Mae nodded her head. "All he does is write? Shit! I wish some of my kids would pick up a pen and paper."

"Mine, too," Pearl said. "Only time mine write anything, it's the next chapter of the jailhouse diaries."

Sissy was quiet. She didn't have any children.

"I don't care what ya'll say," his mother said. "That

shit ain't healthy. He need to go outside. Play with other kids or something. All the time in the house, writing and writing and writing and shit. You know this morning, this fool had the nerve to…to…" She looked at her friends, her eyes pleading for understanding. "Ya'll don't know! You just don't! I was about ready to kill this little boy this morning. Ya'll know how I hate it when people mess up my shit. You know this! You know me!"

They all nodded in agreement on that point. His mother was a serious housekeeper and her domain was always spotless. If she suspected that someone was a dirty person, they were not allowed in her house. "Let me show you what Willmon did this morning." She rose from the couch and led her friends into the hallway. Willmon didn't move.

"Look!" She pointed at the light-blue wall. A short paragraph was written in dark, black ink.

"What is that?" Fanny Mae said.

"He did that?" Pearl asked in a hushed tone.

"I was ready to take him to planet whoop-em-ass and leave him there," his mother's voice rose. "I swear!"

Sissy nudged between the two women and looked at the wall. She studied the writing, looked back at Willmon, and turned back to the wall and started reading.

Mother is God. And glory.
If God don't love you.
If words burn and smoke. In the air.
And glory can't do nothin' but cry.

Missions and Madness

They crept like bandits, moving through the trees and bushes, making as little noise as possible. Paul took the lead, directing Truitt and Mugwump with hand signals and gestures but never uttering a word. They were on a mission and they had agreed to maintain mission silence throughout.

Miss Jones had agreed to meet him tonight.

They huddled together at the base of a tall tree near the side of Miss Jones' house, scouting the area, trying to make certain that no one could see them. Paul noticed that Miss Jones' house was not as isolated as he had imagined. The trees that he thought obscured the lines of sight from the other houses did not seem sufficient anymore. He could see lights shining through windows when he looked through the tree leaves and he could even see into the living room of one of her neighbors through the glass patio doors. *What chances have I been taking!* Strangely enough, this newfound knowledge excited him and he felt a familiar stirring at the thought of being watched.

He shook his head to dislodge those images from his mind…but the feeling remained. Paul had experienced an initial rush of excitement when Mugwump suggested that he leave the curtains open while he was having sex with Miss Jones. His mind had instantly flashed back to when they had watched Jean through her window. Her performance had mesmerized him and inspired him when he discovered the joys of self-pleasure.

Miss Jones had been an extension of that fantasy; the round, full ass, bounceable titties and smooth, flat stomach, and now the desire could go to another level. Paul hoped that the sensations wouldn't overwhelm him and cut his performance short; especially in front of Truitt.

He looked at Truitt and Mugwump huddled next to him in the darkness. They both wore intent expressions, and Paul was glad that they took the situation seriously. Paul beckoned for them to follow him. They crept from their hiding places and made their way around to the back of Miss Jones' house.

Paul signaled for Truitt and Mugwump to wait as he crept across her yard up to the back door. Flattening his body against the wall, Paul slid over to the window and snuck a look inside. Miss Jones was sitting on the couch in the living room with a stack of papers in front of her on a small table. She wore an old, flimsy pair of pajamas that had seen better days and her hair was unkempt, hanging loosely as if she had just woken up. She had her famous red pen in her hand, the one she used to grade the tests that she administered to her students; and she was marking one of the papers stacked in front of her.

Paul had excellent writing skills in which he took great pride, and it was his writing talent that had eventually led him to Miss Jones' bed. After handing in one assignment, Miss Jones read it while sitting at her desk and when the class ended she ordered him to stay so that she could talk to him. When they were alone, she approached him with his homework assignment in her hand and, despite the potential storm that he thought was brewing, Paul caught his breath at the hypnotic curves of her body.

"Paul." Her voice broke him from his lustful stare. A short smile greeted him when he finally looked at her face. "You show a lot of maturity in your writing. Too much sometimes."

"I read a lot, Miss Jones."

"The subject matter and the style that you write with… these two things aren't found in books."

"Yeah. But I think about things, too, Miss Jones. And most of the time, on paper is the only chance that I get to say what I want. You told me that you would never tell me I was wrong. That I…that my thoughts were free to be free. Remember?"

"Relax, Paul." She smiled at him. "I'm not blaming you for anything."

"Yeah. Right!"

"I need to know… Is there anyone helping you with your assignments?"

"No way!" Paul was defensive. "No one but you."

"No one at all?"

Paul shook his head.

"Just a little bit?"

More head shaking. Miss Jones moved opposite of him and took a seat. Regarding him carefully, she held up the paper for him to see and then she began to read. "Sexuality versus love. Love versus sexuality. Are they mutually exclusive or is the contrast comparable to satisfaction versus happiness?" Silence hung in the air for a moment before she spoke. "Pretty heady stuff for a teenager." Paul looked into her eyes. "And this is all yours?"

"You said that my thoughts were free, Miss Jones."

"They are, Paul. They are." Her voice was calming. "I wonder where your frame of reference originates. It's hard to imagine that you would be able to comprehend the concepts of sexuality versus love."

"It's all theory to me, Miss Jones." Paul watched her intently. "I don't have any experience to make it real." He studied a spot on the floor before he decided to take a risk. "As much as I want to." His heart beat wildly as he waited for her reaction to his sly remark. When she spoke, he thought he heard a slight tremor in her voice. "You're very mature. And very smart. You have the intelligence to do anything you please."

"And sometimes I can get deep, too," Paul said.

Miss Jones gave him a look, as if there were something she was trying to figure out, but then she smiled.

Hours of research had been spent on that paper in an attempt to impress Miss Jones and his hard work had paid off. The contents of that paper touched Miss Jones in a way that he could never express straight out, and he hoped that she would understand that he wanted to touch her.

A loud noise in the dark startled him out of his reverie. Truitt and Mugwump were throwing stones at him to get his attention. They were urgently pointing at the front of the house, so Paul inched his way over and looked around the corner. A car was pulling into Miss Jones' driveway; the sound of the tires crunching through the gravel was quickly followed by the slam of the car door. Mr. Valentine, the science teacher, stepped out of the car and stood by the door, taking a long look around. Truitt and Mug- wump ducked back into the trees while Paul flattened himself against the building, too afraid to breathe. Most of the students hated Mr. Valentine because he was an asshole who tried to hide his malfunction by attempting to be cool. Didn't work though—he really was full of shit.

When he heard the doorbell ring, Paul made his way back over to the window.

They stood in front of the door, sharing an embrace. Mr. Valentine tilted her face toward him and kissed her lips. Miss Jones returned the kiss before gently pushing him away.

Motioning for Truitt and Mugwump to join him, Paul turned back to the window. After they hustled over, Paul put his finger to his lips for silence and pointed at the window.

The scene inside took a bad turn.

Miss Jones pushed Mr. Valentine toward the door and gestured for him to leave. Mr. Valentine stood in front of her with his arms stretched out, palms down, trying to calm her. She wasn't having it. With one hand on her hip, she looked him in the eye and pointed toward the door again. A quick step forward and the distance between them closed. Mr. Valentine had his hand around her waist and he easily lifted her off the floor. He spoke to her while he held her in mid-air, but his pleas seemed to fall on deaf ears as Miss Jones struggled to free herself from his grip. Mr. Valentine released her, a derisive grin on his face, and Miss Jones pushed him away, walked over to the door and held it open.

"Get out, asshole," Paul said softly.

"Miss Jones is one fine-ass White lady," Truitt said.

Mugwump and Paul looked at him, puzzled.

"What?" Truitt answered their look. "She is fine. She got a fat booty for a White woman. Paul! I know that she had to let you hit it from the back, right?"

"Shut up!" they both said.

But Truitt wasn't finished yet. "Women with asses like that be liking it from the back. I'm just saying."

Mr. Valentine and Miss Jones stood face to face in the open doorway. He made his final plea. She shook her head no. He snatched her by the wrist and then slammed the door shut. Miss Jones struggled against him but he was much too strong. He tossed her toward the couch and she bounced off of it to the floor. He stood over her and began to unbutton his shirt while she lay there; stunned.

"Oh shit!" Truitt said. "Mr. Valentine finna take some!"

"We have to help her," Paul said.

"How we gonna do that?"

"Oh shit!"

"Wait a minute," Mugwump said.

Miss Jones was lying on the floor but she had recovered now. Mr. Valentine threw his shirt on the floor and barked a command. Miss Jones sat up and removed the top of her old pajamas. A black bra held her healthy breasts at attention and Truitt sighed in appreciation. He barked another command and she wiggled out of her pants. Truitt cursed. Mr. Valentine reached down to lift her back onto the couch before quickly seizing her by the throat with one hand and unbuckling his pants with the other. When his trousers slid down to his knees, Miss Jones brought her knee up viciously into his crotch. Standing outside the window, a single groan could be heard from all three of them when Mr. Valentine's body deflated, his sexual energy evaporated, and Miss Jones struggled to get out from underneath him. Though he was in obvious pain, Mr. Valentine kept a tight grip on Miss Jones' neck and dragged her to the floor with him.

"Mr. Valentine is dead serious," Truitt said.

"Yeah. Wonder what he's gonna do when the family jewels stop hurting?" Mugwump said.

"I don't know," Paul said. "But we have to stop him. He's going to *take* the sex from her."

"Well, it's your woman, so you go in there."

"She is not my woman!"

"You was hitting it, right?" Paul simply stared at Truitt. "Then that's your woman. Go in there and man up!"

But none of them moved. They simply watched in horrid fascination as Mr. Valentine struggled with Miss Jones, ripped her underwear off and flipped her over onto her stomach. Miss Jones yelled out when he roughly thrust himself inside of her and took her sex. Her eyes squeezed shut when a deep grunt escaped from her lips. Then she seemed to look directly at Paul for a brief second before Mr. Valentine grabbed a hand full of her hair and yanked her head back.

They watched. When it was over, they quickly made their way back through the thicket of trees and back home...and they never spoke of the incident again.

Golden Theory

"**D**on't you even try to lie to me, boy!" As soon as the sentence left her mouth, Teresa was struck with the realization that her son was becoming a man. And he was growing up in her absence. Working two jobs left her with no free time, and by the time she came home, she barely had enough energy to fall into bed. His suddenly aloof manner was only one of the changes she had noticed about him lately.

"Ma, I'm not lying to you," Mugwump said.

She was still his mother, and she knew when he was hiding something. "I'm trying to finish off this homework. And it's really hard. Mr. Moore said that we have to decipher this Golden Theory and I'm not even close."

Sighing inwardly, she realized that she was missing her son's life, missing out on his growth. One day she would come home and find a grown man sitting at her table. Teresa had no idea what her son did while she was at work; didn't know where he was going, what he was doing, who he was hanging out with—none of the things that she should know about her teenage son—and she felt a pang inside at her failings as a mother.

"Trouble," she said. "Trouble don't know no names, Julius."

Mugwump looked up from his homework and smiled at her. "This Golden Theory is supposed to be a mathematical equation that is the basis of art, architecture, medicine and all kinds of other stuff. Some people even claim that it is the basis of life. But I can't seem to figure it out."

"Don't play me, boy!" she scolded him. "Now I heard that you've started hanging out on corners. With the drug boys at night. Am I hearing wrong?"

One of her co-workers at the pillow factory, Margie, had given Teresa a full report. Margie was a gossip, but her gossip usually started with a grain of truth and deteriorated with her re-telling.

"I don't get in trouble," Mugwump said. "You know that. I don't do drugs and I don't sell drugs. I'm not interested that way, Ma."

"I don't know what you do when I'm not here."

"So you don't trust me anymore? I'm the radical son now? When did I become the bad guy, huh?"

Something was wrong here. She could feel it. "I know that I'm not around that much anymore. We don't talk like we used to talk. And now you're growing up on me."

"Ma, I'm okay. Alright? There's some things that I have to work out by myself."

Sighing in resignation, she sat in the seat across from him. "And I guess you have to learn your lessons the hard way." She sighed again. "That is one thing you got from your daddy. You got a hard head."

"Ma," Mugwump said. "I got that from you."

Teresa laughed. "Come here, boy!" She leaned forward and folded him in a hug. When he moved back from her embrace, she held him at arm's length and locked her gaze on him. "You still telling lies, though. I know that." Mugwump started to object but Teresa spoke over him. "Maybe I used the wrong word. I shouldn't say 'lie,' but you are not telling the whole story." Change was inevitable, she mused. There was a basic shift in his entire demeanor, the warmth that usually existed between them had taken on a new dimension and she was worried. The streets were laying claim to her son, calling him, and she was helpless to stop it. Her son was becoming a hoodlum. "You still hanging with that evil boy?"

"Oh boy! Here we go again." She had no love for Truitt.

"Don't 'here we go again' me. That boy is a bad influence. And not merely with his actions. He will have you in the same mindset as him. Where do you think he is going to be after he gets out of high school? Right here is where you are going to find him! Right here on one of these corners. A hoodrat with all the trimmings."

A defiant glare flared in Mugwump's eyes. "I've got my own brain. I think for myself."

"Baby. If you hang out in France, you are going to speak French. And that has nothing to do with your mentality. You understand?"

Mugwump looked down at the paper on the table for a moment. "You know, a bunch of people have based some of their understanding of aesthetics—"

"Aesthetics?"

"Their judgment of beauty and such…and related it to this Golden Theory! It's a mathematical equation, is all. So even if it ain't true, it really is. That's the same way that people look at us. Mostly, it's all perception."

"What are you talking about, Julius?"

"I can't really explain it. I know that we go through what we go through to get to where we are. And we have to try to go further than before."

Teresa watched him intently before she spoke. The softness of her words came to him. "Listen. I can't stop you from having whatever friends that you want to have. I know that. But I'm your mother. There's no other person in the world who loves you more than I do. You know this. So I want you to do one thing for me. Just this one thing. Stay away from that boy. Okay?"

Mugwump didn't answer. His mother simply didn't understand. She hated Truitt and he didn't know why. Truitt was one of his best friends and they had gone through a lot together. Truitt always had his back. No matter what. Funny though, how she held Paul up as the saint of the trio and he was the one doing dirt! She was ready to hand Paul a halo at any given moment.

Images of Miss Jones and Mr. Valentine flashed through Mugwump's mind. The scene scared and dumbfounded him. The picture was still fresh in his mind: the moment when he swore that Miss Jones was looking directly at them! It was only for a second, but he was sure that she had seen them watching through her back window.

"I know plenty of hoodlums like him," his mother said, interrupting his thoughts. "They are either dead or in jail right now."

"Truitt is not a thug." His tone was sharper than he had intended, but he was growing weary of his mother talking about his friend like he was a gangster. "What you call thuggery is simply a way of life today. That's the culture we live in. Our reality."

Teresa rocked back, her eyes widened. "I know that you don't really believe that! Tell me you don't?" She moved closer to him and looked in his eyes. "Listen to me. Walking around here with your pants sagging off your behind and talking slang is a passing phase—like when we wore Afros and dashikis, but eventually you are going to have to step up into a grown-up world."

Mugwump looked down at his homework on the table. "It's more than that, Ma. Friendship has to mean something." Teresa was quiet. Mugwump seized the advantage. "And how come you don't never say anything about Paul? He is White, but you don't get down on him."

"Nothing to do with color." Teresa stood up. "His father is my supervisor down at the factory. He's a fair-minded man. Smart and fair."

"And what does that mean?" Mugwump felt his anger rising. She had no idea!

"That means that sometimes you have to see through to the spirit of a person."

"Oh yeah?" Mugwump put his anger in check. His voice was flat, emotionless when he told her, "So what kind of 'spirit' does it take to fuck your English teacher?"

Tinted Life

Truitt quietly opened the front door and stepped softly through. He was still puzzled over the violent episode that had taken place at Miss Jones' house. *Miss Jones is a freak anyway! Has to be! She's giving the sex to Paul, so she has to have some issues with her. Females can be so contrary!*

He would even be willing to bet money that Miss Jones enjoyed it when Mr. Valentine took her. Truitt replayed the scene over in his mind. They had watched in rapt fascination until Mr. Valentine was finished, leaving Miss Jones ravaged and beaten, but she never said a word in protest. She lay there on her back, breathing hard and staring at the ceiling. *Like she enjoyed it.*

His father's voice emanated from the living room. "So, I guess I'm supposed to give a damn, right?"

"I didn't care then and I don't care now, Troy," a feminine voice answered. Truitt wondered which woman his father was abusing this time. His dad was funny that way; sometimes he was a funny drunk, sometimes he was a mean drunk. Truitt didn't know if it was due to the brand of liquor he drank or what.

A woman and her daughter sat on the couch, bearing the brunt of Troy's anger. Defiance flared in her eyes as she returned his stare; her face, however, was drawn and weary. Her brown slacks and lighter brown chambray shirt gave her an air of serenity that belied her wrinkled brow as she spoke to Troy. Truitt could see a faded beauty behind the tension in her face which was barely hidden by the severe pull of her hair into a bun. His eyes shifted to her daughter, who sat stiffly with a mask of indifference worn stolidly on her face. She wore a pair of blue jeans and a loose-fitting sweatshirt and was simply a younger replica of the woman at her side. When she turned to look at Truitt, her dark brown eyes flashed with animosity and he nearly recoiled in surprise. The room went silent as all eyes fell on him and Truitt stood there, waiting. After a moment he finally spoke. "What's up?" Troy turned back to his drink and picked it up from the end table. After taking a big swallow, his voice blared out. "Truitt, this is the whore I told you about! Your mother."

"My mother is not a whore!" the girl yelled at Troy.

"Anna! Patricia took you away from me! She took my little girl."

"I'm not your little girl!"

"Not now. No. She ruined that."

"Wait a minute!" All heads turned at the force of Truitt's voice. He stepped tentatively toward the woman on the couch. Shock was overcome by curiosity as he fully took her in; her chin upturned in defiance, her thin nose that trailed down to her lips that were set in a firm line, her skin the rich brown of walnuts; her beauty was natural. That is until he looked into her eyes. There was no emotion in them as Patricia returned his stare, and a coldness reached out and brought Truitt up short.

In a slightly trembling voice he asked, "You're my mother?" She nodded her head firmly in agreement and Truitt went on. "I have no memory of you. How old was I…like two years old…when you left? I always thought that…" Words failed him, so Truitt turned to her daughter. "And you're my sister? Anna?" She didn't respond but her eyes held the same coldness as her mother's.

"That's right." Troy was getting louder as the liquor was finding its way home. "And now she's back."

Patricia looked at Truitt, her eyes still hard. "Troy, as always, rants and raves without having full knowledge. I'm not 'back.' I will never come back to his madness. Life is much too short." The steeliness of her tone hardened Truitt. He quickly realized that this would be no happy reunion. "My daughter…"

"Our daughter, Patricia! Our daughter!"

"Our daughter," she conceded. "You're right. Our daughter. But you don't know how much I wish that I could change that." Troy glowered at her before tossing down the remainder of his drink and turning back to the kitchen. Patricia stared after him, nodding her head.

"You treated me like I was less than a woman, Troy. You didn't know how to love me. And I was your wife." Troy returned with a full glass in his hand. "You made me hate you."

"But you left me, too." Truitt took the chair, facing her.

"A boy needs to be with his father."

"And that's it?" Truitt leaned forward. "That's the reason? You have got to be kidding me!" Truitt rose to his feet and stood in front of his mother. Hard eyes looked back at him. "You know, he never talks about you; except when he's like he is now. But I never listen to him when he's getting drunk. I figured that there has to be more to my mother than that." He paused to fight against the tremble that threatened to creep into his voice. "Did you ever think about me at all?"

Patricia's expression softened for an instant. "Truitt, you were a baby when I left."

"But you left anyway." Truitt fell back in his seat.

"Damn right she did," Troy bellowed. "And she took my baby girl."

"I'm not your baby girl!" Anna shouted.

"What have you done to her?" Troy growled at Patricia. "What have you done?" His eyes swung back to Anna. "I'm your father!"

"Well, this is not about you, Troy," Patricia broke in. "Or you either Truitt. We came here for a reason."

"I can't wait to hear this." Troy leaned against the

counter in an exaggerated stance of patience. "Why the hell did you bring your ass back here?"

Patricia and Anna exchanged a long look, a solemn silence settling between them. "Anna deserved a chance to meet you, Truitt. You are her brother and I can't stand in the way of that. That's not what I want to leave her with. I can't leave her with that." Patricia paused, seeming to struggle with herself before she continued. Anna reached over and took her hand, urging her to go on.

"What about me," Troy demanded as he watched them with a look of contempt on his face. "I haven't seen my baby girl!" Anna turned a sharp look toward him. "What have you done to her? You spent time putting your poison in her, didn't you?"

"Troy." Patricia spoke to him in a matter of fact voice. "You might not have noticed, but Anna is a woman now. She has her own mind."

"She's not even eighteen yet, Patricia," Troy said. "You call that grown?"

"I'm in my second year of college." Anna's voice was heavy with animosity when she added, "Troy."

"She graduated a year early." Patricia beamed with pride. "She's on her way. She's never going to have to deal with a man trying to destroy her; physically or spiritually." She looked meaningfully at Troy. "Never."

The history between them was too deep to ever be placed in the past; the man she once loved had forever hurt her and the pain would never die. Rising to her feet, she faced Truitt and extended her hand. Truitt noticed that she seemed a little shaky on her feet, like she was tired and was only buoyed by the strength of her convictions.

"Truitt. I'm trying to convince myself that you aren't your father's son. And I'm hoping that you don't resent me for what I did. But it had to be done in order for me to survive." She reached out and took his hand, looking into his eyes and hoping that her words held meaning for him. "I hope that you don't hate me."

Truitt was silent. He needed a moment. All of the day's events came crashing down on him at once, crashing like thunderous rain. He needed shelter, a respite, before heading back into the whirlwind.

Patricia released his hand and stepped away, her hard demeanor returned. "But if you can't find it in your heart to do so, then that's okay, too. Like I said, it's not about you. And it's not about me."

"So what is it about then?" Truitt found his voice. "Ma."

He didn't mean to say that word; it slipped out of his mouth of its own accord, a word he had never uttered before. She turned back to him. When she looked at Truitt, her expression had softened.

"I don't want Anna to be alone in the world." Her shoulders slumped in resignation and she looked to her daughter once again. Anna nodded her head, encouraging her to continue. "You see, Truitt, I've got cancer. And I'm dying."

Truitt

"So what are you going to do now?" Troy set his drink down on the counter.

"Don't try to act like you care," Patricia spoke without looking at him. She watched Truitt, gauging his reaction. "I don't plan on anything but dying."

Patricia had breast cancer and she told them that they hadn't caught it in time. After a series of operations and radiation treatments, the cancer was more widespread than the doctors had originally thought. It had taken her months to come to grips with her diagnoses, but after acceptance came the process of getting her life in order. Death hung in the air...and then everything changed. Truitt felt a sudden pang of being lost, then found, then lost again; a helplessness that was quickly followed by anger—and regret.

"So that's why you came back," Truitt said.

"The only important thing left for me is for Anna to know her brother. The rest is life."

"But what about me?" Troy was becoming irate from being ignored. "I have rights, too! I'm the man up in here!"

"You see," Patricia replied hotly. "That's where you're wrong! You're *a* man up in here, not *the* man! You've always been that way."

"An asshole!" Anna's voice rang out. Troy was taken aback at his estranged daughter's words. "We've had a good life without you. I've had a good life not knowing you. And that doesn't need to change." The calmness of her tone lent even more sting to her conviction and Troy was stunned beyond replying. Truitt watched the exchange wordlessly. His father was no saint but, alcohol and womanizing aside, he still deserved respect as the man who had brought them into the world. The only problem that Truitt had was that there wasn't enough love inside of him to come to his father's defense.

"I wanted to meet you, Truitt," Anna said. "Whether you are interested in meeting *me* is another issue. And if you are really anything like him…" She indicated Troy with a quick nod of her head. "…Then we can cut this short right now."

Truitt looked over at his father. Anna's words had stung him, and Troy turned his back, hunched over the counter and looked down at his drink. Unbidden questions popped up in Truitt's mind. *What happened between his mother and father? What could have been so terrible that she would take his sister and never return?* Ultimately, it didn't matter, Truitt determined. His only choice was to deal with the present, the reality of the here and now.

Turning to Anna, he said, "I'm only me. Please remember that."

"What the hell does that mean?" Troy looked over his shoulder at them. "You can't be like your daddy, boy? I raised you, didn't I? I kept a roof over your head and food in your mouth!" He turned and purposefully walked over and faced them as they looked up at him. "I'm sick and tired of this shit. I have rights and I'm gonna get them."

"What are you talking about, Troy?"

"I'm saying that I have rights also! I'm the father. I have a right to see my daughter; just like you have the right to see your son. That's the law!"

Anna stood to face him. "But I don't want to see you, Troy."

"Don't matter what you want. You ain't eighteen yet and I'm still your father."

"And what does that mean? You haven't been there for me for my entire life. How are you my father?"

"I just am. Nothin' you can do about that. So I get to see you." Troy's voice softened. "You're my daughter. Don't you understand that?" Tentatively, he reached out for her but let his hand drop when he saw the disdain in her eyes.

"You are just the same, Troy." Patricia stood next to her daughter. "You still think that you can make everything the way you want it to be. Make every person fit to your liking." She nodded her head. "You still haven't learned."

"Well, this is the one situation where I can get what I want," Troy mocked her. "You see, Anna's not eighteen.

I can still get visitation rights." He looked down at Patricia. "That is, if you don't take her and run away again."

A small smile played at the edges of Patricia's lips. "I have no intention of going anywhere. We came here for a reason. Truitt, and that's it. You want to try to get visitation, you go right ahead. But you think about one thing. That is, if you remember."

"What?"

"If you remember my baby's birthday."

Troy paused for a moment when the realization hit him. "In two months," he said.

"That's right. And then you don't have any rights whatsoever. So do what you have to do. In the end, it won't matter. It will still be up to her."

A streak of anger crossed Troy's face. "But I can still go to court for my visitation rights! You can't do nothin' about that."

"Go ahead," Patricia said. "But, Troy, what do you hope to accomplish?"

"I want my daughter to get to know me." He looked pointedly at Patricia. "And I mean outside of what nasty stuff you've been feeding her about me."

"Man, this is truly jacked up!" Truitt said. "How do Anna and I get to be brother and sister without a mother and father?" He rose from the couch and walked over to stand by the television. Picking up the remote control, he began to nervously switch it from hand to hand while he spoke. "This is too much all at once. I've never had a mother, or a sister. All I had was my father. I wouldn't even know how to talk to her."

Anna went over to face him. "I know." They watched each other for a moment before Truitt reached out with his hand. "Hey, sis. I'm Truitt."

Anna smiled.

Man Law

"It's a dick thing."

"What?" Teresa couldn't believe what she was hearing from Paul Sanderson.

"Well, that's the way that my son describes it," he said.

She had been utterly shocked when her son told her about young Paul and the schoolteacher. But she was even more stumped by his father's reaction. Anger or denial, she had expected, but what she had received was a sense of puffed-up pride.

"I already know." Paul Sanderson stood and looked out of the glass windows of his office that overlooked the floor of the pillow factory. The sounds of machinery could be heard as the workers manned their stations. "He's been going over there for a while now."

"And you're okay with this? You think that it's okay for this grown-ass woman to take advantage of your son?"

"Advantage? You think that she's taking advantage of him?" Paul Sanderson leaned forward and rested his hands on the desk. Teresa sat in a chair across from him, a look of disbelief on her face. Teresa was one of the best workers at the plant; she was reliable, intelligent and, from all reports, an ideal employee, and young Paul valued her son's friendship immensely. The few times that he had interacted with Teresa, Paul had found her to be easygoing yet sincere and determined; the kind of worker who got things done. He knew that she was a single mother and that she was doing an excellent job raising her son. Mugwump had been a guest at his home on many occasions and he was glad that his son had a friend who had his values in the right places. They both stayed out of trouble and they both worked hard at school.

There were many different ways to find mischief, and Paul was happy that his son hadn't given him any major problems. Part of that stemmed from the company that he kept and, for that, Paul respected the woman who sat in front of him. But this was an issue she couldn't possibly deal with.

"Listen," he said. "What my son is going through right now is what is called *every man's fantasy!* As a man, I can tell you that he's living the dream right now. As the kids say nowadays, it's all good."

Teresa looked him in the eyes. "You're serious?"

"Why would you think I'm not?"

"You don't get it, do you! You think that your sixteen-year-old son is mature enough to enter into a sexual relationship with a grown woman?"

"That's just it. He's not in a relationship with her. The only relationship is between a young man and his sex drive. It's only sex."

"What the hell…"

Paul Sanderson pointed a finger at her as he sat down. "You see, there is a fundamental difference between the way that men and women view sex. Even at sixteen, my son is not bringing any emotional baggage into the sex. It is only sex. No more. No less."

"She's abusing her position. That's sexual assault. Statutory rape!"

"Yet my son keeps going back." Paul leaned back in his chair and regarded Teresa for a moment. "Look, I could see your point if the teacher was holding a gun to his head…" Teresa started to object but Paul talked over her. "Or using force of any kind! But the only thing that she is doing is offering sex to him and he is happily accepting. I don't see a victim here."

Men were crazy when it came to sex and she was beginning to understand where their attitudes originated. It was hard to believe that sex was such an unthinking act to them and that they were absolutely fine with that.

"That's because you're thinking with the wrong head," Teresa said. "No offense."

"None taken," Paul said. "That's what men do; especially when we're sixteen years old."

"Mr. Sanderson?"

"Please. Call me Paul."

"Paul." Teresa smiled. "Paul, that's some bullshit right there."

"Teresa. Would you at least give me credit for being more in touch with what it's like to be a sixteen-year-old male? At least give me credit for having a perspective that you might never understand."

Teresa was quiet. A thoughtful smile played across Paul Sanderson's face. "Okay, Teresa. What would you have me do?"

"Have that hussy put in jail. Under the jail, in fact. Then throw away the key."

"Is that what you would do if this happened to your son? If he came to you to have an honest talk about sex and his sex life, you would have the woman arrested?"

"If she was his English teacher, hell yes!"

"Do you think that he would ever talk to you about sex again after that? Would he come to you for any guidance? Or any questions at all?"

"Yes," Teresa answered hotly. "My son knows he can talk to me."

"No argument there," he answered. "I've met your son, Teresa. And you've done an excellent job with him. He's smart and he has a different type of maturity about him. He's an exceptional young man and I think it had to take an exceptional woman to raise him."

"Thank you."

"No. Thank you," Paul answered. "Your son has been a positive influence on my son and I'm grateful for that. I say all of that to let you know that what we are talking about is not a commentary on your relationship with your son. Not at all. Okay?"

"So, what are you saying?"

"I'm saying that there are aspects of male sexuality that are simply unexplainable. There are going to be issues that, as a woman, you are not going to be able to relate to."

"It's a dick thing," she said derisively. She caught herself getting upset. Was he trying to say that she couldn't raise her son to be a man? Because she was a woman! *Male chauvinism is alive and well!*

"I know it's hard to step outside of your own personal realm of experience, but for your son you may have to." *He's right. Let me listen to what the man has to say.*

"All men are not the same," Teresa said. "I've learned that much. My son has been taught to respect women."

"Understood." Paul leaned back in his chair and rested his chin on his hand. "Thing is…we don't equate respect with sex. Respect. Emotions. All of that really has nothing to do with it. We don't bring those thought processes into the bed with us. Nothing but lust. It's not a conscious decision. It just is."

"Ya'll are slaves to your lust, huh?"

"You say that like it's a bad thing."

Paul Sanderson smiled. Teresa laughed.

"Whatever." Teresa rose from her chair. "But you need to put a stop to it immediately. You're playing with fire and Paul might get burned."

Mugwump

"When we come back around this corner, you better not be standing here." The harsh voice came from the window of the cop car that idled in the street. Mugwump stared back at them with contempt etched across his young face.

"This year two-five, po-po." He watched them with his hands stuffed in the pockets of his baggy jeans.

A look of wonder spread over the cop's face. He reminded himself who this boy was, that he really didn't belong out here on the corner with the hardcore crowd whose future only held bars and lockdowns. "This is my corner, boy! Better you should learn that now. Didn't you see all the little drug dealers start hauling ass when I pulled up? This is my corner. A hard lesson that you gonna learn if you standing here when we come back."

"See," Mugwump said. "You can't put shit like that in the air no more. This corner just as free as I am."

"Woooooo, weeeeee." The cop's chest heaved as he exhaled. He fixed Mugwump in a hard stare before he spoke. "Maybe." He paused to say something to his partner. A cop hat sat on the dashboard and Mugwump took note of the short, military haircut affixed to a large skull and hard, lifeless eyes that bristled in the dark night. A grimace stretched across a severe face like it was supposed to pass for a smile. "You got a choice to make. Play with your freedom or play with God. I don't see you winning—either way—if I pull up around this corner again and you still here. You better find your place, boy. Holla!"

The cop car pulled off.

"Cops ain't shit!" Mugwump yelled after them. When he saw the police car disappear around the corner, the denizens of the night materialized from the darkness as if by the wave of a magician's wand. A few of them sauntered over to Mugwump.

"Man, you better stop fuckin' with po-po like that!" Laylow was the oldest drug dealer on the block. He was born Leonard James but told everyone his real name was Laylow. He was life-long. That's what he always said. "I'm life-long in this game." That was his answer to any question of his street sensibility. He wore a pair of baggy jeans and an oversized New Jersey Devils hockey jersey with a thick gold chain around his neck. His ball cap was twisted at an angle on his head with a gang of braids hanging down to the nape of his neck. Mugwump felt a pang of envy when he noticed the fresh, new pair of Timberlands that Laylow was playing.

"Just 'cause you ain't holdin' nothin' don't mean that

they won't beat you down," Laylow said. He had seen Mugwump's type before; the kind of youngster who would find allure in the action of the corner but who really had no idea what it was to live the life. They always learned street lessons the hard way.

"Go 'head on," Mugwump said. "I ain't done nothing!"

"Like you need to, nigga!" Joe and Togs led a group of dealers who held court on the corner of Headlands and Sunrise. This corner was the hottest spot in the city and every smoker in the area knew it. Unfortunately, so did the police. "Ain't you been watching TV, nigga? For, like the past four hundred years!" Joe and Togs slapped hands and even Mugwump had to join in on the laughter. "They will fuck you up for standing too Black up in this joint," Joe finished. They all looked up and down the block, as if searching for some silent cue that the police would come speeding back around the corner.

They all knew the routine. Every night, like clockwork, the police would swing by to check on the corner, to remind everyone that they were the long arm of the law. Every dealer on the corner knew what time the slinging would have to stop and they learned to fade into the folds of the darkness until the police finished their tour. It was all a street game, a ghetto version of hide-and-seek that they played nightly.

Every one of them knew—except Mugwump.

Mugwump didn't do drugs, either selling or buying. It was a weakness that he never wanted in his life, even though most of his friends liked to get high and called him a nerd. One day he had explained to them why he stayed away from drugs but his reasons fell on deaf ears and soon they began calling Mugwump a hood preacher, which pleased him to no end. A preacher. An injustice reliever. A young man who would spit in the face of the authority that ruled by employing racist wrongs.

Not that he was violent—Mugwump wouldn't credit himself with being able to whip a horsefly in a hurricane—but he did find himself harboring violent thoughts that manifested themselves through his abrasive, biting tongue. He talked a good fight.

Mugwump was a living paradox. He attended Tillman High School and was a serious student, vigorously scrapping for every "A" he could get, taking every class that the programs of study allowed. He could have graduated from high school when he was a junior but instead he stayed in school and began taking classes that would prepare him for college. So he had set tongues to wagging when he began to hang out on the street corner with the thugs.

The drug dealers, many of them guys he went to school with, had threatened him the first night he started hanging out but Mugwump showed no fear, even when they claimed they smelled pork when they saw him.

"I ain't no po-po," he told them.

"So, what you want out here then? You straight?"

"I don't do drugs," Mugwump said. "In any form or fashion."

"You in the wrong place then, homie."

Just then, a police car came cruising up Headlands.

"Po-po," a voice yelled out. Instantly the corner was cleared, leaving Mugwump standing alone when the black and white stopped at the curb.

"What you doing out here, son?" It was a Black cop. The one they called Supercop. He was well known in the 'hood for his dislike of Black folks. Emmett "Supercop" Jones was the most notorious officer on the force and he didn't particularly care how many Black folks he broke in the pursuit of his duty. Supercop kept tabs on the corner hoodlums and he knew that Mugwump wasn't one of them. This kid was one of the good ones, not dirtied by the low expectations of these brainwashed, soon-to-be jailbirds; yet here he was, late at night on the corner at the wrong place, and the wrong time. Supercop knew that the call of the streets had ruined more than one life, exchanging promises for prison sentences; he hoped that he could make this kid see the light.

"My daddy been gone a long time," Mugwump said. "He's one of those statistics you read about. A deadbeat dad. A morally corrupt man." Mugwump paused. "You ain't him, are you?"

Supercop bit down on the bitter response that sprang to his lips. *Here*, Supercop mused. *Here is our future. Even the young, Black men who take advantage of the educational system succumb to the lure of the streets. This kid is a carbon copy of my nephew, Johnny, a good young man with as much street smarts as book smarts. Yet this knuckle- head is out on a street corner late at night; a place where souls go stagnant.* "Real smart," Supercop eyed him. "One of them smart asses." He leaned out the window. "If I was your daddy, I would whup your ass for being out here on this corner. You know what's going on out here. Get yourself home and off my corner, son."

Mugwump watched him.

"If I get out of this car," Supercop said. "There will be some real issues before I get back in." Mugwump raised both of his hands over his head. "Ahhh," Supercop said. "That's the pose right there. Black man spread. Ever since Kunta we've been taking that stance. Physically, symbolically…whatever name you want to put to it. Racially!" He leaned back in the front seat of the car and nodded his head. "Niggas!" he said. "But not all of us, though, I'm glad to say. Some Black folks know how to live and learn. The rest are just niggas."

Mugwump's expression turned sour at that word coming out of Supercop's mouth. As far as he was concerned, Supercop was the epitome of self-hatred. He treated Black folks like cattle.

"Is that you, son? Are you a nigga?"

"All that, because of where I'm standing?" Mugwump pointed at the ground. "From where I'm standing, that makes you something too. An officer…or an overseer. Depending on the system you work in. And me? I can't see much difference between the two."

An angry scowl crossed Supercop's face as he reached

down and wrenched the car door open. He stepped onto the sidewalk when Mugwump spoke. "What you got? A nightstick or a whip?"

Supercop paused with his hand on his baton. He looked up and down the block and saw lights shining from nearly every house on the street. He knew that there were many eyes looking out at him from behind the curtains and glass—not that he cared what they saw, only what they could say on the evening news. He stood in front of the open car door and glared at Mugwump.

"You got a smart mouth, boy. Real smart. But let me tell you something." In a flat, menacing voice he said, "You better get off these streets and back into school before something bad happens to you." Supercop stepped closer until his face was inches away from Mugwump's. "All kinds of things happen out here, *Julius!*" Mugwump's head snapped back when Supercop called him by his real name. "Remember that shit," Supercop continued, "before you come out your mouth like that again. Because you might come up short."

Mugwump was speechless. A shiver of apprehension ran up his spine but he was on a mission and had enough faith in himself to stand tall. This was the road he wanted to travel, to take a stand for what he knew to be right, no matter what force he would have to face, and he knew that if he backed down now, it meant he would be backing down forever.

"Souls can stagnate, you know." Mugwump answered

the menace on Supercop's face with a poetic verse he remembered from a school text. "When your ideals get all dull and void, spiritual growth ceases and your very existence becomes routine."

Supercop arched an eyebrow, puzzled.

"That's why I'm here," Mugwump explained. "So my soul won't ever, ever stagnate. Like my daddy." Mugwump looked him in the eye. "That ain't you, is it?"

Supercop's body tensed as if he had been struck. His eyes narrowed to slits and his knuckles cracked as his hands balled into fists, causing Mugwump to wonder if he had pushed the cop too far. Sparks of anger shot from Supercop's eyes as he fought to calm himself, controlling the anger that he rarely kept contained. Usually, Supercop would have spilled some blood on the ground if anyone had spoken to him like that. All it would have taken was the slightest hint of a harsh remark and this kid was really pushing his luck. "You had your chance," he hissed. "Next time, you go down with all the other thugs." With that, he made his way back to the police car, turned and fixed Mugwump with a steely glare before climbing into the front seat. After mumbling something to his partner the car pulled away from the curb and went down Headlands.

After that confrontation, Mugwump's presence on the corner was accepted and he received an education in street life that settled deep inside of him. He felt a connection to his Blackness, a belonging that made him stand stronger and made him resolve more than ever to make his life count, to live with a purpose—to make a difference.

The street corner taught Mugwump many life lessons. Soon he was laughing with the 'hood, arguing with the 'hood, and sometimes even rapping with the 'hood. There was never a shortage of wannabe rappers stepping to the spot with some lyrical wordplay that needed street corner validation. Mugwump tripped them all out when he first spit because he rapped about subjects that no one understood and he would end up having to explain what his flow was all about. He put feeling into his subject matter, whether it was the first runaway slaves, Thomas Brother Jefferson's Black children, Caligula, Joe Frazier, internal oppression—but they would all laugh and tell him how corny and whack his shit was. Mugwump laughed with them, accepting their laughter as an invitation into a world where his bond was his words. He took a step toward manhood on the corner.

One day, he looked over at Joe, Tugs and Laylow, each in his own slinging position, good vantage points from which they could spot the police from each direction. Mugwump busted out with some rhymes:

"*Speaking of dank!*
Umma smokin' and strokin' prime time playa
Feenin' and scheming and dreamin' like a hay-ya
Mad skills for your windpipe
Like a two-day-old curse
I can even do it! In reverse!

She got golden mounds of delicious
Sexin' muscles, six degrees vicious
Shawtee was halfway up to when-even
Gave her all she wanted—plus seven!

Mugwump finished with a flourish, one hand on his crotch the other raised in a fist. Laylow laughed. "Whack, jacked and corny as all hell!"

"And that's real," Joe and Tug agreed.

"Ya'll don't know nothing about my higher flow," Mugwump said. "It's my pontification of expressed alliteration, allegorical content and metaphorical skills…"

"Po-po!" came the lookout cry. In a matter of seconds the street was empty, except for Mugwump, who stood there alone when the cop car pulled up. The first officer who had warned him off the corner regarded Mugwump for a moment. He took his hat off and slammed it on the dashboard before he finally spoke. "Now didn't we have a conversation earlier." He pushed the car door open and stepped out onto the sidewalk. He slammed the door shut and stepped toward Mugwump, regarding him as if he were a nuisance that could easily be remedied. Mugwump stole a quick glance at the other policeman who was driving the car but he couldn't make out a face. The cop stood over him waiting for a response. "Didn't I tell you to get off my corner?"

"That was a command," Mugwump said. "Like Moses or something."

"True. It was a command. An order. What? You think

that commands don't apply to you? Commands apply to you, too. So why are you still standing on my corner?"

"I'll obey God," Mugwump replied. "And God you ain't."

"Now that is funny," the cop said and moved in closer. "But you don't know, do you?" He paused. "Let me ask you something. Did you not notice that all the little drug dealers scatter whenever we come by? The power to make niggas disappear. Now that is the power of God! Houdini can't even pull that one off." The cop burst out laughing. He reminded Mugwump of his Uncle Jaycee. They were about the same height and complexion and had that same glint in their eyes. But the similarities ended there. His Uncle Jaycee had a calm demeanor and a slow, ingratiating smile that came from his soul while this cop was tripping.

"This corner ain't no church," Mugwump said. "Can I get an Amen?"

"You're welcome," the cop said. He studied Mugwump for a moment and when he spoke next, his voice took on a different tone. "Didn't I tell you to get off this corner before I came back? You really don't know, do you?"

Mugwump had an idea. "So what," he said.

"So what?" The cop was incredulous. "Do you know who you're talking to? This is so what!" A sharp, right punch landed in Mugwump's midsection and dropped him to his hands and knees. "Running your smart-ass mouth."

"Leave that boy alone, po-po!" a voice protested from somewhere in the vast darkness of the alleyway.

"Ya'll always fuckin' with somebody, you dirty bastards," another voice pitched in.

The cop glanced up and down the block, gave a quick check of the alleyway, but quickly turned back to the fallen Mugwump.

"See," he said. "Now you've gone and got the natives all restless." He grabbed a handful of shirt and yanked Mugwump to his feet. "Now get the fuck off my corner." The cop was nose to nose with him, spittle flying from his mouth while he glared with barely contained rage.

This is it, Mugwump reasoned. *Now I'll find out how far my belief will take me. Can I really stand up?*

He measured his words before he spoke. "It takes a punk bitch to punch somebody behind a badge. I bet you beat your kids like that, too, huh? So what?"

A guttural roar rang out and he slammed Mugwump against the brick wall and thrust another blow into his stomach. Pain exploded throughout his entire body— he had never been hit so hard in his entire life—and Mugwump collapsed to the pavement. Agony rocked him as he lay, groaning, face down on the sidewalk. Sucking air through gritted teeth, he tried to will the pain away but he felt as if the punch had passed through his gut and ruptured his backbone.

"Get off that boy, you cop muthafucka!" a chorus of dissenting voices rang out in the night and the cop scanned the alley in an attempt to find the source.

"Somebody need to beat on ya'll like that!"

"A brother can't even stand outside now! Bitches!"

Mugwump pushed himself up to one knee. A slow anger was building in him. His stomach felt as if something had been knocked loose and the pain was not lessening.

The cop stood over him, yelling back at the disembodied voices. "Shut up! I can find each and every one of you, so you better back your nose up out of this business! You better mind your own! Because this could be you next!"

A roar of dischord answered from the darkness and the cop seemed agitated by it. Mugwump felt empowered by the ghetto chants that bombarded the angry cop. His people were standing up for him. Time for him to stand up.

With one foot under him, Mugwump launched himself toward the cop and brought his fist squarely into the officer's jaw, which sent him crashing to the ground. There was a shocked second of silence as the cop lay still on the concrete, not moving at all, but the eerie quiet was shattered when Supercop emerged from the police car. He took in the entire scene in a swift glance and pulled his nightstick from his belt as he made his way around the front end of the car.

"Shit!" Mugwump said as Supercop rushed toward him with the nightstick brandished like a club. Instinct screamed at Mugwump to shrink away, to try to fend off the blows that were surely coming but he disregarded those voices. Instead, he put his hands down at his sides and stood tall. The nightstick came down hard on his shoulder and a blast of pain jolted him, but Mugwump refused to fall. The next blow connected with the side of Mugwump's head and this time he went down in a heap with his head cradled in his hands.

Supercop took a moment to put his nightstick back in the holster before kicking him in the ribs. "Boy, you are more than crazy! You don't hit no cops!"

"I'm bleeding inside," Mugwump groaned and spit out a glob of blood.

"Well here come some more," Supercop said.

Mugwump's body was lifted off the ground with the force of the kick and he rolled over on his back and gasped to the sky. Supercop was moving slowly toward him with a maniacal grin spread across his face. What happened next stunned Mugwump. Supercop went crashing headfirst into the brick wall and Mugwump looked up to see Laylow standing there with a tire iron in his hand.

"Now, muthafucka!" Laylow raised the metal bar overhead, preparing to strike again when Supercop lunged at his legs and tackled him. Laylow was a big kid and he tried to wrestle, but Supercop was bigger and stronger so he quickly overpowered the young man. Using a forearm bar across Laylow's neck, Supercop swung and hit him with a powerful blow to the face that nearly knocked Laylow out. A second blow was on its way when Joe and Tug came flying out of the alley and tackled

Supercop. The two young kids battled with the much bigger man but he was quickly gaining the upper hand. Even in his injured state, Supercop was still hard to handle. He shoved Joe away from him and grabbed Tug by his neck and dragged him to the ground. Before he could do any damage to Tug, Laylow emerged with a rock in his hand, which he brought down on the back of Supercop's head.

Jayrat and his boys came in behind Laylow and soon there was a crowd of thugs flailing away at Supercop. A vicious kick to the face and Supercop flopped against the wall before the blows began to rain on him, pinning his body upright and holding it there while more punches battered him. When he finally went down, a cheer erupted from his attackers as they stood over him and a few people spit on him. A crazed yell rang out and they turned in time to see Laylow come running toward them with a metal trashcan raised over his head. Supercop had inflicted many cruelties on Laylow, often, it seemed, purely for his own amusement. Now a path magically opened as Laylow rushed toward the prone figure and smashed the garbage can across his face.

Mugwump fought against the wave of dizziness that washed over him. A wail of sirens could be heard in the distance and the crowd quickly dispersed, leaving him on the corner with the two beaten police officers. Blood leaked from the corner of his mouth as a coughing jag seized him. He pushed himself up against the wall and fought to manage the pain that throbbed in his side. *I gotta get outta here!* The wail of the sirens grew closer. Mugwump struggled to his feet but lost his balance and fell into the alley. The ground swam beneath him and he couldn't seem to focus so he concentrated on trying to put one foot in front of the other. The alley! He grabbed that thought out of the air and hung onto it. *The alley!*

He reached out for the darkness in an attempt to seize the night and lurched toward it like a drunken zombie. *It's safe. In the alley.* A sudden burst of energy pushed him forward but again he lost his balance and crashed into a pile of garbage cans near the side of the building.

"Shit!" His scream echoed into the silence of the darkness but only night noises responded; harsh contacts of windows slamming shut, the thump of wood meeting wood as doors were firmly closed…the sirens of the police drawing even closer.

End of the alley. Mugwump struggled to his feet and was instantly hit with the odd sensation of dizziness and darkness swirling through his vision. He spotted a green dumpster further down the alley, which his mind grasped and held as if it were safe haven from his troubles. "Got to make it." He felt blood flooding into his mouth with every word but he forced himself down the alley toward the safe, green dumpster. The sirens stopped in front of the store, tires screeched and orders were barked into radios as the crime scene was cordoned off.

Mugwump made it to the dumpster. "Safe." The word tumbled from his lips as he fell behind the dumpster and darkness began to invade his vision. The last thing he saw before he lost consciousness was a cop standing in front of him, greatly obscured by the giant barrel of his gun.

The last thing he heard was a gunshot.

Truitt

Truitt had doubts about which way he wanted to go, which team he wanted to play for, yet he managed to keep his crisis hidden from his friends. He had vague yearnings to experiment, curious to see what same-sex loving felt like; not strong desires, nothing with enough strength to spark him to action, but flashes of lust that pricked his imagination. There was no doubt in his mind, no question at all about his love for women. The attraction was instinctive, primal, and ingrained in his soul, but if he tried to be honest with himself, he had moments of curiosity.

But he would never take that step. He hoped not.

He made his way up the darkened street and stopped at a three-step porch that led to Uncle Dope's apartment. The porch was set out with colorful potted flowers and a red, black and green welcome mat. Truitt pulled the screen door open and looked up at the ornate, brass knocker. He pushed the doorbell.

Uncle Dope swung the door open, grinned at him and ushered Truitt inside. When Truitt stepped through the door, he was reminded that Uncle Dope had the eye of an interior decorator. His apartment felt warm and lived in, comfortable but stylish, and instantly Truitt knew that there would be no slouching and lazing on this man's couch. A love seat was positioned cattycorner with the couch and a decorative single chair was pushed up against the wall beneath the window. African artwork adorned the walls, artistic paintings in expensive frames and various statues of wood and brass stood on nearly every table and vertical surface available. Over in a corner, in a kitchen chair, sat Gloria. Her eyes were glazed and unfocused, the beginnings of a nod settling over her. Truitt felt an old familiar stirring, one that Gloria always brought out of him whenever he saw her. She appealed to his senses. Gloria was an attractive woman with bright, inquisitive eyes and a quick smile that dazzled in its fullness when she was healthy—but drugs had made her sick. The light in her eyes dimmed when she was in the grips of her habit and she never seemed to be happy.

"Sit down, young man," Uncle Dope indicated the plush, light colored sofa. "You know that you my boy and all that?" Truitt considered Uncle Dope his mentor. Uncle Dope was the only adult that kept Truitt in the corner of his eye. Whenever Truitt had issues with his dad, Uncle Dope would appear out of no-where with words of quiet encouragement.

But this time was different. Truitt didn't know if he could talk to Uncle Dope about his mother and his newfound sister. He was really hesitant about discussing something so personal, something so close to his heart that he really wasn't sure if he was honestly evaluating his own feelings. *And what kind of man can't even be honest with himself?*

Uncle Dope stretched out on the love seat opposite Truitt and stretched his legs out, crossing them at the ankles. Uncle Dope was old. But he didn't look his age and definitely didn't act his age. Gloria was at least twenty years younger than he was and she was currently nodding out in the corner.

"And I appreciate it, my Duke," Truitt said.

"I know you do, man! That ain't my point. That ain't what I'm talking about." Uncle Dope paused to rub his fingers over his close-cut hair. He kept it short and wavy but, for the first time, Truitt thought he saw a few strands of gray starting to creep in. It was funny how quickly Uncle Dope was aging since he started chasing after Gloria. "You slippin,' boy." Uncle Dope twisted his lips in disapproval. "I been seeing you."

"Slipping? Slipping how?"

"You done started getting you some draws, huh?"

Truitt smiled shyly. Uncle Dope leaned forward, excited. "Who took your cherry, boy? Huh? You got one of them big-boned girls, didn't you?"

Truitt's smile disappeared.

"I know it! Come on now! One thing that you got to learn is that what you like is simply what you like! Don't you never deny your lust! I don't give a damn what these women out here try to train you to believe, I want you to always listen to your dick!"

Truitt laughed. Uncle Dope chuckled, too.

"He won't steer you wrong! At least, not at first. And since you just starting out...follow your dick. Let him lead the way."

Truitt was lost in thought. *So what is it about then? Ma.*

"You heard me, Truitt?" Uncle Dope was watching him.

"Follow my dick?"

"Yessuh! Full speed. Straight ahead." Casting a quick glance at Gloria, who sat in the corner with her eyes closed, he leaned toward Truitt. "Did she tear you up? Come on, now! The first couple of times can be disastrous. That's make or break time right there. How long?"

Truitt's forehead wrinkled in puzzlement.

"How long did you see her for?" Uncle Dope rubbed his fingers across a scar that ran the length from his shoulder to his elbow. He had been wild in his younger days. Old heads still spoke in awed voices about some of Uncle Dope's past exploits. "You made it past the two-minute mark yet?"

I hope that you don't hate me.

This was one issue that he would have to handle himself. By himself!

"Hell yeah," Truitt said. "I hold my own, my Duke. The girls be liking mine."

"Listen, listen." Uncle Dope waved him off dismissively. "It ain't about like or dislike. You ain't hearing me."

"He hearing you, all right." Gloria spoke from her corner daze. She got up and walked over to Uncle Dope. She stood in front of him for a brief second, giving Truitt a full view of her firm backside. Her body was fantastic, curved and pleasing to the eyes and she knew it. Uncle Dope spread his arms and Gloria moved into them, settling comfortably on his lap before turning back to face Truitt. "Truitt is hearing the only thing he can hear right now. The loud roar of his sex thing waking up. Like bam! Bam! Bam!"

"You see, Truitt!" Uncle Dope pulled Gloria tighter into his lap. "Don't let nobody tell you nothing like that! You see, my main problem when I was your age was that I had no guidance in dick matters. Nobody told me shit! It was the worst trial and error lesson…" Truitt started to object, but Gloria was watching him with a smirk on her face, so he stayed quiet. "Listen," Uncle Dope went on. "Ain't nobody in the world can prepare you for the feeling of sex. It's like blackout heaven. It's like there's nothing left in the world but an orgasm that you gotta have and you are in mad pursuit. That moment, the moment that you catch it! That's when most people realize that there is a Gawd! Yessuh! Ain't nobody but Gawd can make an orgasm."

"Check you out," Gloria said. "But Truitt already got a reputation. A friend of his already calling him Thick Dick Truitt. She talking already."

Truitt's mouth hung open.

"Can you excuse us?" Uncle Dope looked at Gloria. "Me and my boy got some business to discuss. Why don't you go lay in the bed and I'll be there in a minute. Alright?"

"Yeah, baby." She kissed him and hopped off his lap, making a beeline for the bedroom. But not before flashing a sexy smile at Truitt.

"Women," Uncle Dope said once the door closed behind her. "It's hard to talk to them about man sex. Listen. My main thing to tell you is this: you have to maintain control. You take control of the sex; don't let it control you. Which ain't as easy as it sounds, is it?"

Truitt nodded in agreement.

"Every stroke you take leaves you a millionth of a second away from skeeting all inside of her. One extra movement, one muscle twinge, one hint of a touch and skeet, skeet, skeet!" He looked meaningfully at Truitt. "Skeet!"

"Yeah, man," Truitt said. "I got it. Skeet!"

"So you gotta learn how to love that moment. Learn to appreciate that one millionth of a second, learn how to ride it and enjoy it and conquer it...but you can't cross it. Ain't no turning back if you do."

Truitt remembered his first time with Jackie, the instant rush of intensity that ripped through him which he was helpless to stop. "That's a tall order right there, my Duke."

"It is." Uncle Dope nodded his head. "It is. But you can do it."

"How so?"

"Practice," Uncle Dope replied, smiling. "Lots of practice."

Gloria came out of the bedroom clad in only her bra and panties. "How long you gonna be, baby?"

Her nearly naked body was everything that Truitt had imagined. His blood rushed from the sight and he felt a blush creep up his cheekbones, but he couldn't tear his eyes away from the scantily clad figure before him. Shifting in his seat to cover his hardness, he watched as Gloria found her way back onto Uncle Dope's lap. When their lips met, Truitt felt an odd sense of envy for the passion and fervor that was displayed. Uncle Dope broke from their embrace and looked at him.

"Don't worry about it, youngblood. These women out here..." He paused while Gloria worked her body against his. "They know the power that the visual has on us. The lust of the flesh. The lust of the eyes." He nodded his head in silent agreement. "A woman's curves. That's a powerful drug."

Gloria uncurled from Uncle Dope's grasp to speak to Truitt. The look in her eyes scared and thrilled him. "Men," she said. "Ya'll don't know how to admit that we got the good shit."

"Bullshit," Uncle Dope said.

"Yeah," was all Truitt could muster.

"Ya'll full of shit, too."

"Can't help that, baby," Uncle Dope said. "I think it's genetic."

"Told you." She worked her body again.

"Hard-wired into our DNA and shit."

"I got something I want you to code real hard."

"Oh. Now you talking nasty, huh?"

"We got nasty to do." She stroked his cheek. "What you got for me, sweetie?"

Uncle Dope reached into his pocket with an eye on Truitt. Their bond had exceeded friendship and crossed the boundary to family, closer than many blood relatives that he knew, but every man has his secrets, his own private joy that remained hidden from view. Gloria's fingertips trailed along the scar on his arm. Uncle Dope had never told Truitt the story of how he had gotten the long slash on his arm. Probably never would. Some hard lessons life has to teach. He handed Gloria a dollar bill.

"You see," Gloria said. "My baby pays attention, but just enough to be hardheaded. I gotta give it to him; he has that good desire."

Uncle Dope started singing in a sharp, clear tenor. *"My desire. Tells me all the things I need to know about you."*

"So what you know then, baby?"

"You're the one who's tearing down my heart."

"Truitt." Uncle Dope looked deeply into Gloria's eyes as he spoke. "It's all about pleasing your woman. Taking those steps to keep her happy." Reaching behind the sofa, he pulled out a baggie full of white powder. "Coke. Yeyo. I use it for fun. For my girl."

"I don't mess with drugs, my Duke, and you know

this." Truitt had never had the desire to get high. He had only recently experienced his first taste of beer and he still wondered what all of the fascination was about. The beer that his friends, Hawes and Macher, had given him was warm and nasty and he decided that he wouldn't drink another one.

"Yeyo ain't nothing," Uncle Dope said. "Like I said before: control. You gotta maintain control; whether it's white powder or this here chocolate tight."

"Naw! That's cool, my Duke." Truitt waved off the offer. "I'm gonna try to do my thing without that. I don't need it." Gloria got up and went over to the stereo to retrieve an old Earth, Wind & Fire album cover. She put it on the table and dumped the powder from the baggie on top of it.

"Shit! I don't need it either." Uncle Dope watched her. "But it is so much more fun. Ain't it, girl?" He pulled out a credit card and handed it to Gloria, who used it to begin forming lines of white powder on the album cover. They were all quieted by a knock on the door.

"Who dat?" Gloria called out.

"Me!" a feminine voice answered.

"Who dat say 'me' when I say 'who dat'?"

"Me say 'me' when you say 'who dat.'"

"They play this game all the time," Uncle Dope told Truitt. "Gloria, get the door, huh."

She bounded over to the door and, when she swung it open, in stepped Diamond. Diamond and Gloria were occasional get- high buddies, even though their friend-ship was a lifelong one, forged since childhood. Diamond's life had taken her down a rough path and she had ended up with two kids that she supported by stripping at a club downtown. Diamond was a thick stripper and her assets had that extra half-second of jiggle that enticed men to pull money out of their pockets. She was wear-ing a baggy pair of jeans and a tee shirt with "Sunshine" written across it, but Truitt still saw the sway of her full body. She came in the room and sat on the couch next to him.

"I'll be damned," Uncle Dope said. "It's like you got powder radar, Diamond! Every time we about to partake of some yeyo, here you come."

"Ease up, hoss." Diamond held up her hand. "I think that you exaggerating. Shit!"

"I called her and told her to come over, baby," Gloria said.

"I ain't staying too long." Diamond looked over at Truitt. "I know how you like to get your freaky deaky on when you get high." She shared a quick laugh with Gloria. "And you know that's right!"

She darted a quick peek at Truitt and a knowing smile curled the corner of her lips. Diamond was a grown woman with a taste for teenage boys that were on the cusp of manhood. She yearned for the feel of their hard bodies and reveled in their newly awakened hunger. Her two children had different daddies that were both sixteen years old when she began sexing them. Diamond considered herself a teacher and her body was the classroom where her young students learned the pleasures of manhood. That was why Gloria had called her: to help train the young man Jackie called Thick Dick Truitt about the power and joy of sex.

"You don't have to go." Gloria bent over the table and snorted a line of coke through the rolled-up dollar bill. "When we finish, you can stay out here and school Truitt." She handed the bill to Uncle Dope, who also snorted a line. "You think you can do some- thing with that, Truitt?"

Truitt felt a blush burning up his cheeks and he looked down at the floor.

"None of that, dammit!" Uncle Dope sniffled a few times. Truitt's eyes fixed on the older man. "Ain't no shame, no shyness, concerning what you like or what you can do with yours. You a man now, Truitt. You hear me?" He caught Truitt in his stare. Truitt met his glare without batting an eye. Message received. "We handle ours." Uncle Dope extended a fist, which Truitt bumped with his knuckles.

Truitt turned to face Diamond. She watched him expectantly. "In all honesty," he said and gently took her hand. "This is exactly what I want." He brought her hand to his lips and kissed it while looking directly in her eyes. Truitt had seen a guy do that once on television and the girl had gone crazy. Diamond barely cracked a smile. Truitt leaned forward and gently kissed her lips. This time, Diamond smiled.

"Let me get some of this," she said.

"My boy don't play." Uncle Dope passed her the rolled-up bill. While she snorted a line, he spoke to Truitt. "You sure you don't want to try none?"

"Naw, my Duke. Control."

"Hope you got plenty," Uncle Dope said. "'Cause she sure don't look like she got any."

"Shut up," Diamond said. "I got plenty." She looked over at Truitt. "Especially for a gifted young man. Is that you, Truitt?"

Truitt learned many lessons that night. That lust is insatiable. And that cocaine gave him strength and stamina. All he needed to do was maintain control.

Mugwump

Mugwump woke up in prison. Pain laced his body when he tried to move, so he decided to lay still and breathe. He looked up at the slate gray ceiling, saw nothing familiar and then lowered his eyes to take in his surroundings.

He was in a small room. The closeness of the walls and the stillness of the air struck him as the echo of a distant hum registered faintly in his brain. His arms and legs felt heavy, his thoughts were sluggish and, when he tried to move, his body refused to react, as if it were encased in heavy slush. Anxiously, he looked up again and his eyes settled on the steel door. A small, rectangular pane of glass was set into the middle of the doorframe that seemed hard and heavy. A handle was welded into the door in place of a doorknob and he noticed that there were no hinges on it; it didn't swing open, it simply slid back into a recess in the wall. He had seen those kinds of doors before when he had gone to visit his Uncle Rudy at the Coxsackie Correctional Facility upstate.

A frightened gasp burst from Mugwump's lips as the

stark realization of his situation came hammering home. *This is prison!* Tears slowly slid down his face as his dreams of the future shifted from one of great promise to that of a flame extinguished. Life hadn't prepared him for confinement or the toughness needed to survive in a world of violent men who played by their own cut-throat rules. He wasn't hard like that, wasn't built that way, and at that moment he felt as if he had nothing left to live for.

He wasn't unfamiliar with prison life. More accurately, he was familiar with the effects that incarceration had resulted upon where he lived. Brothers who had been away upstate for a while never spoke of their experiences while they were locked up, but Mugwump always saw the desperation in their eyes. That despair was some-thing, an emptiness, that he could never live with.

Thoughts of suicide danced across his mind. Anguish overtook him and, strangely enough, his desperation took on the shape of hope. *Death is better than this.* A deep sleep would become the ultimate escape. His eyes darted around the room. What he saw nearly made him cry out in surrender.

There was nothing.

There were no chairs, no charts with pens attached to them, no sharp objects…nothing. Had he been able to get up from the bed, there was nothing in the room that would have helped him bring his life to an end.

A fleeting memory of a book he had read in the eighth

grade, *Johnny Got His Gun*, came to him. A young man who had been anxious to go to war had found himself lying in a bed with no legs, no arms and no face. His face had been blown off. His mutilated torso lay in a hospital bed, unable to see, hear or talk, his only connection with humanity being the nurse who cleaned him each day. He only had his thoughts to keep him company as he marked the passing of days by the sunshine that came through his window and warmed his body and the allure of death was his only hope. His mind needed the peace that his soul was craving. Johnny got his gun.

Mugwump gasped aloud as he fought against his tears. As he pushed himself up into a sitting position, a searing pain traveled up his arm and he froze, waiting for the ache to fade. His breaths felt slightly restricted by the bandage that was wrapped around his ribs, but when he exhaled he felt a painful reminder of the blows he had taken from the Supercop.

The room had no windows.

The dank smell of the room overwhelmed him, moved through his spirit with a finality that, once crystallized, became his new reality. He was not going home.

The electric hum of the overhead lights droned on endlessly.

"Where am I at?" The words hissed between his clenched teeth. "Fucking jail! Shit!" He ran his hands gingerly down his bruised ribs, checking the swelling beneath the bandages. His face was swollen and bruised and his left eye was swollen so badly that it was nearly closed. "I gotta get out of here. Why am I?" Breaths came at a heavy price for Mugwump; the pain rushed around through his ribs with each heave of his chest. He lay still for a moment.

The corner. He cringed when he thought about his last night of freedom: spent on the corner. The drug spot. Chilling out with dealers and hustlers…a hell of a place for him to find a principle worth standing for. A location that placed him in the eye of a drug war in which idealism had no role and, in fact, the only reward that Mugwump had received for his efforts was a cop-punch to the face. And a free trip to jail.

The tears started again.

The steel door stared back at him.

That steel door was the condition that he fought against. *Any man that was worth being a man had to fight to become one.* That sentiment had struck a deep chord in his young soul and found a place in his psyche until it became a part of him.

He sobbed aloud.

"But this is real life! Right here? This is real life! I'm locked up?" His chest heaved as he fought to manage the pain. "And I didn't do anything." Tears streamed down his face. "But this is jail, though! Real talk! I'm locked up! That cop hit me! Shit!" Images of the cop's face flashed across his mind. "He didn't have a right to do that." Mugwump quickly glanced around the solitary room. "Now I'm lost in here. They are gonna keep me in here. Forever!" Mugwump collapsed. And for a moment the only sound that could be heard were his wrenching sobs that echoed off the drab walls of his cell.

Through his tears, it occurred to Mugwump that his life was over. He had entered a new reality. One that created hard times and hard men. Dreams died behind bars and nightmares took the form and shape of menace. No one emerged unscathed from prison. There remained a greater distrust of the justice system, a suspicion greatly honed by the harshness of incarceration. The hardened criminals who had gone away when they were young returned to the streets carrying within their souls a callous indifference that permeated their every waking moment. They were the ones who caused Mugwump the most fear, the ones who caused him to dive face-first into his schoolwork, and the reason he held education as the key to changing his lot in life. And the real hardcore thugs were the examples of what he swore never to become, until now.

Heavy voices sounded outside the door and, when it swung open, a tall, dark-haired police officer stepped into the room, followed by a uniformed guard. The door clanged shut behind them. The police officer had a bland face, no outstanding features, just bland and pale. His uniform gleamed, however, the polished brass shining even in the fading light as he walked over to the bed and looked down at Mugwump, who met the man's stare and said nothing, waiting.

"This?" The cop looked back at the guard standing by the door. "This little motherfucker here beat down on Supercop? Get the fuck out!" Inching closer, he bent down so that their faces were close enough for Mugwump to see the rough cut of the officer's jaw. "So how about it, son? You got a bullshit story of how you didn't do it? Even though we found you unconscious, hiding behind a dumpster? I, for one, cannot wait to hear this one. You see, I need a good story to tell to the world. I have to tell them why I am even bothering with a kid, no, not a kid, because you are being charged as an adult, with viciously beating two cops. Huh?" He cocked his head toward Mugwump. "I didn't hear you!"

Mugwump looked into the cop's eyes for a long moment. "Okay, officer. What happened?"

The cop nodded his head in agreement. "What?"

Mugwump contemplated before speaking. "I need *you* to tell me everything that happened."

"You need me! To tell you…" The officer chuckled. "Now that's rich! You need me to tell you. If I were you, I would stop playing games with me. Are you high? What kinds of drugs have they got going into you?"

"Officer," Mugwump said. "Overseer? I don't hurt people. I don't remember. It's like my brain is short-waving, clicking in bits and pieces but I can't get the whole…thing! I get the dots but I…I…I can't connect the dots."

"So you're going with that story, huh?" The cop looked down on him.

"I've got one image that comes in strong and frequently, though," Mugwump rushed on. "You might not like it, but I'm going to give it to you straight. This thing that keeps sticking in my brain." Mugwump looked the policeman in the eye. "The Supercop was swinging at me. He hit me. Right here." Mugwump touched his bruised face.

"So you maintain that the police assaulted you?" He glanced at Mugwump's beaten body.

"I practice non-violence," Mugwump said.

"Two of this city's finest police officers are now lying in intensive care at Columbia Memorial Hospital. Both beaten so severely that they lapsed into a comatose state." He turned and headed for the door. "You better pray to your non-violent God that they wake up."

Two Years,
Five Months,
Twenty-Five Days

Mugwump stepped out into the sunshine determined to never look back. The midday sun beat down hot and heavy, but he basked in the glorious heat that bathed him with freedom. It had taken two years, five months and twenty-five days of blood and fear, but he had finally been released. His case had received national attention from both the media and Civil Rights groups who kept pressure on the municipal government to free him, yet the wheels of justice had ground slowly as Mugwump languished behind bars.

When the time came for his trial, a parade of witnesses, drawn by the spotlight of the media, testified before a grand jury about the events of that night but the proceedings dragged on. Eventually, all charges against Mugwump had been dropped and he now had a lawyer who filed charges against the city's police force for violating his civil rights.

None of that mattered to him as he walked away from the facility that had housed him for nearly two and a half years. There was no looking back, his vision lay ahead at his future, the life that had been suddenly put on hold was now ready to be lived.

Mugwump had learned serious life lessons while he was in lockup. It had been tough for him in the beginning: he had doubted that he would make it a week. But he had been fortunate to be roomed in a cell with a man named Donald Fears who went by the name of Brother Black. Brother Black was a quiet man, hard spoken but sincere, and he hated anyone who wasted words. "Say what you mean," he told Mugwump. "Or shut your mouth and save my ears the trouble." He was ten years into a life sentence when Mugwump arrived at his house. Mugwump sat on the hard mattress, afraid to move under the unblinking eye of Brother Black. Books lined three shelves of the cell, each shelf attached to the wall near Brother Black's prison bed. The wall was papered with snapshots from his life before the jail bars closed in on him.

"You see this over here?" Brother Black's voice was hard. "You don't touch none of this over here." He glared at Mugwump through eyes of steel. Brother Black had spent time in the gym and his muscled physique was evident, but what Mugwump noticed most was the serious set of his jaw and the menace he presented. His head was covered with a thin sheen of hair that could easily be mistaken for no hair at all and his face was flat and thin. An aquiline nose, thin lips, and a slightly tilted forehead that poked out over his flat, black stare convinced Mugwump that this was not a man he wanted to anger. Deciding that silence was the better part of valor, Mugwump lay down on the concrete-hard mattress and stared at the ceiling.

"If you're gonna be in here, you are going to act like a man," Brother Black said. "You will carry yourself like a man and you will think like, and be, a man. You hear me?"

Mugwump said nothing.

"A man gonna speak up and be heard."

Mugwump turned his head and looked at him. "I'm gonna be in here forever." A tear escaped out of the corner of his eye and he made no move to wipe it away. Brother Black took a seat on the bed and watched him. "It's like this is not real. Can't be."

"This is as real as it gets, bruhman," Brother Black said. "And let me tell you right now...if I ever see another tear come out of your eye, I'm going to beat you down my damn self. Don't ever let me see that again. You heard?"

Mugwump wiped the tear away and he started talking. He told Brother Black his entire story, from his conflict on the corner until he woke up in the prison hospital. Brother Black listened without interrupting, hearing the entire story before he said a word. "One thing that you have to realize, bruhman, is that I don't care. Nobody does. You're here. With the rest of us. You have to learn to just...be!"

Brother Black took Mugwump under his wing, kept him out of harm's way and, after a while, even let Mugwump read some of his books. Brother Black had connections; he could have any book that he wanted delivered to his cell, and when he discovered Mugwump's love of reading he read some novels that Mugwump recommended.

One night they were talking in their cell and Mugwump asked Brother Black why he was locked up. This was a question that he knew he shouldn't ask, but Mugwump's curiosity got the better of him. He had to know. Brother Black regarded him for a tense moment and Mugwump thought that he had overstepped himself.

"Because I fit the description," Brother Black said and then told him his story.

❊❊❊

Before I was sent here, I was in my third year of medical school, studying to become a surgeon. I was the pride of my family, the only one of eleven children who had even attempted to go to college. One day on campus, I met Tonya. One look and I was hooked. Not many times in life do you come by someone so definite, know something so surely, that you never have any doubt. It was quick and perfect. Tonya was pursuing her MBA and I was studying to become a doctor. Like I said, perfect. Three months later, against the wishes of both of our parents, we got married. She was a purposefully compassionate woman and she planned to use her degree to open businesses in the Black neighborhoods that she had grown up in. She believed that there was money there, in the ghetto, but that Black folks didn't know how to become financially empowered as a single entity. So she wanted to develop a Black Think Tank—that's what she wanted to call it, the Black Think Tank—with Black intellectuals who wanted to establish commerce in the urban communities. Wanted Black folks to achieve financial stability in the place where they worked and lived. She was on fire with her dreams.

One day, I went down to her office and saw Tonya in action. She was sincere about her dreams and chasing them; like I said, she was on fire. Soon, I found myself caught up in Tonya's zeal and rediscovered my racial identity, found myself re-evaluating my own purpose. I jumped in with both feet, igniting myself from Tonya's flame and, as a result, she made me an important part of her staff. I immersed myself in the inner workings of Tonya's world, venturing back into the very projects that I had desperately tried to escape, meeting with leaders of the community, talking to doubtful and disbelieving residents about economic empowerment. Our message was peace and unity through financial well-being—a message that was met with indifference and apathy.

We ran into many brick walls, but through each fight,

I was becoming empowered. I discovered my true calling. So I changed my course of study; there weren't enough hours in the day for me to follow my new dream of making a social difference while attempting to become a doctor, so I decided to get my MBA.

Tonya and I became a force; our mission became a movement that quickly began gaining momentum. We had a business model in place which, if successful, would establish economic stability on a level rarely seen in the Black community.

We were also drawing the attention of the business community outside of the projects. Historically, Blacks spend most of their income on goods and services that are totally disconnected from their neighborhoods. Our plan was to change that. We planned to build a network of Black businesses that would keep project dollars in the projects with the final phase being that, with a conglomerate of business owners, it wouldn't be a project anymore. The prospect of the potential loss of millions of dollars in revenue was not lost on the affluent business owners of the city. As a result, they sent representatives to meet with community leaders to further their own agenda. Armed with big promises and big dollars, they had us thoroughly outmanned and outgunned. We met with many defeats but we shrugged off the disappointments and kept pushing forward. We were really idealistic. We would let nothing stand in our way.

There was no surprise when the threats started coming.

"This is what we signed on for, baby," Tonya whispered in my ear one night as we lay in bed. "Our purpose."

I could only look at her. Our intimacy was as deep as the moonlight, as if the darkness intensified my love for her. If anything ever happened to her, I knew that my soul would never recover.

"Yeah, baby." I reached for her. "But I love you. A lot, lot!" Tanya laughed at my foolishness. "You mean more to me…" I stopped to kiss her. "I probably couldn't live without you."

Tonya ran a finger softly across my lips, and after a moment she laid her head on my chest. I felt her breath on my skin before she kissed my neck. "We were meant for this, baby. You and me. That's a part of our love, too. You and I can stand up to it. And if we can't…" She gently reached down and touched me. "I'm going to love you until I can't anymore."

The rest of that school year was a tireless, unending struggle as we continued trying to expand our network, fighting tooth and nail against the established business community and the influence of their spending efforts in the Black community. By the time spring break rolled around, Tonya and I decided to take a much needed rest. I had secretly been saving money for the honeymoon that we had never taken and surprised Tonya with a trip to Jamaica. The last semester had been particularly grueling, so she grudgingly agreed that we both needed a week to unwind.

On the third night there, I walked in the front door and saw a man standing over the bed looking down at my naked wife. He had a knife in one hand and his dick in the other. As soon as I stepped inside, I was hit in the side of my head, nearly losing consciousness when I slammed into the wall. I barely saw the outline of my attacker rushing toward me, but I was able to get one knee underneath me and swing. A high, pitched squeal escaped from the man as he bent over, frozen in pain and clutching at his family jewels.

The other man turned and looked at me as Tonya came awake and quickly rolled away from him off the bed. He looked down at his partner rolled up in a fetal position on the floor and came toward me. The metal pipe that hit me lay on the floor next to his writhing partner and I scrambled over and picked it up. The man with the knife was nearly on top of me when I turned toward him. He was swinging the blade wildly. I was still stunned from the blow to my head but I managed to avoid the knife. I jumped away, but felt it tear through the front of my shirt and slash through the flesh of my stomach. I managed to twist away and came back swinging the pipe with every bit of strength I had left, catching the man in the forehead. The blow knocked him backward and he landed facedown near the bed. A painful grunt escaped from him and he rolled over on his back with the knife sticking out of his stomach. His eyes were glazed over with fear when I walked toward him. I felt hot blood leaking down my stomach, which reminded me that he had sliced me, but I didn't feel any pain so I figured that the cut wasn't too deep. At least I knew I was doing better than this guy!

"Tonya!" I called out. "Tonya! You alright, baby?" Tonya had run into the bathroom and, at the sound of my voice, she poked her head out of the doorway. "You alright?"

I sighed with relief as she rushed toward me. "Yes! Yes!" She was nearly in tears as we held each other and collapsed to the floor. "Baby..." She pulled me closer and the tears began to stream down her face.

We both turned at the sound of the man struggling to his feet by the bedside. A look of deathly pain danced across his face, his body trembled and his eyes were bugged out in disbelief. A thin sheen of sweat formed on the swollen knot on his forehead while his lips jerked as if he were struggling to speak. Ragged breaths escaped his body as he turned from the bed and stumbled toward the door. His partner shakily rose from the floor when he saw the man stumbling toward him and managed to catch him before he crashed to the floor.

As he helped his partner toward the door, he cast one long look at me and Tonya, still huddled on the floor, then gathered his partner under his arm and carried him toward the door. He stopped in the doorway, reached down, grabbed the handle of the knife and yanked it out of his partner's stomach. He threw the knife back into the room and they stumbled out into the night. A second later…they were gone.

"What the fuck was that? Shit!"

"Baby, you all right?" Tonya ran her hand around the swelling on the side of my head.

"My head," was all I could get out.

"Does it hurt bad?" Tonya moved from my embrace. "They tried to kill us, baby!" she said. "Oh my God! Somebody's trying to kill us! He had a knife! What are we going to do?" She was getting hysterical.

I reached out to her. "Tonya. Baby. Help me over to the couch."

When she saw that I needed her help, I saw a calm determination settle over her. "Okay, baby." She came to my side and helped me to my feet. I stumbled over to the couch and she sat next to me, gently pushing my head to the side to examine the swelling that had formed there.

"You know something?" I said through clenched teeth. "My head doesn't really hurt that bad. It feels kind of numb." I paused to look at her. "It's my stomach that is paining the shit out of me."

Tonya looked down at my torn shirt for the first time and saw the blood soaking through it. A sharp intake of breath was followed by a shocked gasp. "What did they do?" She held her hands in front of her face.

"Not that bad," I said. "I don't think."

"Let me call the hospital." Tonya jumped up from the couch and reached for the phone.

"No!" I shouted. "No hospital!"

Tonya picked up the receiver and started pressing buttons.

"Tonya! No!" I yelled and made a feeble attempt to snatch the phone from her hand.

She turned to look at me. "What?"

It was more than a question and I immediately began to explain. "No police. I think I killed him. You see where that knife hit. He's dead."

Tonya paused with the phone in her hand when the realization of my words hit home. The thought of her man in jail, the very possibility of it frightened her and that stab of fear jolted her back to reality. She hung up the phone.

"Baby," I said. "You know that if I get caught up in the system…there is no getting out. I am not going. I can't do time for this. We haven't finished what we were put here for." A flash of pain shot across my abdomen and I winced at the sting of it. "You told me that," I finished.

She paused for a moment. "Lay down."

She helped me slide my body down on the couch until I was lying flat on my back. Rising to her feet, Tanya hurried back into the bathroom and turned on the faucet. Cabinet doors were yanked open and slammed shut, curses uttered in exasperation as the moments ticked by before Tonya emerged with a small bucket of hot water and a towel. She flopped down on the couch and sat the bucket on the floor before helping to unbutton the blood-soaked shirt. The knife had cut a long, thin slash across my stomach and she dipped the towel in the hot water, wrung it out and began dabbing at the wound.

She recoiled from the painful inhalation that hissed from my lips. "Baby," I told her through clenched teeth. "That stings, okay. Just a little bit." Beads of perspiration dotted my forehead but I tried to sound calm and in control. "That water's hot, Tonya. Water needs to be warm." Tonya looked at me with a frightened expression on her face. "Make it warm, baby." I put my hand on hers. "Bet you never thought you would hear me say that, huh? Make it warm, baby. Make it warm."

Tonya laughed aloud at my corny joke but the laughter carried the sound of a hysterical cry. She sat there for a second and I watched as my woman regained control of the situation. I saw that fire come back into her eyes. She stood up and carried the bucket into the bathroom and filled it with warm water. When she came back to me, she soaked the towel and squeezed off the excess before she placed the entire cloth over the length of the cut. I howled in pain but Tonya held the towel firmly to my stomach as my body bucked against her. I collapsed; trembling with agony, fists clutched above my head as she stopped the blood from flowing and soon my body adapted and the hurt became manageable.

When I stopped thrashing around, Tonya got to her feet and walked toward the front door. Surveying the damage from my struggle with the two men, she began to clean up the mess. The metal pipe and the bloody knife still lay on the floor. She took a long look at the open door and bent down to retrieve both of the weapons. Quietly, she moved over to the doorway and peered outside with the pipe poised to strike—but they were gone. After easing the door shut, she moved back into the room for a quick check on me. The towel on my stomach had turned a dark red so she gently eased it from my grasp and hurried to the bathroom to rinse the blood out.

The slash on my stomach was not bleeding as heavily and we could see where the flesh had been torn. The cut was thin, straight and precise, as if it were the slash of a straight razor. She sighed while gently pressing the towel to my stomach. I winced when the cloth made contact. Tonya sat on the edge of the couch next to me and took my hand.

"They lucky," I said after a moment.

"Lucky?" Tonya looked at me.

"Yeah, lucky. If they had hurt you, I would have killed them both."

Tears welled up in her eyes.

"Without the slightest hesitation. You're worth it to me." I reached for her. "Now, can I have a dab of sugar?"

Tonya laughed through her tears and leaned down to kiss me. "So what are we going to do now," she said. "My God! Can you ever forgive me for this?"

"What are you talking about?"

Silent tears began to make their descent down her face, and her voice was barely audible in the suddenly quiet room. I reached for her and wiped a tear away.

"Truth be told," I said. "I wouldn't go through this for anyone else but you. And I mean forever."

"I love you, Don."

"I know," I said. "Now how about helping me over to that bed."

We spent the rest of our vacation inside the cabana while I healed, with Tonya leaving only to get pain medication and bandages. On the day that we were scheduled to leave, Tonya bandaged my stomach, which was healing well as long as I didn't move my torso and break the scab, and we headed for the airport. I moved slowly as I exited the cab and made my way through the airport. Though I tried to mask my anxiety, I breathed a deep sigh of relief when the plane was airborne. Every bounce of turbulence that buffeted the plane brought on a fresh bout of pain to my stomach. I felt even more relief when the plane touched down back in the states after the torturous flight. Life returned to normal once we were back at school. The only reminder of that night was a razor-thin scar across my stomach, so Tonya and I moved on.

I was sitting in class when the police came in and took me out in handcuffs. They charged me with the murder of Arnold Conn, the owner of a chain of grocery stores who had been one of our most outspoken adversaries.

Someone had bludgeoned him to death down on Lark Street, the dark side of town, after he had left the house of his mistress. The assailant had been seen running from the scene of the crime and I fit the description. A highly publicized arrest was followed by a speedy trial and I was sentenced to life without parole.

✪✪✪

Without Brother Black, Mugwump doubted that he would have been able to survive the two years, five months and twenty-five days.

"Man," Mugwump told Brother Black before he was released. "I owe you my life. And I know I can't ever repay you."

"Yes, you can," Brother Black said.

"Name it."

"A life for a life."

"A life for a life?"

"Yeah. Just take your life…and live it. Don't waste it."

Willmon

The formative years of his life had been spent in a mental haze as he wandered into his young adulthood chased by the frenzied echoes of his youth. Willmon didn't know what to do with himself, had no greater expectations of himself and no master plan other than trying to live with the voices that bounced around in his head. Strange thoughts gripped him and they sometimes obscured his vision, his reasoning, and he always felt off balance. Willmon didn't do life. Life did him.

It was on his first day back at school that Willmon had his first experience with the Dead Eyes. He was in gym class watching his classmates play basketball. Willmon loved gym class because no one ever bothered him. All he did was sit off by himself because he was never chosen for a team no matter what sport they played.

His head was throbbing that day, worse than usual, the pain so intense that Willmon could do nothing more than sit with his back against the wall and close his eyes.

"Willmon!" Coach Tucson called him. Willmon closed

his eyes tighter as the coach's coarse voice bounded through his skull. The pounding of footsteps coming closer wasn't enough to get Willmon to open his eyes. "Willmon!" Coach Tucson stood right above him now, yelling at the top of his voice, angry at having been ignored. When he finally opened his eyes and looked at Coach Tucson, an anguished scream tore from Willmon's throat, a sound so raw with fear that the other students froze.

Coach Tucson had no eyes!

Both of his eye sockets were empty, and blood red orbs rotated in their stead.

Coach jumped back, startled, as Willmon curled up in a ball on the floor, eyes shut, while he cried hysterically. "What's the matter, Willmon?" Coach spoke gently to him. Willmon screamed again. Students began to gather around as Coach Tucson knelt down near Willmon. "Willmon." His voice was soothing. "Calm down. It's all right. It's okay. Come on. Calm down."

Slowly, Willmon's struggle eased as he began to think that maybe he had imagined that Coach didn't have any eyes. Maybe that was it. Since the bicycle accident, his mind had been playing tricks on him. Sometimes voices. Sometimes visions. Cautiously he opened his eyes to look up at the man bent over him.

He screamed again when he saw the glowing, pulsing Dead Eyes staring at him.

Coach called the nurse and they sent Willmon home.

It was days before Willmon would look anyone in the face after that episode, and when he did, he breathed a grateful sigh when he saw that their eyes were normal. Soon he convinced himself that it was his imagination that had scared him. That he had scared himself. But he never forgot the horror of seeing a man with no eyes. Dead Eyes.

One day Willmon discovered a remedy: Cannabis. Whenever he smoked weed, the constant confusion in his head seemed to disappear. The fog that hovered within him lifted and he was able to see things clearer. His mind opened up to new thoughts. He wondered about things the doctors had told his mother about his brain; why it wasn't working the way that it should, the reasons that they couldn't do anything about it.

"Your son is not sick," the doctor said. "He had an injury to his brain. When the injury healed, there was nothing else we could do. There are so many things about the human brain that we don't understand."

"But why is he acting so crazy?" his mother asked. "He's like a mental patient or something. Sometimes he's all right and other times I'll find him staring at the walls or something."

"There are things about the human brain that we don't know," the doctor repeated. "We can treat him with medication—"

"I can't afford your drugs, doctor. And I don't want no zombie walking around my house."

"But you can't afford to leave him in his present state either, Mrs. Angel."

"And how can I get him to stop writing on my walls?"

His mother ignored the doctor's warning and spoke to the matter that was bothering her. Willmon listened to this exchange but found no meaning in the words. His head had started hurting again, a steady throbbing that only eased when he closed his eyes and shrouded his brain in darkness.

His first encounter with marijuana had been the result of a joke. A few classmates were getting high during lunchtime at school down by the softball diamond. Willmon often went down to the field to get away from his schoolmates who tormented him with their name-calling and bullying. When they spotted him sitting by himself, they hatched a plan.

"Yo! There go Willmon the Retard."

"That dude is weird. Like he crazy or something."

"He probably on some drugs or something."

"Yeah. I bet you they got him on some serious pills."

"What you think he will be like if he smoke some weed?"

"That would be some shit right there! What if weed made him normal and shit?" They all laughed as they passed the blunt around. "This is some good shit here, though," one of them said after a while. Willmon hadn't moved from his spot on the grass down the third base line. "Let's get the retard zooted and see what happens."

They approached Willmon as if they were on a great adventure, urging him to smoke the rest of the blunt.

"No!" Willmon shook his head vigorously. They pushed the blunt in his face, letting the smoke waft up his nose. "No, no" Willmon said as his eyes followed the cigar that they held in front of him.

"Listen," one of the boys demanded. "You are going to smoke this blunt, retardation. Now!"

Willmon did. And after a moment, his head stopped hurting. Clarity settled on his brain and the random sounds in his mind died down to a dull roar. He lay on his back and looked up at the cloudless sky, taking in the fullness of the air and the warmth of the sunshine. He was elated to have his mind back, pain free, to be cognizant of the feel of his imagination, and he remembered the friends that he once had. Real friends like Truitt, Mugwump and Paul who used to play with him and hang out with him. Willmon had lost those memories and he was happy to have them again, even if only for the moment. The weed had made him free. There would be no looking back.

His mother never noticed the difference in him. Some days he would come home with a clear mind and watch her, never letting her know that he had found his cure. One day he walked in the house after having smoked a blunt and found his mother lying on the couch, watching television. Her eyes were dull and glued to the TV and, as usual, she did not acknowledge his presence. A head wrap was tied around her head, knotted in the back to hold her hair in, which meant that she was going out to the club. An ashtray lay on the floor in front of her with a cigarette burning and sending up curls of smoke. A bottle of cola sat next to the ashtray and Willmon could see peanuts floating around in the dark liquid. She wore an old housedress that covered her thick legs and blue slippers that lay on the floor where she had flung them off her feet.

Willmon watched her for a moment. "Ma," he said.

His mother let loose with a loud, wet fart that startled him. "What you want, boy?"

She never took her eyes off the television. Willmon opened his mouth to answer when the smell assaulted his nose. He was used to his mother's farts but she had put some extra stank on this one! He stepped back.

"Ma," he said again.

She turned her head and shot him a warning glance. He knew better than to bother her while she was watching a television program. Willmon ignored it. "Something I always wondered. Why did you name me Willmon?"

"Get on away from here, boy!"

Willmon stood his ground. "For real. I would like to know."

"Well, look who's doing all the talking today." She looked at him with her lips wrinkled in distaste. He had asked her questions like this before, even questions about his father, but his requests had always gone unanswered. The denials always started with the distastefully wrinkled lips. "You better get out my face right now," she calmly replied. "I told you before about bringing me this foolishness. You better get on."

"I'm sixteen now," Willmon said. "I'm old enough to know now." Willmon moved closer. "So what is my daddy's name then?"

His mother's head snapped around. Sitting halfway up on the couch, she warned him. "Make me get up! Hear?"

"What's his name?" Willmon looked down on her. He felt the fog returning but it felt different this time. There was no throbbing to it. His vision remained clear. "How come you can't tell me? It's only a name. It don't mean nothing to me. And it damn sure don't mean nothing to you. So what's the problem?"

She pushed herself off the couch and was suddenly standing in front of him. For the first time in his life, Willmon stood face to face with his mother, yet unafraid, armed with a newfound freedom. This was his moment of truth, the first step toward finding his true self.

"You the problem, boy," his mother said. "You a big problem. Always gonna be a big problem. A big problem 'cause you got a big head." She paused to scratch under her armpit. "Ever since you cracked your head on that concrete back there you been twisted in the head. I'll be glad when you get on away from here."

"Who am I? To you. Who I be?" Sometimes he felt so utterly alone. No man is an island and he had no connection to human warmth, no knowledge of sincere compassion and his only choice was to build an oasis in his mind. In fact, loneliness became his oasis, a place of refuge where he huddled to view the world as it passed him by.

Over the years, Willmon had built a father he never met, displacing the negativity of his life by projecting an image of make believe into his reality, a visage that he held onto when he had no one else and nothing else to hang onto. And now, as he stood in front of his mother expecting answers that weren't forthcoming, he knew, deep inside, that she would never tell him what he needed to know.

"Who I be?" he asked again.

"Shut up, boy!" His mother had that shut down look in her eyes.

"You know," Willmon said through the pain that was growing in his head. "I could never understand why you won't never answer me about where I came from. Who I came from! But that's okay. Umma be a man soon. I can handle it. But I want you to know something. You did me wrong. You did."

Willmon flinched instinctively when his mother stepped away from him, disbelief flashing through her eyes.

"Boy, I gave you life!"

"And that's it? That's all you had to do? What about me? What about my mentals?"

"What the hell is 'mentals'?"

"Me, Ma. My mentals is me." Willmon watched his mother sit down on the couch with a stunned look on her face. "I needed help sometimes." He stared at her. "From you and only you. Nobody else. And I never got it."

"You got the same thing as everybody else." She lay back down on the couch, her indication that she didn't want to be bothered with the conversation. When she turned her eyes back to the television, Willmon moved to stand in front of her, blocking her view and forcing her to look at him.

"Who is my daddy?" His voice rang out much louder than he had intended. His mother's eyes narrowed to angry slits and her lips turned down in anger.

"Who you yelling at," she said. "You better get out from in front of me. You see me watching this program."

"Why you won't tell me?"

"Get out from in front of me."

"Why?"

"Your daddy was just another nigga!" she yelled. "That's all!"

Willmon bent down to eye level with her and said, "A nigga that you laid with."

His mother moved with a speed that he didn't know she possessed and slapped him, the sound echoing with resonance in the sudden silence. The pain descended on his brain and stayed there, throbbing and blurring his vision. His reality shifted and suddenly he was back in a world of hazy fog. His mother watched him for a second as Willmon held his hand to the spot on his face where she had struck him.

"I'm going out." She walked over to the stairs. "You old enough to stay in this house by yourself. I'll be at the bar. You heard me?" Willmon sank slowly to the floor. When she was satisfied that he understood, she started up the stairs. "Me and Leon going out tonight, so you better be in the bed when we get back."

Willmon sat there for a moment, listening to his mother bustle around as she prepared to go out to the Half-Moon, her favorite bar, to meet Leon. The throbbing in his head returned along with fantastic colors, and words began to crowd back into his imagination. *I need to write!* He stood up and stared at his favorite wall. A clean wall stood before him because she had made him scrub it clean from the last time that he had written on it. *Yes!*

When his mother came down the stairs she was dressed to kill, her face made up and her hair hanging in curls down to her shoulders. A black dress hugged her figure, her thick legs were encased in panty hose and she wore a pair of dark, high-heeled shoes that made her seem trimmer. She noticed him standing in front of the wall and warned him not to write on it. He smiled at her and told her that he wouldn't. Willmon watched as she walked out the door and reflected on how much he loved his mother.

An Intense Desire Called Passion

Truitt discovered his sexual nature, an intense desire called passion that became the spark of his personality. He had needs and he had lust; sometimes that dynamic duo would keep him awake at night.

He'd had a lot of sex, mostly great sex, but there never seemed to be enough to keep his eyes satisfied. Truitt often quoted his creed to his conquests: "If a woman can satisfy my eyes, not my sex or my mind, but my eyes, then she can have me forever."

Emerging from his bathroom, Truitt crossed the living room and grabbed his beer from the coffee table on his way out to the patio. He pushed through the screen door and stepped outside. The patio ran the length of the ground floor apartment and was fronted by two sliding glass doors that led to his bedroom. A four-foot wooden wall that was built around the perimeter gave him some sense of privacy as he looked out over the well-manicured lawn that stretched out through the entire complex. He would often sit out on the patio in his lawn chair and watch the neighborhood kids play football on the large expanse of grass that sat right in the middle of the Four Horizon apartment complex. During the nights, he would come out on the patio with a few blunts and a twenty-four-ounce bottle of beer so that he could relax in the darkness. Tonight was the start of the weekend and he planned to get groovy. He set his beer on the flat top of the wooden rail and pulled a vanilla flavored blunt from his pocket. He paused to look around; a cement pathway ran about five feet away from his patio. Once he was satisfied that the coast was clear, he pulled a lighter from his pocket and lit up, pulling on the blunt until his lungs were full of smoke.

The club is gonna be jumping tonight!

He could feel sex in the air, lurking out there, waiting for him to prowl, stalk and attack. Women were everywhere. For every three women he met, two would be interested and one, at least one, would let him sample the draws.

The acrid smoke from the marijuana filled his lungs and stung his eyeballs. "It's gonna be a beautiful night!" The beer bottle was quickly tilted to his lips and the cold liquid cooled the smoke that stung his throat.

He counted himself lucky that he had found this apartment; it had a spacious bedroom and the other areas were exactly to his liking. He had a fireplace in the living room set neatly into the wall across from the medium-sized kitchen. There was a counter that separated the kitchen from the living room and he had brought three stools from Wal-Mart so that the kitchen counter could also serve as his kitchen table. After landing a job with an Internet service provider as a technician, Truitt found that he could now afford to live an upgraded lifestyle. So when he walked into the apartment and took note of the spaces and the view from the patio, he felt, instantly, as if it belonged to him and he signed the lease right away.

Truitt took another hit off the blunt as he looked out into the quiet night. Since his life had fallen so neatly into place, he now had time to pursue his favorite pastime: sex. Exhaling a thin stream of smoke, he paused to take a swig of his beer and contemplate the subject. Many people considered his mission to be an impossible fantasy, with great expectation placed upon an unsuspecting woman, but Truitt didn't see it that way.

Truitt sought perfection; the perfect orgasms with the perfect woman.

The perfect woman for him wouldn't even be aware of her perfection. She wouldn't know that the curve of her neck would draw him close enough to touch it with his lips or that the feel of her hands on him would keep him at home or that every nuance of her body would become a part of his memory. She would make his chest heave. She would make him close his eyes and immerse himself in her sensations, maybe make him describe them in emotional colors like Passion Blue or Dark Red Lust or maybe Mango Orgasm. She would make him open his eyes and witness the physical love fight that their sexes would wage, carnal beauty that would move in nature's time. In. Out. Twist. Up. Down. Deep. He would watch her sex envelop him, hold him still before he would breathe and stop, holding himself there and bathing himself in her lust for him—because inside she couldn't lie. Her desire would hold syncopation, squeezing tight, then tighter, then a secret spasm that only they two would share, and then she would be there…at the crest of an orgasm that he would watch her ride. "Sex" was a word that didn't completely describe the object of his passions, didn't encompass the width of his grand pursuits.

Truitt took a big hit off the blunt before putting it out. Weed seemed to turn on a switch inside of him, one that pushed his mind to another plateau. Good thing that the drug dealer lives across the hall, Truitt mused.

"Girl, we gonna be up in the club tonight!"

Truitt turned toward the distinctive sound of femininity that approached; his curiosity peaked as he anxiously waited to see who would come around the corner. There were three women. His attention was instantly drawn to the big girl of the group. Truitt liked his girls thick and healthy and she fit the bill perfectly. She was shapely; her big hips and big chest made Truitt want to leap over the railing and pull her soft body to his body. She looked up at him and their eyes met. She smiled shyly and looked away. He could tell that she wasn't used to being looked at that way, especially when she was in the company of the smaller, curvy women who accompanied her. One of them was a model issue girl, thin, with a lithe figure and hips that could be held in the palms of rough hands. Her dress was short and form-fitting, gliding gently along her petite figure. Her thin face was warm, with high cheekbones and thin lips framed by her long, curly hair. Her eyes were bright and eager and her skin looked soft and supple. The third woman was gorgeous. Body banging, face flawless, and she was too beautiful for her own good. Her feathered hair opened up to reveal a classic beauty; skin that was unblemished, each feature of her face was perfectly placed, including her lips which were full and inviting. She wore the infamous little black dress that was form-fitting but not really tight. A light jacket covered her shoulders but not so much that her firm breasts were hidden from Truitt's gaze. Both women looked at Truitt when they rounded the corner, but he kept his eyes on the prize.

Truitt considered himself a handsome man. He had a dark, penetrating stare that lent itself well to the brooding, intense features that drew women to him. But he felt that his biggest asset was his honesty. One lesson that he had taken from his father's failure was to never lie. Life experience had also taught him that the only way to attain success was to charge forward strongly and to hell with the consequences.

"Hello, ladies," he said, greeting them.

"Hi," two of them replied in unison. Truitt kept his eye on the big girl. He watched her intently until she finally looked at him. She reminded him of Diamond.

"Listen," he spoke to her. "Can I ask you a question?"

She stopped dead in her tracks, surprised that he was talking to her. Truitt took his time and waited for her answer. She was round and curved in all the right places, proportioned the way he liked his women: big and sweet. Her friends held no interest for him; Truitt had always liked women with a little weight—meat on their bones all the way around. Mugwump and Paul called him a "chubby chaser" but Truitt didn't mind. He felt that he needed a lot of woman to love and there was always joy when they loved him back.

"You want to ask *me*?" She looked at him doubtfully. Truitt appraised her. She was pretty with long, straight hair and eyes that glinted under his intense stare. He could see the fullness of her hips from where he stood and her breasts were heavy and full. An image of him and her in the bed, butt naked, flashed through his mind, him behind her, hitting it doggy style, pounding, as he watched her ample ass flow with each thrust. It took a lot of woman to handle what he carried but he imagined that she would be able.

"Yeah," he said. "I can't let you walk by without asking you your name. You got a man around here?"

"Damn, you bold," one of her friends said.

"More than," the other chimed in.

"Not really," Truitt replied. He noticed that she hadn't answered, so he tried another approach. "But I don't want you to get the wrong idea. My name is Truitt. I want to introduce myself because in seconds you will have walked by me. I think that you are a very attractive woman and I at least had to say hello."

She blushed at his compliment and looked at her friends who looked at Truitt skeptically. Truitt leaned forward on the patio wall. "You gonna tell me your name?"

Pausing to glance at her friends she turned back to Truitt and said, "Kim."

"Kim," Truitt said. "Listen, I know you out with your friends and all but what is the possibility of me ever seeing you again?"

Kim didn't answer but he saw the interest in her eyes.

"I mean," Truitt went on. "Is it possible?"

"Well," she said. "What's the possibility that you could come out from behind your wall and I could see what you look like?" Truitt smiled. He knew what she wanted to see and he wasn't afraid to show her. He worked out regularly to keep himself in shape; while he wasn't the biggest man in the world, his body was muscular and tight.

"Tell you what," he said. "Why don't all of ya'll come inside and we can have a drink?" He paused to smile at Kim. "And maybe I can pass your inspection." He pointed up the walkway that led to his apartment. "It's around there." He walked back through the patio, through the living room and met the girls at the front door. Pausing with his hand on the doorknob, Truitt made a quick inspection of his apartment. A sofa sat facing his large, floor-model television and a plush armchair sat at an angle next to the sofa, its back to the barely used fireplace along the far wall. The one picture that he owned hung above the fireplace; it was an abstract piece that he had bought at a garage sale. Various shades of colors, including blues, blacks, grays, and deep purples swirled across the canvas, sweeping and flowing toward the center where all colors dissolved and formed two clasping fists. The rest of the room was neat and minimal; a real-life bachelor pad. There was no sign of a woman's touch in his residence but Truitt was glad that the apartment wasn't messy.

He pulled the door open and they were standing there waiting with Kim in the front. "Welcome." Truitt greeted them. "Welcome to my abode." Kim was the last in the door and Truitt stood there watching her. Kim looked him in the eyes and Truitt smiled back at her.

Ushering the women inside, he told them to have a seat and offered each a drink.

"What you got?" the first girl asked.

"I've got some soda, water, orange juice and beer." Truitt grabbed four beers out of the refrigerator and gave one to each. He sat in the armchair facing them and popped the top on his can. "You said your name is Kim, right?"

"Yes."

"So what you wanna ask me?"

She paused to look around the living room, at the bare walls, the sparse furnishings and the television. "You don't have a woman here with you, do you?"

"No woman. No."

"And you wouldn't ever lie to me about that, would you?" Her voice was heavy with sarcasm. Truitt was silent. "Because men do, you know."

"Do what?"

"Lie!" her friends replied.

Truitt smiled before he responded. "So you want complete and total honesty from a man?"

Kim cut her eyes at him. "It would be nice."

"Damn right!" The other two women nodded their heads in agreement.

"That's why you don't have a man," Truitt said.

Kim raised her hand in front of her face to hide the smile that threatened to break out. Her friends recoiled in shock. They pulled out their 'hood cards, neck-popping and finger-snapping, and were about to break on Truitt. He held his hand up to silence them. "Now, I'm not saying this to be vicious or anything. But to ask a man to be completely honest is a little outside the box." He looked at each one of them intently. "I'm true, though. About the things that matter."

"And that's probably why you ain't got no woman," the model answered, unwilling to let the slight go unanswered.

"Yeah," the sexy girl joined in. "He probably thought that the game was what mattered. When his woman asked him what the score was...that was the only time she would get the truth."

Truitt noticed that Kim didn't have much to say at this point. She was watching, measuring him and his reactions in handling her girlfriends' attitudes. He laughed out loud. "Ya'll are tripping! Complete honesty is a very rare thing. Life is a combination of truth and good intentions, well, sometimes, bad intentions. Well, you know, sometimes outright lies...but I'm as good as I can be."

"Yeah right," the model said.

"That shit sounded good, though," the sexy girl said. "Needs work, but you got the foundation. Build on that."

"Okay." Truitt raised his hands in surrender. "Men lie. It's a given. So the nature of our deceit should be what you worry about." Truitt grabbed his beer and took a sip. The women sat next to each other on the couch, dressed to tempt and ready for a night on the town. The model had a gentle body, slim and shapely, but pleasantly firm. The sexy girl had more of a physical presence; her body was stacked and loaded like an ultimate weapon. Truitt noticed a spark of interest when he looked in her eyes. Kim sat next to her, a big, beautiful woman that was stirring the lust of his imagination with the fullness of her body. His eyes were caught on her swollen breasts packed inside her bra.

"What kinds of truths do you think matters?" he said.

"Why don't you have a woman?" the model asked. Truitt noticed her expressive eyes. There was a mystery there. "And you mean to tell me that you don't have any kids running around here?"

"I don't have a woman, but I'm looking for one." A look of purpose crossed his features. "The right one. And of course, no woman, no kids." There was a general disagreement with that sentiment as they went on to defend all of the single baby-mama's of the world and cursed at lowlife men who helped put them there.

"Truitt," the sexy girl said. "Let me ask you a question." She straightened up and sat erect on the couch, her full breasts thrust out in their healthy splendor. She was gorgeous slash sexy slash damn slash fine! He noticed that Kim shrank away and he couldn't help but smile. "Do you know how to make love to a woman?"

"Sometimes," Truitt said.

"Sometimes?" She rocked her chest from side to side. "A woman needs love. All the time! You need to know that."

"Well," Truitt began. "I can do combinations. Sometimes love. Sometimes straight fucking!" He directed his gaze at Kim. "Sometimes love leads to straight fucking."

"Now, I know that's right!" Kim finally broke her silence. Her friends gave her a questioning look. "Shit! Don't make me lie! A good back cracking is what the doctor ordered sometimes." She looked at Truitt. "Do you have a back cracker?"

The ensuing silence filled the room as they looked to

Truitt for an answer. A small smile curled at the corners of his mouth as Truitt and Kim eyed each other. Truitt knew not to comment on his sexual prowess to women. Most of the women that he knew told him that too many guys talked the talk but came up short when it came time to walk the walk. He had adopted the stance of showing rather than telling.

The sexy girl broke the silence. "You ain't saying nothing," she challenged. Truitt took a drink of his beer. "You got a little pee-pee? A tiny, whiny boo-boo?"

He nearly spit his beer out as he joined the laughter. He nodded his head before deciding on his answer. "Actually, my dick is magnificent. I have never, ever gotten a complaint about Little Petey."

They all fell out laughing. "Little Petey!"

"That's his name. Little Petey! See, it's not an ordinary tanga-lang. Okay? See, I have length on my shit...I definitely touch bottom. Believe that. But I also have width, so I fill you up both ways. Wide and deep. Which makes it very hard for the clit to hide from me."

The women were silent. Truitt didn't know if that was a good thing or a bad thing, so he quickly explained himself. "I'm honest about what matters."

Ophelia, Charlene and Kim

"So how would you decide which one of us you would want to hook up with?" Charlene said. Truitt knew better than to answer that question. Charlene was the model and Truitt couldn't help noticing the classic touches of her face: the high cheekbones; slim, pert nose and flawless brown skin. "You see," she continued. "I think that we've misled you by letting you kick your game. Because we're really not out here looking for relationship-type shit."

"Let me guess then," Truitt said. "Sugar daddies?"

"Nope," they answered in unison.

"Baby daddies then."

"Hell-to-the-NO!"

"What then?"

"Something you say you've got," Ophelia, the sexy one, said. "A magic stick."

"And we don't mean no imaginary stick neither," Charlene said. "So don't play yourself."

Women! I'll never figure them out.

Truitt stood up from his chair and went back into the kitchen to get a bottle of wine that he kept for special occasions; a White Zinfandel that he kept in the cabinet because he knew women liked it. He retrieved three wineglasses and opened the freezer for the ice tray. He cracked the tray and shook out the cubes, filling each glass with as much ice as possible; he liked his wine cold and hoped they did too. As he handed each one of them a glass and poured their wine, his pulse raced but he fought to maintain his composure. He looked into each woman's eyes before returning to his seat and calmly sipped his beer. "So what are you guys saying?"

"We're saying, if you can't come correct, then don't come at all."

"I'm still lost," Truitt said. "Sometimes I'm slow like that. Break it all the way down for me."

Ophelia turned to the others. "May I?" They nodded their heads in agreement and she started talking. "You see, Truitt. We are modern women. These are modern times. We don't sit around and wait. We go and get what we want. Be it riches or be it pleasure, we've decided to go ahead and get ours."

Truitt felt himself becoming aroused as Ophelia spoke. She had a sexiness about her that demanded a reaction and he shifted in his seat as he felt his manhood thickening from the sexual images flashing across his mind. "Get your what?" he asked.

"Our pleasure. Can you handle that?"

"Handle all three of ya'll pleasure? I've always been able to in my fantasies. I mean, I've got the power."

"Yeah," Charlene said. "You popping your gums over there. Your mouth writing a check that your ass may not be able to cash."

"Ya'll ain't bullshittin' me, are you?" Truitt looked from one of them to the other for confirmation.

Ophelia stood up and walked toward him. "We can show you better than we can tell you." Charlene and Kim joined her by the kitchen counter. "Do you have a pen and paper?" Truitt retrieved both items from a kitchen drawer. "Write a number between one and ten—don't let us see it!" Truitt stepped away and turned his back to them and quickly scribbled on the paper. He turned back and waited expectantly as the three women watched him.

"This is how we do it," Charlene said. "We are going to 'do' you. But you had better be up to par."

"I am." Truitt was finally beginning to understand what was happening. These girls were going to run a train on him! He thought about who he would relate this wonderful, beautiful experience he was about to have...but then he realized that no one would ever believe him.

"And we have only one rule," Kim said. Truitt looked at her. He hoped that she would be first because he had the greatest desire for her.

"What's that?"

"You have to do whatever we want you to do."

"Okay," Truitt agreed. He would go along with anything at this point; they didn't even have to ask. "Nothing goes up my ass, though! Matter of fact, try not to go near it. Aiight?"

"Boy!" Ophelia said. "You truly are a trip. Do you agree to our rules or not?"

"Of course I do."

"Good." They all looked at one another and smiled before walking back to the couch and picking their drinks up off the coffee table. "Kim, you wanna put some smoke in the air?" Kim nodded and went into her purse. "Spark up that blunt, girl." She did. Truitt went back to the patio and retrieved the blunt he was smoking earlier and lit his up too.

Charlene looked at Truitt and said, "I think homeboy is going to need all the help he can get."

"Maybe not. Maybe so." Truitt was all smiles. "Who's to tell?"

"You seem to be in pretty good shape. Do you work out?" Ophelia paused when the blunt was passed to her. "Have you got stamina?"

"Well, I'm drinking milk now." Kim and Ophelia laughed. The blunts were taking them to the feel-good place. "I work mostly by feel, and instinct. I got something for all of ya'll."

"Well, get ready then," Charlene said. "Seven."

"Five," Ophelia said.

"Two," Kim threw in. Truitt took a moment to catch on; they were guessing the number that he had written down. He picked it up and held it out for them to see.

"I picked eight," he said. An insidious grin spread across Charlene's face. "That means I get you first. Good luck," she said. They all laughed. Truitt joined in.

"Well, let's get busy then." Truitt took a final hit from the blunt and placed it in the ashtray. As he and Charlene headed for the bedroom, he looked back at Kim and Ophelia. "I'll be back," he said. Little did he know that he would never be the same again.

✪✪✪

"Why are men such dogs?" Ophelia lowered the volume on the television as they watched the Soul Music Video channel. Truitt and Charlene had finished their sexual encounter and she was in the bathroom taking a shower.

Charlene had been an angry fuck; both aggressive and needy while also being incensed about needing a man for satisfaction. A man-hater! He had been relieved when Charlene achieved an orgasm and the act was over. Not that he didn't enjoy himself, but the encounter had been labor intensive, lacking the usual joy and gusto that he was used to. She had lain in the bed for a while after they had finished and Truitt had patted himself on the back for a job well done while he showered. Charlene had been very demanding but he felt as if he had been up to the task and, secretly, he was grateful that she had waited to take a shower—he needed the time to recharge.

But he felt like he had the power and, as he looked at Ophelia, her full breasts and healthy hips worked their magic on his sex drive and he felt himself reawakening. She was next.

"No answer," she looked at Kim pointedly. "Even men don't know."

Truitt watched the women before he spoke. This was the woman question; a question that no man could fully explain and no woman, at least not one that he had ever encountered, could fully comprehend. To him, it was like trying to explain racism to a white person. Instead, he got up and went into the kitchen. He had another blunt that he wanted to smoke.

"For real, though," Ophelia said. "Ya'll walk around drooling and slobbing after every woman you lay eyes on. Like dogs in heat."

"Arf! Arf! Arf!" Kim sounded like a toy poodle. Truitt chuckled.

"And ya'll nasty, too! Men will do and say anything to try to get some."

Kim solemnly agreed with that remark. Truitt tried to keep a straight face.

"Some what?" he said.

"Pussy!" they replied together, and then looked at one another and burst out laughing.

When the laughter died down, Ophelia spoke again. "And you're one of them. And like any dog, you don't know why you do what you do. Do you?"

"Excuse my manners," Truitt finally said. "Can I offer you two a drink?"

"Answer the question!"

"Trying to throw alcohol on the conversation!"

"Just like men do," Kim said, nodding her head. "What you got? Some more wine? 'Cause you know that wine makes women horny, right?"

"Ya'll do get real horny on that wine, though," Truitt said. "And I do mean wild, too!" Both women started to object and Truitt laughed. "Ya'll are tripping. I'm only messing with you." Retrieving the blunt from his hidden stash, he came back into the living room. He reached over the side of the couch and picked up the lighter, flicked the flame and lit the blunt before he spoke again. The bathroom door opened and Charlene emerged. "Well," Truitt said. "I'm not like the others."

Charlene went over and sat on the couch. Her hair was damp from the shower but her face was cleanly scrubbed, her skin was smoothed with lotion, and she looked as if she were refreshed. Truitt thought that she looked like a freshly-satisfied woman.

"Heard that too many times before," Kim said.

"Only in the fact that I know exactly what I want," Truitt continued. "There really is no reason for me to lie about it. And I always give a woman a chance to respond to my honesty. Other than that…I'm the typical male. Swinging dick and all." With that, Truitt passed the blunt to Ophelia before he went into the kitchen to get a beer from the refrigerator. He looked over at the women sitting on his couch. "I've got the rest of that Zinfandel in the 'frigerator, chilled and ready. You sure you don't want a drink?"

"Arf! Arf! Arf!" Ophelia barked.

Kim laughed and told him to bring the bottle.

Truitt pulled his second ice tray from the freezer and cracked it. "To tell you the truth," he said as he stacked the ice cubes in their glasses. "I bought this for me. I like wine, especially white wine. It tastes even better when it's really cold." After refreshing each of their drinks, he went back to his chair and sat with his legs stretched out in front of him. He reached behind his head and set the empty bottle on the kitchen counter and then sat back in his chair. Charlene passed him the blunt and their fingers touched. A look passed between them and Truitt smiled. *Yeah. I did an excellent job on her!*

Taking a big pull from the blunt before he spoke, he exhaled and let the thick cloud of smoke drift in front of his face. "What ya'll don't have is the right type of man in your lives."

"And you know that, how?" Kim said.

"Because you sound bitter," Truitt said. "I would never make you bitter."

"So what…" Kim took a sip of her wine. "What exactly do you want, mister man?"

"Me? I'm looking for the perfect orgasm." A stunned silence hung in the air. "And I do mean perfect."

"What are you talking about?" Kim said. "A perfect orgasm?"

"This nigga trippin' right here," Ophelia said.

Charlene seemed amused.

Kim looked at him, her expression thoughtful. "And what constitutes a perfect orgasm?" she said before leaning back into the cushions of the couch and tipping her glass to her lips.

"Probably means he wants to hit it doggy-style," Ophelia offered. She paused and added thoughtfully. "Now you know that might make it perfect." She exchanged high-fives with Charlene.

"Yeah," Kim said. "For a dog."

"A few minutes ago you said that men are dogs…"

Kim cut him off. "So what are you saying?"

"I'm saying that I agree," Truitt said. "I have to agree. But let me tell you something." He set his beer on the floor between his feet and spoke. "We can't help it."

"You can't help it?"

"Nope."

"Yeah. You can help it." Charlene became the speaker while the other two co-signed. "You don't want to help it. That's where the dog comes in. Dog in. Dog out! I mean, for real. What kind of state are you in, what kind of life are you living, where any piece of flesh can control your state of mind? Can't help it?" Charlene looked at her friends. "Men don't have no self-control is what you're saying."

"Actually, it's the opposite." Truitt smiled. Women don't understand men, Truitt mused, that was a given, but the problems start when women want men to think like women. And that would never happen. Truitt took the blunt and hit it before he started. "There's two sides to every man…"

❋❋❋

Truitt waited in the living room while Ophelia showered. She had been a vainglorious lay and he had spent their entire encounter together idolizing her beauty, obeying her directions, and meeting her performance requirements. He had nearly lost interest. Almost. Until he watched her body move, then his excitement returned and he found himself anxiously awaiting her next command to suck this or lick that, but his enjoyment went no deeper than the moment. Truitt found her beauty to be only skin deep.

While Ophelia showered, Charlene was rooting around in the kitchen, looking through the phone book until she found an Indian restaurant. She ordered Tandoori Chicken, Tandoori Shrimp, Lamb Tikka, curried rice and flat bread.

"I'll be right back." Charlene came around the kitchen counter. "I'm gonna run across the street and get us a bottle of wine to go with this Tandoori."

"A white wine!" Truitt yelled out. Charlene snorted

in response and went out the door. Finally, he had a chance to be alone with Kim.

"How are you?" Kim said. "You tired yet?"

He was, but there was no way that he was going to miss his opportunity with Kim. Besides, he reasoned, by the time they all sat down to eat, he knew that he would be re-energized. And he wanted to give Kim his full attention, wanted to show her that she was the best and that her sweetness was his weakness. "No. I'm aiight," he said. "Honestly, you are the one I've been waiting for. You are going to make this night right for me."

"But my two friends couldn't? They couldn't make the night special enough for you?" She crossed her legs and waited for Truitt's response. They watched each other knowing that this was their moment. Nothing stood between them but the raw truth and a chance to be real with each other.

"I think that you are more my type," Truitt finally answered. "We need to get to know each other better, is all."

"But we have to do the sex thing first, right?"

"Do you want to do it the other way around? Is that what it will take to make you my woman?"

"No," Kim said. "It's going to take much more than that." She stood from her seat and looked down at him. "Tell Ophelia and Charlene that I'll see them later. I'm out of here."

"You're leaving!" Truitt jumped to his feet. "Why?"

He rushed over to the door and faced her. "Couldn't you see that I wanted to get with you from the jump? Can't you feel that there's something happening between us? Come on. I know that I'm not alone in this."

"Maybe I did feel something." Kim reached for the door. "But that was before you went into your bedroom and laid with my friends!" She realized that she was yelling at him and she purposely took a moment to lower her voice. "You really are like the rest," she said. "You're only as good as the sex in front of you. And that's all."

Truitt was quiet as she opened the door.

"I'm honest about what matters," she said and walked out.

Take Control

Paul knew from his first day of work at the pillow factory that he was destined for something better. *Bigger and better, actually!* He would have been long gone to a school in another state if his father could have afforded it, but they barely had enough money for him to attend State University. Even then his father had insisted that he take a job at the pillow factory in order to bring in a paycheck.

All things considered, Paul had to admit that he had it pretty good. His father had turned the basement in the house into an apartment for him and left him to his own devices; letting him be a man is what his father said. The only conditions that his dad insisted upon were that Paul maintain good grades at the university and keep his job at the pillow factory. So far, neither of those requirements had been a problem.

Looking out over the factory floor, he saw Miss Teresa, Mugwump's mother, at her station. He could only imagine the joy that she was feeling because Mugwump was released from jail last night after doing two years for the incident with the cops. Paul knew that Mugwump was innocent. It was a well-publicized case and there had been an uproar in the Black community when the story broke. Paul had even participated in a few of the many protest marches that took place to demand Mugwump's release. When the police arrested a sixteen-year-old boy for the beating of two cops, the people of the community had rallied behind Mugwump. Numerous eyewitnesses had come forward to testify that the police had beaten him, verifying Mugwump's version of events, but the justice system moved slowly and by the time the bureaucratic wheels had turned, more than two years had passed before Mugwump was set free.

Paul left his desk and made his way over to Teresa's station.

"Hi, Paul," she greeted him.

"Hey, Miss Teresa," Paul answered.

"I guess you know that my baby is home, huh?"

"Yes, Ma'am." Paul smiled. "And it's about damn time."

"You ain't never lied," Teresa said. Small worry lines stretched across her face, lines that hadn't been there before Mugwump was arrested. She had maintained a strong front, but Paul had often caught her in candid moments when the strain showed on her face. "Are you going over to the house to see him? He's been asking about you."

"You know that, Miss Teresa," Paul said. "In fact, I'm going over there right now."

"Did you get permission from your father?"

"I don't need no stinkin' permission!"

Her eyebrows rose.

"Well, yeah. I did," Paul conceded. "But you know that I was going over anyway. Nothing is going to stop that." Teresa nodded her agreement. "So how is he? Still the same Mugwump?"

Teresa turned away from him. "No. He's different. Changed. He went away a boy and came back a fully-formed man." She looked at Paul. "He asked about you, though. He'll be happy that you stopped by."

"Has Truitt been over yet?" Paul said. A frown passed over her face before she answered. Teresa had never approved of Truitt.

"Yeah," she said. "He did."

An uncomfortable moment of silence settled between them. "Well, I'm out of here," Paul said. "I'll see you later, Miss Teresa."

Paul went back to his dad's office and said good-bye before leaving the factory. Retrieving his bike from the rack on the side of the building, Paul took off down the block toward Mugwump's house. He preferred riding his bicycle to driving his car whenever possible; on most days, it was the only exercise that he would get, and today was a nice day to ride. Mugwump only lived a few blocks away from the factory and, in moments, Paul was knocking on his front door.

While he waited, he wondered how much of the old Wump was still there. What had he gone through for the past two years? Was their friendship still strong?

Paul shook his head to clear his lingering doubts. He decided to place his faith in the strength of their years of friendship, years of brotherhood, really. Seconds later, the door swung open and Mugwump stood there.

"Whiteboy Paul!" A huge grin was on his face. "What the hell took you so long, son?"

"Wump!" They shared a warm embrace. "Man! I'm glad you're home."

"Me too, bruh. Me too." They stood back and measured each other. Mugwump had put on some weight. He looked healthier. Paul figured he had spent some time in the jailhouse gym. His face looked as if it had taken on some years, a prison maturity and an outlook that Paul would never comprehend.

"Yo!" Mugwump said. "Let's squat out here on the porch. I'm loving the outdoors right about now."

"No doubt." Paul sat down on the stairs. Mugwump settled down next to him. "How have you been, Wump?"

"How have I been?"

"I mean, how are you feeling? I know that me and Truitt missed you like crazy, man. Our lives were never the same with you gone."

"I hear you," Mugwump said. "But you and Truitt made it. That's a good thing. All good."

"But what about you?"

"What about me?"

"You okay? I mean, you lost a few years for something that you didn't do. Aren't you angry?"

"Anger doesn't matter. It doesn't help."

"It doesn't?"

Mugwump looked at Paul. "Imagine being angry for two years." He leaned back on both elbows and looked up at the sky. "I actually did something much more productive than that."

"Well, I was angry for you," Paul said. "A lot of us were. Pissed, as a matter of fact. They took you away from us. For nothing! They took my brother."

Mugwump extended his hand and they tapped fists. "I did my time. Time didn't do me." He paused to take a pack of cigarettes from his pocket. Paul looked on wordlessly as Mugwump pulled a lighter from his pocket and lit it. "Moms said that you started at the university. You like it?"

Paul wanted to ask Mugwump about the cigarettes—things had changed—but instead he said, "So far, so good."

"Have you figured out a major yet?" Mugwump blew out a stream of smoke.

"Not yet. I've got a few years to figure that out. Right now it's more fun than business. The classes are pretty easy...and the women!" Paul jumped to his feet. "Aw Lawd, the womens!"

Mugwump laughed. "So you got yourself a piece of ass up there at the school?"

"Yeah, man," Paul said. "This girl named Cara. She's pretty nice."

"You hitting it yet?"

"Wump, it's not simply about sex."

Mugwump arched an eyebrow at him.

"Okay," Paul said. "Yes! I am knocking it down!" They laughed and slapped hands. "But she's not experienced. She really doesn't know that much in bed."

"What! And you do?"

An awkward silence hung between them until Teresa came around the corner. "Just took a break to come and check on my son. Is that okay with you?" She smiled at Mugwump.

"It's all love." Mugwump stood and kissed her cheek. "As you can see, Paul is catching me up on things."

Teresa went up the stairs and paused at the front door. "Did you eat something?"

"Yeah, Ma. I ate already." He nodded at Paul. "We were getting ready to take a walk."

"You coming straight back?"

"Definitely, Ma." To Paul, he said, "Let's walk." They headed down the street past Gallo's grocery store and across Madison Avenue. Mugwump spoke first. "Man, it's humid out here today. It's like wet sunshine out here. Or is it just me?"

"Who cares, man? I'm glad that you're out here to get wet with me. Man! It wasn't the same for me after you went away. It was just me and Truitt." They rounded the corner on South Street toward the library.

"Oh yeah," Mugwump said. "But life goes on. We're all grown up now." He paused to take a last drag on his cigarette. "Doing grown man things."

Tossing the cigarette on the ground, he crushed it underfoot. They walked past the old, dilapidated basketball court that had no nets left on the rims toward the library where Truitt was sitting on the back of one of the lion statues. "Me Tarzan in this joint!" he yelled.

"Truitt still as wild as hell, I see," Mugwump said.

"Worse," Paul said. "Matter of fact, I think that he has lost any control mechanisms that he had in place."

"You know that I ain't never had no controls," Truitt said as he hopped down the stairs and slapped hands with his two best friends. "Just ask the womens! And they like it."

"Which reminds me," Mugwump said. "Something I have been wondering about." He turned to Paul. "Whatever happened with Miss Jones?"

Paul and Truitt exchanged a quick glance.

"I never heard anything about her after that night at her house. I was waiting for Mr. Valentine to be coming up in the joint, but I never heard anything about him. What happened?"

"Miss Jones left and never came back."

"She didn't even say good-bye," Paul said. "She just packed up and moved away."

"She didn't charge Valentine?" Mugwump said. "He raped her and she didn't say anything?" Paul was looking at the sidewalk. "She didn't even give you a heads-up?"

"Fuck that bitch!" Paul said.

Mugwump was taken aback. "Damn, Paul!"

"I'm serious," Paul said. "Fuck her. In fact, if you think

back on that night… Didn't it look like she was enjoying herself? She looked like she was liking it to me."

"Well, you would know that look better than we would," Truitt said. He walked over to a low-hanging tree limb, jumped up and caught it with both hands and started doing chin-ups. "Miss Jones sure was fine, though. I woulda roughed her up if she woulda asked me."

"Me too, bruh," Mugwump said. "Me too."

"Fuck her," Paul said.

"Why you sound bitter, Paul?"

"I'm not bitter. She showed me a lot."

"Schooled you, is what she did," Truitt said. "You should be glad for the lessons."

Paul didn't respond. Miss Jones had taken his manhood. And he would spend the rest of his life taking it back.

Like This

Paul picked Cara up from her dorm room and they went directly to the hotel. Cara was a PK—preacher's kid—who was getting her first taste of independence and she was as wild as a newly freed woman could possibly be. Her long, brown hair hung down past her shoulders and her soft, gray eyes suggested an innocence that was unspoiled. When Paul met her, her walk instantly drew him; the way her hips swayed enticed him and their rhythm called his nature. Her smile suggested hints of sexuality, an intrigue that he was determined to explore further.

Cara's total sexual abandon had surprised Paul, yet she was eager and willing to bow to his every desire, allowing him to unleash every pent-up fantasy that he hadn't had the opportunity to express. She didn't like it in the beginning when Paul would get rough with her, sometimes leaving her sore and spent; but she learned to submit to his needs. After all, he was good to her, attentive and much more mature than the other guys at school that she had dated. Sexually, he had much more endurance than any man she had shared her body with, always making sure that she was satisfied before the sex was over. The only issue she had was that he always wanted to fuck which was good for her most of the time, but sometimes she wanted to make love, to have an intimacy that meant more than bumping and grinding. She yearned for the afterglow at times, wanted that warm feeling in her center, a relaxing post-orgasm that would gently sway her to sleep. Cara wanted it all and she knew that if she was patient she could change him into the steady lover that she craved.

"Get in the bed!" Paul ordered as soon as the door closed behind them. "Take off your clothes."

"What?" Cara knew that he liked a little resistance. He reached for his belt buckle and slid it through the loops of his pants. "I like your body, Miss Jones." Paul was getting excited with the fantasy of his role-play, even though he knew that Cara didn't care for his "Miss Jones" scenario. But when he told her that it was part of his fantasy, like she was, she went along with it in order to please him. "Take 'em off," Paul said. Cara started a slow striptease for him. "Wait a minute!" Paul jumped up from the bed. He went into the bathroom and turned the light on, came out and turned the bedroom light off. "You are so much sexier in the shadows, Miss Jones." Quickly, he undressed while he watched her dance.

Cara was thick and full-bodied. Most of the guys at school considered her fat because she carried one hundred forty-five pounds on her five-foot, nine-inch frame, but Paul told her that she was all woman. Regular visits to the gym kept her fit, she spent at least an hour a day on the treadmill, and her body was firm. She told him that she didn't really want six-pack abs because she thought that a muscular stomach was too manly, yet she wanted sexy so she kept it sexy. By the time she finished her striptease, Paul was standing at attention and stroking himself while he watched her. "Oh shit," he whispered.

She climbed into the bed and waited. Paul took her doggy-style. He grabbed her by the hair and yanked it. Massaged her ass before spanking it. Cara responded, losing her inhibitions and discovering the thin line between pain and pleasure as she pushed back against him, meeting him thrust for thrust, cursing him while commanding him to do it harder and harder. The sight of her flesh was intoxicating and Paul found himself nearing an orgasm, so he pulled away from her and lay down on his back.

"Ride me, Miss Jones," he said. Chest heaving, his breath caught in his throat as Cara slowly lowered herself inch by inch onto his pulsing erection. She settled into a steady rhythm until he reached up and put his hand around her throat. "I said, ride me, Miss Jones!"

Cara's eyes popped open. She was in control now. She grabbed his arms and started bucking wildly. "Oh yeah? Fuck me then!" Cara rode Paul hard, the sound of their pounding flesh growing louder in the darkened room. She felt an orgasm wash over her but she didn't stop. Paul yelled out and she felt his eruption inside of her, hot and heavy, but she kept on riding. The head-board banging against the wall punctuated her curses and his stream of grunts until they both collapsed in a worn out heap of flesh. After a moment, Paul took Cara in his arms and she nuzzled into his embrace with her lips gently brushing the skin of his neck. They lay there for a while with Paul stroking her sweat-drenched hair until their breathing returned to normal.

"Paul?"

"Cara."

"You don't hate me, do you?"

"Not at all! I like being with you. You feel so good to me."

"Umm."

"Am I making you feel good?" Paul looked at her. "I mean, I felt you tremble. Inside. Were you faking it?"

"No!" She hit him lightly in the chest. "No faking. I don't think I know how to fake it anyway. Not yet."

"Really?"

"Really."

Paul smiled and moved her over so that she was lying on her back. Their eyes met briefly before he lowered his mouth down and took one of her nipples in his mouth. Cara held his head, guiding him as she felt his tongue flick across her stiffening nub and a tremor surge through her body. He could have her any way he wanted. She wanted him that badly. But one day he was going to tell her all about Miss Jones.

The Ache Returns

The ache returned and this time the pain was much worse. It started at the base of his skull and lingered daily in the front of his brain. The haze had also returned and sometimes Willmon felt as if he were floating in his own brand of hell. Reality would fade in and out for him, each waking moment was spent trying to grasp onto what he thought was a piece of the real world. Strangely enough, he found his mother to be the anchor of his existence. She was real and he found that he couldn't live without her.

Even the weed was losing some of its effectiveness, only holding off the sluggishness of his mind for an hour or two until he found himself craving those precious hours. He had finished a blunt earlier and was sitting in the recliner in his living room with his head leaned back, staring at the ceiling and enjoying the pretty colors that swirled around on the white surface while his mother and Leon argued.

"I can't talk to you while your retarded son is in here," Leon said. The top of his balding head was glistening with sweat and his lips quivered beneath the heavy mustache that he wore. His wide, flat nose matched the rest of his dented face and the ragged sideburns that never grew in fully. Dark, flat eyes peeked out from beneath a jutting forehead and when he spoke, Willmon thought of sandpaper being dragged across his vocal chords.

"He ain't paying you no attention," his mother said. "So forget my son and tell me what you got to tell me." Willmon heard the tension in his mother's voice, a timbre that he knew all too well, and a smile flashed across his face because he knew that Leon was about to get his.

"I done told you about talking to me like that," Leon said. "That's the main reason that we don't get along. You got too much mouth."

"Oh, *now* you want to complain about my mouth, huh?"

"Because you got too much, that's why."

"How about you get to what you got to say? You been hemming and hawing all night long. Like you scared of something. I been around long enough to know when a man is up to something. What happened? You done got tired of this? Spit it out. Try being a man about yours."

"Now what the hell do you know about being a man?" Willmon heard Leon get up from the couch and walk around the room. When he next heard Leon's voice, it sounded like he was standing right over him. "You sure don't know how to pick none. If you did, you wouldn't have this bad case of retard son you got."

"What does Willmon have to do with this?" His mother paused to take a deep breath and the next time she spoke her voice was deadly calm. Willmon knew that aspect of his mother too. It usually happened right before the storm. He closed his eyes and tried to concentrate. A poem popped into his mind, right before his eyes. *The ache. The touch. My soul knows only the two.* He felt himself exhale and opened his eyes. Leon was standing there looking down at him. And he had the Dead Eyes! Blood-red sockets moved like rolling liquid staring down at him and Willmon screamed.

"Shit!" Leon jumped. He pointed angrily at Willmon. "See! That boy is crazy!"

Willmon lay back in the chair with his eyes closed, crying hysterically.

"Leave him alone!" his mother said.

The haze was still there but this time it felt familiar and Willmon felt strangely safe; he felt himself calming down. The throbbing in his brain was growing louder and getting bigger. He felt his mind reach out for his mother.

"What!" his mother shrieked.

"You heard me," Leon said. "You gave me the claps."

"I ain't gave you shit! I ain't been with nobody but you. And you know it."

"That's what you say!"

"Who else you been out there screwing, Leon? Huh? Who, you sonofabitch!"

"You the one who gave me the claps," Leon said.

The claps! The word stirred up memories in Willmon's mind. Back and far away. When he was younger. Back in the day, before his accident when he used to hang out with the fellas. *"I'll kill the bitch." "For real." "Somebody got to pay for that." "I'll get me a gun and shoot that bitch."*

Slap!

"Get the hell out of my house!"

Willmon's eyes popped open in time to see his mother throw another punch that caught Leon in the face, rocking him. He stumbled back a few steps before straightening up and glaring at Willmon's mother.

"And don't you ever step foot around me again," she said.

"That ain't no problem, bitch." Leon turned and walked toward the front door. "None at all."

"Tell your story walking, apple knocker!" She rushed to the door and slammed it after him. Silence filled the room and Willmon studied the dark colors that swirled behind his eyes. The last vestiges of his high were fading and he was holding onto his version of mindplay for as long as he could when he heard a loud cry. Slowly, he eased open his eyes and glanced to his left. His mother was sitting on the couch with her head cradled in her hands. Her body started shaking as wrenching cries escaped from her lips. Willmon watched as the tears rolled down her face and soon he felt an unfamiliar wetness stain his cheeks.

"No!" his mother cried out. "No!" More sobs escaped her. "I know that this trifling man didn't do this to me."

"*I'll kill the bitch.*" "*For real.*" "*Somebody got to pay for that.*" "*I'll get me a gun and shoot that bitch.*"

The thought gave him strength.

Willmon wiped his tears away.

She Got Game

Mugwump and Paul were sitting on a bench in the park when David Valentine came walking toward them. Mugwump nudged Paul when he saw him approaching and they instantly flashed back to that night long ago when they had watched through the window as Mr. Valentine raped Miss Jones.

Paul had often considered confronting Mr. Valentine about the incident but always experienced an inexplicable anger that overtook him, a rage at the man who violated the woman who had introduced him to intimacy.

David Valentine stopped and stood looking out over the fence that circled the park at the river. He had his back to them. With a touch of curiosity, they watched David Valentine as he stood there, seemingly lost in thought, oblivious to their presence. His shoulders slumped as if there were some heavy weight placed upon them. He half turned and glanced at them but decided to look back at the swirling waters of the river.

"Miss Jones called me." His voice sounded hollow, as if it were echoing off the waters. Paul and Mugwump were silent, unsure if David was speaking to them. "Who are you talking to?" Paul's voice was sharp. "I know that you're not talking to me?"

David slowly turned and faced them before he spoke again. "She called me a few days ago and told me to find you guys." Pausing to look at the ground, he waited a moment. "She knows that you guys were there that night. She saw you."

Paul rose from the bench. "What night was that? The night you raped her?" David looked at Paul and said nothing. "That's right." Paul's voice rose. His clenched fist was by his side and he leaned forward until his face was inches away from David's. "Yeah, I saw you. You're a rapist."

Mugwump laughed out loud. "I can't believe that you would violate a woman like that! That's weak. Real weak. But I know why you did it, though."

"Because he's a rapist," Paul said.

"And she doesn't have to like it, right?" Mugwump regarded him.

"You were there, too," David said. "She told me that she recognized all of you. And where is your friend, Truitt?" He looked around as if he expected Truitt to jump out from behind a tree. "She wanted me to…told me, really, that I had to talk to you guys about what happened that night. Because, in reality, you don't know what you saw. I can't even explain it. Sometimes there are things between a man and a woman."

"Man! Talk about trying to justify your actions!" Paul

was hot with anger and Mugwump was taken aback by his aggressive stance. He looked at David Valentine.

"You took that pussy, man. Simple as that. What more can you add to that?"

"Much more," he barked at Paul. "Now why don't you back away from me, Paul." Their eyes locked, and for a moment, Mugwump thought that Paul was going to hit David Valentine, but then he walked back over to the bench and sat down. "Anyway, I was ordered to talk to all three of you."

"For what?" Mugwump said.

"By the way," Paul said. "Whatever happened to Miss Jones? She went away right after you *raped* her."

"I don't know. She called me on the phone. She wouldn't give me any more information."

"My man." Mugwump took a pack of cigarettes out of his pocket and thumped one out. "Tell me this one thing: why did you have to take the ass? I mean, don't you have any rap skills at all?"

"Nothing's real." David seemed distant. "It's all smoke and mirrors when you have to deal with a woman; especially certain types of women. Like Nina."

Paul and Mugwump exchanged a look. "What in the hell are you talking about?"

"I have to apologize to both of you. Tell Truitt when you see him," David said. "Miss Jones thinks that you may have been adversely affected by what you saw that night."

"But not you, huh?" Mugwump said. He seemed to

be enjoying David's discomfort. "And what took her so long to realize this?"

"I don't know. And I could care less if you were traumatized for life."

"So why are you here?" Anger had crept back into Paul's voice. Mugwump knew that Paul had been having sex with Miss Jones, but that was years ago and he figured that Paul would be over it by now. Yet it seemed like he hadn't moved on.

"That bitch forced me to do this." David slammed his hand on the fence. "She threatened to go to the police if I didn't." He glared at them, his eyes narrowed to angry slits. "She especially told me to make sure that you were okay, Paul. As if you are the only one who can intellectualize the events of that night. So! Are you sexually repressed from watching me hit that? Why were you watching me anyway? What were you doing there?"

Paul jumped to his feet. "What were you doing there?" They stood face to face, and though David was an older man, he wasn't much taller than Paul. His hair hung down over his face, giving him the look of a wild man and veins stuck out in his neck as he stared at the young man in front of him.

"Paul. Calm down, man," Mugwump said. "It ain't that serious." He went over and pulled Paul by the arm back to their spot on the bench. "I met plenty of dudes like him when I was away. One thing I learned is that there is something inherently and genetically twisted about a man that would force intimacy on a woman. Right, Mister Valentine?"

David looked at Mugwump, a thoughtful expression finding its way to his face. "Yes. I guess that is true. It's a violation, a spiritual violation that can damage the soul." He was pensive as he leaned back against the fence and looked up at the sky. "But you still didn't answer my question. What were you doing there? Were you guys like peeping tom perverts? Huh? Was that it? You took your little weenies around town peeping into windows and pounding your puds?"

"What I can't figure out is why Miss Jones didn't have you locked up," Mugwump said. "You could have gone away for years; especially if we would have testified as witnesses. You would have been gone. So why didn't she?"

"We should report you to the police ourselves," Paul said. "That probably wasn't your first time anyway. You're probably like Jack the Raper."

David Valentine finally exploded. "That's bullshit!" His face was haggard; he had bags under his eyes as if he hadn't slept in days, and he looked as if he hadn't shaved in a while. He angrily swept his hair back over his head. "Nina simply wanted me to talk to you, to check on you, so that I could reassure her that you were okay. I told her that you would not be too willing to talk to me but she insisted."

"Looks like you are Miss Jones' bitch now. She'll probably have you washing her dirty drawers."

"And painting her toenails," Paul added.

David snorted derisively, turned and took a few steps away from them. He moved stiffly, which seemed to add a few years to his tired frame. "I didn't rape her."

"What?"

"I said that I didn't rape Miss Jones."

"Sure you didn't."

"I don't have to rape women."

"We saw you, man! With our own eyes."

"Of course." David turned to them. "Sometimes your eyes don't see what you think they see. You see, what you saw was a game that we played. Me and Miss Jones. On more than one occasion she even made me wear a mask, a ski mask, like I was robbing her. It was one of many games that we played. Games that turned her on." He paused to look at Paul. "And for some reason, I think that is something you would know about."

Paul stopped for a second, caught off guard by David's insight. He looked at Mugwump who was lighting a cigarette. "Is that how you are going to spin it," he said after he recovered. "Is that what helps you sleep at night?"

"It was all a game, Paul. A game!"

"You're going to have to sell that dream to somebody else. Because I'm not buying it."

"Miss Jones is a freak?" Mugwump exclaimed.

"Very uninhibited," David said. "Sometimes she liked it rough and she knew that I would give it to her whatever way she wanted. I had a serious hard-on for her."

"She had you whooped." Mugwump laughed. "Ain't you ever heard? You supposed to pop that coochie! Pop! Pop! Pop!"

"It was all a game to her," David said. "And I lost."

Street Games

"Do you think he's lying?" Mugwump looked over at Paul.

"I think that he's scared." Paul stared straight ahead as if he were afraid to meet Mugwump's inquisitive look. Paul was flustered; his calm demeanor was gone, replaced with an unreasoning anger.

"But he didn't have to come and find us, Paul."

"He's scared."

"Scared! Scared of what?"

"Jail." Paul pointed at Mugwump. "Us."

"You're not thinking straight. He has only one thing to be scared of; Miss Jones! That is, if you really believe she told him to come and find us."

"Hell no!"

"But Paul," Mugwump said. "How else would he know that we were there?"

Paul stopped and looked at Mugwump as the realization began to sink in. He turned and looked up Central Avenue at the buildings that lined the street. Four lanes of traffic streamed through the intersection that led over

Northern Boulevard and the bridge that connected it to Clinton Avenue. They stood in front of the entrance of a small grocery store and Paul stepped aside as a young, pregnant girl pushing a baby carriage went inside.

"Did Miss Jones ever call you?" Mugwump said. Paul turned and followed the girl into the grocery store without answering, leaving Mugwump outside to ponder why his friend was acting so strangely. The Front Page Bookstore occupied the building next to the grocery store and Mugwump took a moment to look through the display window and peruse some of the titles that crowded the shelf. There hadn't even been a Black bookstore in the city five years ago and now the shelves were crowded with publications. *We finally coming up!* Mugwump mused.

Traffic began backing up at the intersection further up the block and a crowd was gathering, talking and pointing at a disturbance in the middle of the street. When Paul came out of the store with a soda in his hand, they continued up the block toward the cars stopped at the intersection. Irate drivers were now angrily pounding their car horns at the blockade and a few were even leaning out of the windows and yelling at the cars ahead of them.

"Paul, you have to tell me what all this anger is about," Mugwump said. Tipping his soda to his lips, Paul remained silent as they neared the corner and then he looked with interest at the problem with the traffic. "For real, man." Mugwump's curiosity was now piqued and he strained to see what was going on.

"I'm good, Wump."

"But she never called you, did she? She left and took a piece of you with her. She didn't even bother to say good-bye."

There was someone standing in the middle of the intersection, blocking traffic in both directions but ignoring the drivers who were waving at him to get out of the street.

"Paul, that was just sex, man. Nothing more. At least, not to her."

"And how would you know that?" Paul said. Mugwump had changed a great deal but Paul had grown up too. Long gone were the days when he heeded the advice of others simply because they thought that their opinion was the right one. Manhood meant that he had to take control of his own life.

The uproar grew in intensity and when they finally realized what was going on, they gasped in disbelief. "Is that Willmon out there?" Paul said.

"What?" Mugwump said, though he recognized him, too. "Hey, Willmon!"

"What is he doing, man? Come on!" They pushed their way through the crowd, making their way out into the street as they ignored the comments of the onlookers.

"That is one crazy dude!"

"Look at him! What is wrong with him?"

"He smokin' that crack."

They moved people aside and rushed over to Willmon. Sirens could be heard in the distance as they approached him standing there with a dazed look on his face. Willmon had changed since the last time they had seen him. He was growing dreadlocks, though they were still so short that they didn't reach past his ears, and his frame had filled out a bit even though he still appeared somewhat fragile. His expression was unfocused, as if he had no idea that he was standing in the middle of a busy intersection, and when he saw them approaching there was no indication that he recognized them. Blue jeans sagged off his hips as he stood there with one hand jammed into his pocket. His shirt was dotted with red splotches that looked like blood. Mugwump pulled up short and stuck his arm out, barring Paul from getting any closer.

"Willmon." Mugwump kept his voice calm. "It's me, Mugwump. And Paul."

Willmon cocked his head at them.

"You know Willmon ain't right anymore," he whispered to Paul. "Since that accident, he's been sick."

"I know," Paul said. "But I hear the police coming. We have to get him out of the street."

Mugwump inched forward.

"Willmon," he said. "Let's go, man."

"Kickball!" Willmon said.

"Yeah. Remember we used to play? In the alley behind the house?"

"Yeah! Yeah!" He looked past Mugwump. "Paul. Whiteboy Paul!" A big smile broke across his face and he threw both hands in the air as he rushed to embrace Paul. Paul patted him on the back and said, "Come on, Willmon. Let's get out of here, okay?"

"Okay." Willmon followed them across the bridge on Northern Boulevard toward Clinton Avenue, then down Third Street where they turned back and went under the bridge and waited until they heard the commotion overhead die down. Willmon was oblivious to the incident he had caused, talking a mile a minute the entire time that they were supposed to be hiding from the police.

"Willmon, man," Mugwump said. "What's going on with you?"

Willmon pulled a blunt out of his pocket and lit it. The pungent aroma floated up in the air as he puffed heavily, trying to get a good burn on the tip of the cigar. Paul stood up and walked a few feet away. He didn't care for drugs of any kind and was taken by surprise when Willmon passed the blunt to Mugwump, who took it and started smoking, too.

"Jesus, Mugwump!" Paul said. "You do it all now, don't you?"

"Everything but the seeds, the stems and the sticks," he replied, then blew out a plume of smoke. "What I'm wondering about, Willmon, is what were you doing in the middle of the street, man?"

Willmon didn't answer; he simply leaned back against the stanchion of the bridge and waited for Mugwump to take two and pass. "I don't know, Wump," he answered when he got the blunt back. "I don't know. Sometimes, in my mind, I just leave."

"That's exactly what Mugwump is doing now," Paul said. "Leaving."

"Paul, you tripping."

"That stuff kills you, Wump. It's a gateway drug."

"Kill!" Willmon yelled. "I'm gonna kill that bitch!"

"See what you started," Mugwump said. "Weed doesn't kill. Now, Miss Jones? That's what kills."

Willmon started laughing.

"That's hilarious," Paul said. "Willmon, man, we haven't seen you in a long time. How have you been?"

Willmon took a deep hit off the cigar and then he seemed to visibly relax. The fuzzy, faraway stare faded from his eyes as he looked at them. "I ain't been doing nothing, man. Just chillin' and shit, looking to take care of business."

"What business you got to take care of?"

"My mother's business, you know." Willmon fidgeted, happy that the pulsing pain in his head was ebbing away. "You know something? Since I had my accident, all the medicine the doctors gave me? Only thing that works is the buds." He looked at the cigar in his hand. "I see more clearly then." He passed it back to Mugwump before putting his hand in his pocket and running his fingers along the barrel of the gun, triggering the memory of how it had come into his possession.

His mind had been clear then.

He had been stealing money from his mother's purse for weeks and hiding it in his room until he thought he had enough money to buy a gun. His mother hadn't been the same since the incident with Leon; she didn't care about anything anymore, so she never noticed that her money was coming up short. If she did, she never said a word to him about it. Armed with sixty-five dollars, Willmon went down to lower Swan Street—a place that was called The Sewer—to buy a gun.

It had been easy. A dealer named Peace did business out of a house that sat on the corner, a few doors down from France's Grocery Store, on the corner of First and Swan Streets. Willmon went through the wrought-iron gate that surrounded the grassless yard and knocked on the unpainted, wooden door.

"Who?" came the reply.

"Willmon."

The door opened a crack. "What your crazy ass want?"

"It's me."

The door opened wider and Willmon stepped inside. A head-ache moved in his head as he followed Peace downstairs into the basement. "What your crazy ass want?" Peace said again.

Willmon stood there and waited for the pain to pass.

"You hear me?"

"I want a burner."

Peace laughed. "Get outta here with that!"

"For real. What? You ain't got no more?"

"I ask the questions, little nigga." *Everybody knew that this kid was crazy, but he had always been harmless. Now he wanted a gun.* Peace figured that he probably didn't know the first thing about a gun. "How much you spending?"

"I got fifty dollars."

Peace laughed. "And what you want to get with that? We don't sell no peashooters up in here."

"I don't want no peashooter. I want something that shoot bullets."

"Well, you gotta come better than fifty dollars, little nigga. Much better than that."

"Okay then. I got sixty."

"Well then, nigga!"

"Let me see first."

Peace went back into a closet and pulled down a box which contained a brown, canvas bag. There were three guns inside; one of them was a semi-automatic that had misfired when they had gone on a job in the city and the gun no longer worked. He would have been dead if he had needed to cap somebody but, luckily for him, his boys had his back. Willmon wouldn't be able to shoot any bullets with that gun. Besides, Peace figured that Willmon wouldn't know that he would have to cock the gun anyway.

Turning back to Willmon with the gun in his hand, he demanded the money, which Willmon pulled out of his pocket and gave to him. Peace then raised the gun and pointed it, inches away from Willmon's face. "See, little nigga! This what it gonna feel like when you point it at somebody." Pressing the gun into Willmon's forehead, he said, "Can you feel that?"

Willmon smiled. "Yeah. So give me my gun."

The hard smile faded from Peace's face when he saw that Willmon didn't flinch from his threat. He lowered the gun and handed it to him, glad that he wasn't selling him a gun that actually worked. "You really is crazy, ain't you, nigga?"

When Willmon left the dealer's house with the gun in his pocket, the haze had returned. He had five dollars left in his pocket and he knew a guy who still sold nickel bags on Swan Street so he quickly purchased one and headed back home. By the time he got to the corner on Central Avenue, his brain was on fire. He had lost his place in reality when Mugwump and Paul had found him in the middle of the street.

"I'm gonna kill that bitch," Willmon said.

"Who you planning on killing?" Mugwump was feeling the effects of the smoke.

"The bitch."

"I know what you mean." Paul came back and joined them now that the blunt was gone. "Make you want to hurt someone."

Mugwump said, "You don't want to do nothing crazy. You don't want to do what I did. I went away for a long time. You wouldn't want to do that. You wouldn't make it in there." He took a closer look at Willmon. Gone were all the vestiges of the wild innocence of that little nappy-headed kid that used to look up to them. The young man who stood before him was troubled and angry, on a road that Mugwump had taken himself. He remembered his promise to Brother Black that he would make his life count and here was his opportunity to fulfill his vow. "Hey, Willmon," he said.

Willmon extended his arm with his fingers poised, mimicking a gun with his thumb as the firing pin. "Click, click, bang!"

"Willmon!"

"Knock 'em down. Set 'em down."

Paul reached out and pushed Willmon's hand down, his eyes filled with the same concern that Mugwump felt.

"Tell you what," Mugwump said. "I'm going to come get you tomorrow. Okay? Let's go up to the park and chill out for a bit. Get you away from some of this madness. You down for that?"

Willmon nodded his head and raised his hand again. "Click, click, bang!"

"Willmon's out of it." Paul was watching him closely. "It's that weed."

"No, I ain't," Willmon said in a surprisingly calm voice.

"Yeah. You are," Mugwump said. "You gotta get away from all the madness."

"Let us stop this madness. Let us stop this madness," Willmon said in a singsong cadence. "Let us. Stop. This. Maaaddddnessssss!"

Paul and Mugwump exchanged a puzzled glance.

"A poem I heard the other day," Willmon explained. Mugwump stood in front of Willmon and looked directly into his eyes.

"What was up with that episode in the middle of the street, Willmon?"

Willmon answered, "I'm gonna kill the bitch."

Ménage

Enough! To hell with Miss Jones! Cara's anger surged to the forefront when she realized the extent of Paul's infatuation with the schoolteacher. He had gotten to the point where he couldn't be with Cara without Miss Jones being in the bed with them. It was an emotional ménage à trois and Cara was getting lost in the shuffle.

"I'm not doing it anymore, Paul." She sat up in the bed looking down at him after another session of sex. Paul had been especially vigorous, pounding himself into her angrily, heedless of her satisfaction, until he climaxed violently and tossed her aside. Usually an attentive lover, he now lay on his back staring blankly at the ceiling, lost in his own little world. "Paul!"

"Stop yelling, Cara. I hear you."

"No. You don't hear me. You aren't even listening to me."

"Yes, I am."

"No, you're not."

"Okay." Paul turned to her. "I'm sorry. What did I not hear?"

"I can't do this anymore. It's not fair to me and it's very, very disrespectful."

"Okay, Cara," Paul said. "This is where I came in. Am I doing something wrong?" Seeing her incredulous look, Paul cut her off. "Let me restate that. What did I do wrong?"

"Come on, Paul! This ain't rocket science here. Your obsession with this Miss Jones. What is that?"

"What is that?"

"Yes! What is the obsession? Don't you want me? Am I enough for you?"

"What do you mean?"

"Me!" Cara said. She took a second to calm herself. "Me. I… I mean this woman in front of you. I want you to want me, Paul. Can you do that?"

"Of course I can do that," Paul said. "In fact, I am doing that."

Cara leaned toward him and looked in his eyes. "Paul, I am not Miss Jones. And there really isn't any room in this relationship, or this bed, for Miss Jones. I hope that you can see that."

Paul pushed himself upright until he was face to face with Cara. He liked her a lot, she felt good in his hands, but he was the man in the relationship and he knew that if he gave into her demands then he would always be the submissive partner. "So what are you saying then? We can't see each other anymore? You're not happy with the way things are?"

"I'm saying much more than that, Paul."

"Am I being the dense male again? Or are my mind-reading skills not up to par?"

"I can't believe this." Cara was exasperated. "You don't get it, do you? Let me put it this way. Next time we have sex, I'm going to call you Mister Pitt." She lay down on her back and started moaning, "Yes, Mister Pitt. Give it all to me, Mister Pitt. Every inch. Harder! Harder!" She stopped and opened her eyes. "Now do you get it?"

Paul's eyes went hard. Steely, shattered glass reflected the emotions that he struggled to keep in check. All of his trust was out the door, scattered outside, along with the feelings that he had for Cara. "I got it," he said. "I got it."

Cara was taken aback by his calm acceptance. Silence filled the room. Moving closer to him to rest her head on his shoulder she felt him flinch. The warmth was gone. "I'm sorry," she said.

"You're honest. I can't ask for more than that."

They settled into bed and watched television for a little while. Paul didn't even object like he usually did when Cara flipped to the Lifetime Channel, and he soon found himself caught up in the movie that was playing.

"That woman is crazy as hell," he commented as they watched the jealous woman put the wife's cat in the dryer, set it to sixty minutes, and leave it for the couple to find when they came home.

"We can get crazy sometimes," Cara said.

"Not that crazy! She drugged the husband, had sex with him, videotaped it and sent copies to the wife and the wife's parents. That is playing hardball. Can you say *therapy?*"

"That was an excellent dramatic presentation."

"Now I feel like a drama junkie."

Cara slid a hand under the covers and gripped him. "Are you hooked?" She stroked him firmly. An image of Miss Jones flashed across his mind and he felt himself respond, springing fully erect.

"If you'll be my therapist," he said. "Cara."

Miss Jones

Men ain't nothing but drama! Little egos with a penis attached. Nina Jones had learned that lesson at an early age and had taken it to heart. She had learned the power of her femininity and it molded her into a thrill seeker.

Charles Jones had loomed large in her life, raising a daughter by himself after Nina's mother had died. Her father was a big, strapping man, ill-equipped to deal with a daughter and not especially in touch with the sensitive side of his personality. He spent over thirty years working for Two-Man Construction and he brought his hardhat philosophy home with him every night. The job was his life. He'd started working as a gopher, grunting his way through day after day of grunt work and, after years of dedication, he had clawed his way up to foreman. He lived hard and raising a daughter hadn't changed his demeanor one bit, but Nina loved her dad. As a result, she emulated his mannerisms and adopted his outlook on life, becoming a tomboy, disdaining dolls and dollhouses, opting instead for tree houses and mud pies. However, as she grew older, her body obtained the fullness of womanhood.

She had the ruddy complexion of her father, but she inherited the graceful beauty of her mother. By the time she reached adolescence, Nina had achieved the sexual magnetism of adulthood and the maturity of a woman with full knowledge of her sexuality. She learned about men by watching and listening to her dad.

"Women know that we are all hunters." Nina sat at the top of the stairs and listened to her father and his drinking buddies, their voices getting louder with every swig of liquor. She loved eavesdropping when her father and his friends had what she called their "Man Club" meetings. She especially took pride in the authority with which her father spoke on such a wide range of subjects, from sports to current events and even politics. She decided that she would be as well-rounded and knowledgeable as her dad. "The pursuit of orgasmic perfection is intrinsic in our beings."

"What the fu—?"

"In other words," Earl said, "men are beasts who are led around by our peckers."

Laughter and agreement followed.

"An oversimplification," Charles said, followed by a loud belch. "But true. So very true."

"I don't agree with that," Mike Easley said. Mike was the real scholar of the group, a Columbia graduate who returned to his hometown often to visit his old friends.

"You never do," Earl said.

Mike continued, "Men are honorable. We pursue more than the fleshly lust."

"You're drunk," Earl said.

"Don't kid yourself, Mike," Charles said. "It's in our DNA."

"Again, I disagree."

"It's true that there are some…" Charles took a quick sip of his drink. "There are some genetic deviants out there. There are some men who can have a woman once a month and be satisfied with that. That's not normal." He pointed a finger at Mike. "Just watch *Oprah*!"

"Yeah," Earl pitched in. "If it's on *Oprah*, it's gotta be true." Earl and Charles laughed as they clinked their glasses together. Mike's voice was an octave higher when he spoke.

"Television rarely has anything to do with reality. The reality is that there are good men, doing good things every day." Mike wore a big smile on his face. "Not simply following their erections around like Willie the one-eyed wonder worm."

"You see…" Charles tottered a step toward him. "That's a conditioned response right there. Society has taught you that, Mike. Sex and goodness are not mutually exclusive."

"Where in the hell did you get all of the big words today, Charles?" Mike laughed. "I'm impressed, though. I must admit. But you have us in the vein of cavemen."

"Your point being?"

"We're better than aminals."

"What the hell is an *aminal*, Mike? All that college and you're an aminal."

"That's the liquor," Mike said. "I meant manimal."

"You know what I think," Charles said. "You know what I would appreciate? A woman with an attitude."

"No more liquor for that man!" Mike said.

"Yeah," Earl agreed. "A woman with an attitude? Is this some new type drink?" He looked suspiciously at his glass.

"Honestly…" Charles held his drink in the air. "Women should treat sex like men do. Sex and love are two different things. And please don't confuse the two."

Mike regarded Charles. "I'm sure that you don't want your daughter to be like that. She's already turning into a beautiful young lady."

"Watch yourself now," Charles said.

"And she's going to need all the guidance that you can give her. And that won't be the garbage you are spouting right now."

"My girl is going to be a strong woman. She is going to stand on her own two feet. Not depending on anyone. So when I'm not around, she'll still be okay. Still strong."

Nina made her way back to her bed with a renewed purpose. She resolved to be strong…for her dad. She would make him proud.

She was a senior in high school when she met Chris, a freshman who transferred from Bolton High School in Louisiana. Chris had a tanned complexion, long, dark hair and the mysterious glint of a rebel in his eyes that had the other girls scheming when Nina decided to conquer him. She had reached womanhood with a dark, smoldering beauty that she carried with a self-assurance that bordered on conceit, but she remained casually aloof. Nina was a loner, her attitude toward girls her age was biased by her days of tree climbing and rock throwing with the boys. She considered the others silly and weak. Nina had only one female acquaintance, Margie, and the only thing they had in common was that Margie was a loner too. They were distant friends with similar pursuits.

"The new guy is sexy. Kinda dark," Margie told her one day when they were sitting at the lunch table. "He has some really good hips for a boy his age."

Nina said nothing. She had already decided that Chris would be her first. He was the answer to the blossoming sexuality that thrummed inside of her every day; a sexual cauldron that bubbled daily, one that she was barely keeping the lid on with her fingertips. Though Chris was a freshman, he was nearly six feet tall, sturdy and strong, but Nina knew instinctively that she had better tread carefully.

Nearly a week later, they had a secret rendezvous and she gave Chris her virginity.

They met in a tree house that she had helped to build when she was a kid, back in the woods, down the hill from Columbia Park. Moonlight glowed as Nina climbed up the wooden blocks nailed into the tree which served as steps, crawled into the tree house and found Chris waiting inside with a thick wool blanket spread out on the floor. She sat next to him and they listened to the night sounds of nature: crickets' chirping was accompanied by the occasional rustling through the underbrush. They found comfort in the absence of human sounds. She stood up and looked out of the tree house window.

"You can't tell anyone, Chris," she said after a moment.

"I won't, Nina," Chris said anxiously. He fidgeted on the floor. "I love you, Nina."

She turned to look at him. "But you can't say anything to anybody." She pointed a finger at him. "Ever!"

Chris was quiet.

Nina turned back to the tree-house window. "And I'm going to make sure that you don't." From the tree-house, Nina could see past Columbia Park to the projects across the street. She saw no one. She turned back to Chris. He had told her that he had sex before but she doubted it. He was watching her nervously, as if he didn't know what to do next. It was time for her to take control. "Come on," she said. "Take your clothes off. Let me see it."

Chris unbuckled his pants. "What about you?"

"Don't ask questions." She watched as Chris stepped out of his pants and stood naked in the moonlight. She reached out and touched him and his hardness lengthened. She smiled at the effect she had on him. "You take this thing." She squeezed it gently and felt him grow even more. "And you do what I tell you to do with it."

Somewhere In Between

Somewhere in between, Nina's sex turned from enjoyment to dominance...and she thoroughly relished the feeling of power.

The transition was subtle but indelible. Nina was in her junior year at State University, one year away from obtaining her teaching certificate, and she was feeling the pangs of loneliness. College had been a long, solitary journey for her; she had donned social blinders after graduating from high school, determined to reach her goal.

After leaving high school, Nina had left Chris behind, too. He cried and begged her to continue the relationship; and she had to admit that he had been as good as his word, that he hadn't betrayed her trust, but in the end she had to move on. He had served his purpose as her horse, for that is what men had become to her, simple animals that she would ride to her heart's content and then put out to pasture. Chris had been a stallion; she had ridden him to college, but that was where the romp ended.

Years had passed and now Nina was feeling that itch again.

She met David Valentine outside of the student lounge on campus and their physical attraction was instantaneous. David was a serious young man who aspired to write the next great American novel and Nina sensed vulnerability in him. His soft-spoken manner and quiet smile sparked a heat inside of her as she imagined what she would do to him.

She stood next to him, reading a menu that was taped to the cafeteria wall.

"It's much more interesting out here."

Nina turned and saw David standing there, unsure of what to say but deciding to brave the storm. "Is it?" She smiled at him. "What makes it so interesting out here?"

"You do." They watched each other until David said, "Can I walk with you?"

"I have a few minutes before my next class," Nina said. They walked around the sprawling campus and Nina found David to be introverted yet intelligent. He had an air of simplicity that immediately piqued her interest and inwardly she began to make plans for him.

On a hot Friday night, they went on their first date. David Valentine was the perfect gentleman, striving to make a great first impression. Nina appreciated his gestures while she took her time and made her plans. She carefully dropped sex hints for David, looking into his eyes as her lust seeds sprouted into raging fruit. He picked up on all of her clues but was anxiously patient as he waited for her to select the moment that they would be together.

When they eventually spent the night in the hotel, Nina made the experience unforgettable. She made David Valentine pleasure her, and made him hold back his own release until she gave him permission. He used his tongue until his jaws ached, his fingers until his wrists tired, and his sex until he begged for mercy. But still, she said no. And David held on.

She tied him to a chair and danced for him, her sex a hair's breadth from his hardness, teasing him to no end. She was harsh, then gentle; rough, then soft. She blindfolded him, commanded him to keep his erection while she dressed, walked out the door and went to the store to buy a beer. She returned fifteen minutes later with the drink and a bucket that she got at the desk, which was filled with ice cubes.

"Your orgasms are not your own," she warned him before putting the ice in her mouth. She plunged on him, taking his hardness in her mouth and watching him jump with the shocking coldness. She rode him until the ice melted and David Valentine was straining against the ropes.

She stood and watched him, finding comfort in his agony. He was where she wanted him. Somewhere in between the grit and the glamour, between the pain and the pleasure of her whims and desires, Nina felt a wetness between her legs as she watched his erection pulse with a want of its own.

"Please!" David grunted. His plea sent Nina into a frenzy. She tore her clothes off and mounted him. Tearing the blindfold from his eyes, she kissed him and ran her tongue roughly across his face. Pulling away from him she said, "No." She began her grinding motion. "You please."

David Valentine went for his, bucking so violently that the chair scratched and bucked against the floor. A scream accompanied his release, which spewed from him, leaving him limp and breathless as Nina's juices mingled with his and they listened to the silence for a while.

After Nina untied him, David took her hand. "Let's do that again," he said.

Sex Lessons

Paul dropped Cara off at her dorm room and decided to grab a bite at Charlie's, a local pub that served burgers and fries. She had left him feeling angry and cold. He didn't care about her anymore. It wasn't his fault that Miss Jones was stuck in his imagination and Cara should understand that. Miss Jones had been his first and he still carried the hurt of her moving away without a word to him.

Yet his desire for her remained. It burned fiercely—damaging any relationship that he had since she touched him. She had been the perfect answer to his teenaged lust, sexing and loving him in every way, creating a perfect feeling throughout his entire being.

Miss Jones had touched him and he couldn't let go.

He remembered when they had started seeing each other and Nina had taken him to her bedroom for the first time. He remembered like it was yesterday; it had been their third time making love—the first time had been on the couch, with Nina bent over the coffee table giving him an exquisite view of her round softness. The second time they had made it as far as the stairs. Nina reclined with her back arched and her legs open, inviting, as Paul stood there motionless. She taught him patience, allowing him to barely enter her as she wriggled her hips beneath him. His eyes felt as if they were melting because he wasn't allowed to reach down and touch the firmness of her body. Miss Jones knew how to work it.

Paul felt himself swell at the memory.

Standing at the entrance to Charlie's, he paused to take in the calm warmth of the night before he stepped into the pub. Patrons crowded around a circular bar, some standing, others sitting at tables, watching games on overhead televisions. Paul sauntered over to a table and began flipping through a menu that was wedged between the salt and pepper shakers. After settling on one of Charlie's famous pepperoni sandwiches, he looked up and spotted David Valentine sitting at a nearby table.

Paul hated the man on sight.

Valentine had crushed the best thing that Paul had ever had in his life. *It couldn't be that there were no other women out there for Valentine to date!* Paul reasoned. *He was a good-looking guy with a good job—all the things that women loved. So why did he have to take the pussy from Miss Jones?*

Paul got up and walked over to David Valentine's table, flopping down in a chair.

David Valentine's eyes registered surprise but he didn't say a word as he gazed at Paul sitting across from him. A waitress arrived with a plate of hot wings and a bottle of Corona.

"What do you want?" David asked when the waitress walked away.

"I was out taking a walk," Paul said.

"And you ended up here?"

"Is that a coincidence or karma?" Paul picked up a menu. "Guess where I was going to end up?" David arched an eyebrow in question. "The police station. I was gonna tell them that I witnessed a rape."

David fell back in his chair. "I told you. It wasn't a rape. You didn't see what you thought you saw."

"And I'll be a perfect witness, too!"

A smile crossed David's face before he took a wing from his plate and bit into it. He waved it in the air while he spoke. "You think I don't know, but I know. You fucked her too. Your little, young, underage ass was having sex with her too. Your English teacher! But you got involved. Emotionally. You should have done what any other red-blooded, American male would have done in that situation. Hit and run!" He took another bite of the chicken wing and washed it down with a swallow of Corona. "Wham, bam, thank you, Ma'am. Hit it, split it, and then quit it. That's a lesson most young men don't need to be taught, but you seemed to have missed that class."

"I don't really care about either one of you," Paul said. "Really, I don't."

"Yes, you do." David smacked his lips. "You care. That's why you won't tell."

"Whatever helps you sleep at night."

"If I go to jail, she goes, too," David said. "And what good would that do? Look. In life there are these things called Sex Lessons. The Lessons teach you that there are some pleasures—like sex—that you can't explain and you have to live with the fact that the pussy was one hundred percent mind blowing! And you loved it. Take it in stride. Get out there and get the rest of your Lessons." David took another swallow of beer. "You never, ever graduate, though."

"You're wrong," Paul said. "I will tell the police everything I know about that night. But her name won't come up; I mean, me and her didn't have sex. So I won't lose her, too. Question you need to ask yourself is, do you want to bet your freedom on a Sex Lesson?" Paul watched David Valentine as he paused with the beer halfway to his lips. "I've heard a lot about prison and I could only guess that they would have you wide open like a twenty-four-hour convenience store."

David Valentine placed his beer back on the table, assessing the measure of Paul's resolve. "You're really serious about this," he said.

"Where is she? You know where she is. Where is she?"

"Okay. Sure. But if I tell you, then you forget about what you think you saw that night. Deal?"

Paul leaned back in his chair. "Deal."

Willmon

Willmon Angel gently ran his fingers along the barrel of the gun in his pocket. He dug deeper, reaching past the trigger until he felt the plastic-wrapped Now & Later. He pulled it out, unwrapped and popped the sugar-coated candy into his mouth. Looking up Columbia Street past the Half-Moon Bar, past the people sitting out on their porches, beyond the kids playing football in the street, he saw only one thing: The Hole. That's what they called the local gambling and drinking spot. It sat across the street from the CC Club, a big brown building that had a dancehall inside where Willmon had once watched a stripper dance, after sneaking inside. He paused to contemplate his mission. He was going to kill the bitch. Leon. The muthafucka who diseased his mother.

The sweet taste of sugar rolled over his tongue as he gripped the gun tighter and pulled his book bag into the crook of his arm. Sweet.

For a brief moment, he thought about the homework assignment that was inside of his tote bag. The teacher told them that they each had to read a short story of Greek mythology and hand in a report at the end of the week. She thought that he hadn't been paying attention, but Willmon read the story about Ares, the god of savage war. He had smoked a blunt and he was clear when he picked up the book. He had a fondness for mythology and the image of Ares, god of savage war, appealed to him. A pang of regret raced through him as he realized that he would never finish that assignment. He was going to kill the bitch. Leon.

"Willmon!" Brother Jeffrey stood across the street in front of the CC Club wearing his football jersey. Brother Jeffrey was one of the few people who was kind to Willmon. He talked to Willmon like a man, even joking with him sometimes when other people were around. Willmon took his hand from his pocket and crossed the street to meet him. "Where you going, man?" Brother Jeffrey asked him. Willmon looked at him, but the words stuck in his throat. He didn't want to lie to Brother Jeffrey but he knew that he couldn't tell him the truth either. "So you not doing nothing, right?" Brother Jeffrey went on without waiting for an answer. "You want to go make some money? All we have to do is move this refrigerator for this old man and he will pay us twenty dollars. I'll do most of the work."

Brother Jeffrey waited for him to answer while Willmon panicked. Across the street, he saw Leon walk around the corner and step into the passageway between the two buildings that led to The Hole. "Gonna kill the bitch!" Willmon said. "Kill." Brother Jeffrey stepped away. "Okay," he kept his voice even. "Okay. I guess that I can do it by myself." He regarded Willmon with concern. "You okay, Willmon?"

Willmon didn't know how to answer. When Brother Jeffrey called out to someone down the street and walked away, Willmon turned to face the passageway. Two brick buildings that stood side-by-side, one blue, the other red, had been constructed separately, leaving enough room for people to pass through. Feeling the cold steel of the gun for reassurance, Willmon trudged across the street and down the alleyway. Rounding the corner he was nearly overcome by the smell of The Hole. There was a mishmash of odors: human funk, liquor, weed and piss, all fighting to gain prominence in his nostrils.

"What you doing down here, boy?" Blue's husky voice startled him and Willmon stumbled, nearly stepping in a puddle of vomit on the side of the walkway.

"Looking," Willmon said.

"Yeah," Blue said. Despite his thunderous voice, he was a reed-thin man, balding with wrinkled skin that lined the area around his deep-set black eyes. "They told me that you was a crazy one." He bustled down the pathway and around the corner. Willmon took a moment to calm the pounding of his heart. The remnants of a headache began to creep into his brain and he shook his head in an attempt to fight off the haze that he knew was coming. He knew that he had to be clear in the head when he faced Leon. With renewed determination, Willmon marched around the corner and ran into a group of men standing in a circle playing dice. None of them took notice of him as he stood there and took in his surroundings.

A grassless yard stretched from the back of The Hole to the alley that ran behind Columbia Street. An old, rusted truck rested on blocks that were overgrown with weeds and the front seat of the cab was filled with empty beer cans. The back porch was three steps up from the ground and the handrail looked as if someone had staked posts in the ground and pushed two by fours through holes in the top of them. The doorway to the Hole had no door, and the open space glowed a bright red as if it were an open invitation to forbidden land.

A loud roar emanated from inside of the building and Willmon panicked as he wondered how many people were in there. The thought that other people would be around had never entered his mind. His plan needed some revisions. Quietly, he slipped away, back through the yard into the alley. He walked deeper into the shadows until he was sure that no one would see him. When he was satisfied that he was alone he pulled the gun out of his pocket and examined it. The cold metal gleamed dully in the muted light of the moon but Willmon felt strength in its weight. He hefted it in his hand, growing accustomed to the feel of it, imagining the spark and flash of its fire. His mind's eye pictured the gunslinger's stance that he would assume right before he pulled the trigger. Willmon spread his feet apart and gripped the gun with two hands like he had seen in countless movies and television shows.

"I'm like…like… like…Ares!" Willmon posed with his arms raised, victorious. "God of war!" He listened as raised voices echoed down the alleyway and decided that he liked the sound of his new title. "Ares! God of war," he pronounced again. With a renewed sense of determination, Willmon tucked the gun inside of his book bag before proceeding back to The Hole. He marched determinedly into the yard, and then up the stairs of the porch until he stood in front of the open doorway. When he stepped inside, there were four men and a woman sitting around a large table playing a game of poker. The game stopped as they all looked at him in mild surprise. Leon was at the table, still wearing the blue jumpsuit that he had to wear at the auto shop where he worked. Across the table from him sat his woman, Rita.

"Hello, young man," the woman greeted Willmon.

"Hello, ma'am," Willmon said.

"So respectful," Rita said.

"What are you doing in here, young fella?" A man in a dirty blue shirt sat next to Leon with a puzzled look on his face.

"I'm looking for Leon."

Leon sat at the far corner of the table—farthest from

Willmon. He would not be able to reach Willmon without coming around the table. By then it would be too late. He had smoked some weed before he went on his mission but he felt the high starting to leave him. His vision faded for a moment and he only saw Leon as a gray shadow.

"What the hell do you want, retard?" Leon spoke around a cigar that he was chewing. "Do you have an appointment?" A few of the men guffawed.

Willmon moved back until he felt the wall behind him touch his shoulder blades. He glanced around him and saw that he was standing alone; no one was near him.

"You killed my mother," Willmon said in a low voice.

"What?" Leon looked down at the table and reached for a pile of bills in front of him. After throwing his bid on the pile, he looked at Willmon again.

"You killed my mother," Willmon said in a clear voice. "You diseased her." Calmly reaching into his book bag and moving into a corner, he pulled the gun out and pointed it at Leon. "Now. I came to kill you." His woman, Rita, screamed at the sight of the gun. The men at the table froze. Leon's eyes widened, and then narrowed as he studied the teenager who pointed a gun at him.

In a calm voice, he said, "Now, son…"

"I ain't your son!" Willmon yelled and dropped the book bag. "I ain't nobody's son anymore!" He pointed the gun at the woman. "You! Back out of here! All of ya'll get out; except for Leon. Close the door behind you!" She remained frozen with her eyes glued to the gun. Willmon pointed it at her head. That woke her up. "Right now!" A frenzied scramble followed and in seconds the room was cleared. "You killed my mother," he said, again when they were alone. People started screaming through the open doorway, hysterical voices rose in panic, but Willmon heard none of it. The pain in his head was starting again.

Leon was at a loss. "I didn't... I don't... What the hell are you talking about?"

"You gave her the disease." Willmon's voice dropped into a monotone. "Now I give you a bullet. Umma wet you."

"Nigga, please!" Leon snorted. "Umma wet you!" he said in a mocking tone. "Umma wet you!" He paused. "What does that mean, son?"

Willmon swayed on his feet. "That means that when I shoot you, all kinda wet blood gonna come out of you. And then you gonna die. Just like you killed my mother with the AIDS."

"Do you know what AIDS is, son?"

"Yes, I do." Willmon wiped the sweat from his forehead. "And I ain't your son!"

"AIDS is some grown-up shit. Son! You ain't equipped, mentally, to deal with nothin' like..."

"I know one thing, though," Willmon cut him off. With his free hand he wiped at the sweat pouring down his face. "You ain't leaving this room still breathing."

Willmon was having trouble catching his breath.

Leon smiled and nodded his head. "I don't care, though." He leaned back in the chair and crossed his legs. "You ain't shootin' nobody. No. Body. You hear me?" He kept a smile on his face as he spoke. "Do you know how easily I could come over there and take that little gun from you?" He slowly leaned forward and glared at Willmon. "Do you?"

Willmon began blinking rapidly. His eyes felt like they were itching and the constant batting of his eyelids gave the room a strobing effect. He focused on Leon and his heart froze. Leon had the Dead Eyes! His eyes were gone and red orbs of fire pulsated in his eye sockets, but Willmon managed to control the scream that threatened to tear from his throat. *No more fear!*

With his back against the wall, he lowered the pistol to his side. "I don't care either, do I? Because I made a plan! I ain't leaving this room breathing either." He stood upright and spread his legs apart, assuming a shooter's stance with both hands gripping the gun while looking down the barrel with one eye squinted shut. "I'm Ares. God of War!"

"Put that gun down, boy!" Rita was standing in the doorway with Leon's shotgun in her hand. He kept it in the trunk of his car because of some trouble that he'd had at The Hole before. Willmon never took his eyes off Leon. Nothing else mattered to him. He decided to take Leon before the pain caused him to lose his concentration.

I'm gonna kill the bitch!

"It's over, retard," Leon said. "She got her sights set right on you. Come on. You not gonna shoot nobody no way."

"Put it down! Now!" Rita's shrill voice rang out.

Willmon could only hear Leon. He could only see Leon. His image began to float in waves, cresting in black and falling in gray, moving back and forth in the chair.

And the Dead Eyes!

"You ain't leaving here breathing," Willmon panted.

"Don't you see that she got that gun pointed—"

"You ain't leaving here breathing!"

"Put that gun down!" Rita was screaming now but Willmon never looked in her direction. Leon was fading from view.

Suddenly Willmon's vision went black. First there was light, then there was nothingness. *This is death!* Willmon panicked at the darkness.

Leon rose from the chair.

Willmon squeezed the trigger. *Click!* Nothing.

A deafening explosion shattered the night. A welter of blood and bone blasted open on Willmon's chest as the bullet tore through his side and out of the front of his torso. His body was flung against the wall and he was dead before he crumpled to the floor. Leon looked down in disbelief at Willmon's body twitching in its final death throes. Rita was standing in the doorway with her eye still sighted down the barrel of the shotgun. The color drained from her face when Willmon's body bucked in the air and a thick stream of blood shot forth from the hole in his chest. She dropped the shotgun in horror, her body began shaking violently, and a horrific scream pierced the air. Leon rushed over to her and pulled Rita into his arms while shielding her from the grisly sight of Willmon lying on the floor. He knew that he could never tell her that she didn't need to shoot him. That the gun hadn't fired. That knowledge would stay with him for the rest of his life.

"None of this matters, Rita," he whispered to her as he led her out of The Hole. "None of it."

Blood Soaked

M ugwump woke up in the morning with the sunshine streaming through the window and he knew that it was going to be a good day. Dressing quickly, he went into the kitchen and, to his surprise, his mother was cooking breakfast. She told him that she had a rare day off from work and that she was going to celebrate by sleeping and doing nothing. It felt good talking to his mother; they hadn't seen much of each other lately and he missed the talks that they once shared, so they spent a few hours catching up with each other's lives. They were friends again—as mother and son.

They were sitting on the couch in front of the television when Mugwump told her that he was going to pick up Willmon Angel and take him to the park and chill out for a while.

"Willmon is not the same little boy who used to hang around here, is he?" Teresa said.

"Nowhere near," Mugwump said. "I think some quiet time in the park, the peace and quiet, the nice, warm sun…

I think that would be a good starting point. A chance for me to see what's up with Willmon."

Teresa regarded him sternly. "He's not your responsibility. He's not."

"Yeah. I know. He needs some help right now. It'll be all good." Mugwump rubbed his palms together and smiled. "Matter of fact, that's where I'm getting ready to go right now." He jumped to his feet. Teresa smiled as she rose and stood in front of her son. "Julius, I'm so proud of you."

"Proud of me? For what? All I'm doing is helping a friend out. Like I'm supposed to, right?"

"That's why I'm so proud of you."

"Thank you, Ma."

Mugwump was out of the house fifteen minutes later and walking down Clinton Avenue toward Willmon's house. Clinton Avenue was packed tight with tall, brick houses, each unit fronted by a tall set of steps that jutted out into the street like an angry tongue. Most of the buildings were at least three stories high and they were also very old and in need of repair, but the streets were alive with ghetto sounds. Children played under the stairs on some of the buildings while at others old men sat in chairs, lounging in the shade. Everything about Clinton Avenue seemed exciting and dangerous to outsiders, but for Mugwump it was all as it should be; another day...another day.

When he finally made it to Willmon's house, he knocked a few times and waited but there was no answer.

Frustrated, Mugwump sat on the porch for a few minutes, wondering where Willmon could have possibly gone. "He knew I was coming!" he said aloud. But then he remembered the way that Willmon had been behaving on Central Avenue, standing in the middle of the inter-section while oblivious to the backed-up traffic. He got up and knocked on the door a few more times and waited. No one answered. He was walking down Clinton Avenue when he ran into Brother Jeff, who was coming out of the corner store with a cocoa bread beef patty and drinking a soda.

"Whattup, Wump?" Brother Jeffrey stopped him at the corner. Brother Jeffrey was a hustler. "Make Money" was his mantra because he said that he enjoyed money, liked the feel of it in his wallet and in his back pocket… and he would do whatever job was necessary to ensure that his pockets stayed fat.

"Nothin', bruhman. Nothin'."

Brother Jeffrey had known Mugwump since they tried out for the Pop Warner football team and both dropped out after one tryout. They had become good friends and Brother Jeffrey had seen that look of concern that crossed Mugwump's face on many different occasions. Brother Jeffrey preferred the positive things in life and always tried to help his friends conquer the negatives. "Man," Brother Jeffrey said. "What's up with you? What's wrong, man? You look like somebody stole your wallet or something."

"It ain't always about money, Brother Jeffrey."

Brother Jeffrey nearly choked on his beef patty. "I know that for some it's not. You know, earlier today, old man Brother Hooknose up the street wanted me to move some furniture for him?"

"Come on now, man." Mugwump suppressed a smile. "You know good and well that man's name is not Brother Hooknose."

"Sure it is," Brother Jeffrey said. "The man has a hooked nose, man. Brother Hooknose! Anyway, I couldn't do the job by myself...and he was paying! Twenty dollars! To move some furniture. Dude! Anyway, it took me nearly two hours to find someone to help me go get that money."

While Brother Jeffrey took a breath to take a bite of his sandwich, Mugwump scanned the streets hoping to spot Willmon. He figured that Willmon might have gone on an errand and was on his way back.

"Yo! Wump. Peep this." Brother Jeffrey washed down the sandwich with a swallow of soda before looking earnestly at Mugwump. "I tried to get your boy Willmon to help me a little while ago but he was tripping. Like bad."

"You spoke to Willmon? When?"

"A little while ago. He was talking crazy, Wump. I didn't know how to take him."

"What did he say?"

"He was talking crazy. Real crazy. Talking about he was 'gonna kill the bitch.' I had to leave him alone."

"Where was he?"

"Down by the CC Club. Wump, he was wildin'. He was more out there than I ever seen him before."

"Did you see where he went?"

"Yeah. I saw him. Before I got halfway down the block, he was crossing the street and going straight down to The Hole. I hope everything is all good with him," Brother Jeffrey said. "Hope nothing happens to the brother. He's good people."

Mugwump hurried down Clinton Avenue toward Columbia Street, his apprehension growing with each passing second. Something was terribly wrong, he could feel it. By the time he rounded the corner of the CC Club, he was at a full sprint but he pulled up short when he saw people standing around the pathway. Pushing his way through, he sprinted down the path between the two buildings only to see another crowd gathered around the open doorway of The Hole.

"That little dude is fucked up!" A voice was heard above the murmuring of the crowd. "That's Willmon." A shout rang out. Mugwump forced his way through the bodies until he was standing in the doorway. Leon was standing in the doorway with his arm around a woman who was crying with such anguish that a hush fell over the The Hole. His other hand held a rifle, which only intensified Mugwump's fears, and when their eyes met, Leon's lips trembled as if he were trying to say something but no words came out. Finally, he turned his head and began whispering comforting words to the woman he held. Mugwump fought back his fears and crept up to the doorway, cautiously taking a look inside.

His knees gave way at the gruesome scene in front of him and his heart felt frozen. Willmon lay on the floor in a pool of blood and Mugwump knew instantly that he was dead. His cries of agony joined the woman's as his mind fought to accept the reality of what his eyes were seeing, that his friend was lying there, lifeless. The wound in his chest looked like shredded meat issuing forth a stream of blood that didn't seem as if it were going to stop. His arms lay at an odd angle, one twisted behind his neck, the other pointed straight out into the room. His book bag lay on the floor, blood pushing against it in a crimson wave which also flowed around a gun that somehow glinted dully in the darkness. Mugwump moved into the room and got his first smell of death, a stench that could be felt in the air. The sudden pain of loss brought him to his knees again. Willmon's lifeless eyes were open and vacant, staring out into nothingness, the spark of Willmon's spirit long gone.

A harsh cry tore from Mugwump's throat, guttural and heart-wrenching as it echoed eerily through The Hole. Willmon's body shuddered once more in a final spasm, startling Mugwump into a second of disbelief, but then the tears started anew. When he looked up again, through his blurred vision he noticed that the body had shifted and Willmon was now pointing at the discarded book bag and the blood-soaked gun.

Nina's Embrace

Standing across the street from Miss Jones' house in the shade of a tree, Paul watched and waited. Curiosity burned inside of him, wondering what she was doing, and who she was doing it with. He had seen her pull up in her car, and when she opened the door she stepped out looking sexy. A tight skirt hugged her curves, her hips sent those curves swaying, and Paul felt the swelling of desire. Her blouse clung to her breasts; the small buds stood up nicely, reminding him of soft touches. He found himself wanting her again.

He had to have her.

Patience! he reminded himself. This time it had to be perfect.

A red, two-door sports car pulled in behind hers and Paul was surprised to see David Valentine emerge. He followed Miss Jones up the walkway and together they went inside her apartment.

That dirty dog! Paul's anger surged. *He's still sniffing around!*

Apparently, David hadn't taken Paul's warning seriously.

Paul paced back and forth, wrestling with the decision that he had to make. The more he paced, the angrier he became. Paul thought that he had made it quite clear that he wanted Miss Jones to himself. *Well, to hell with that! The wait is over!*

Paul spun on his heels and headed straight for Miss Jones' front door. He purposefully knocked and waited. When the door swung open, David stood there. A brief look of surprise flashed across his face, quickly replaced by a benign smile.

"You finally made it." He stepped back, opening the door wider for Paul to enter. "Nina thought that you wouldn't come. She doesn't know everything, does she?" He closed the door and walked back into the house. Paul followed him into a comfortable living room. A woman's touch was evident by the soft ambience that pervaded the space; it had the soft darkness that lent itself to a sensual vibe.

"She's in the shower," David said as he plopped down on a plush, dark sectional that spread across the room. "Have a seat. Make yourself comfortable."

Paul moved to the end of the couch. "We had a deal."

"You wanted the address," David said. "I gave it to you." Paul said nothing. David Valentine was right; he hadn't made a good deal.

"Some things I don't have to tell you. Sex Lessons. Remember?"

David Valentine smiled. "At least you were listening."

He leaned over toward Paul. "I told Nina everything. I told her that you were coming to pay her a visit. And I have to tell you…she didn't really seem to care one way or the other."

"Is that your version of reality?"

"In fact, she took me right into that bedroom right there." He pointed to a doorway. "She seemed excited by it. Thank you."

"That's not anything for me to worry about," Paul said. "Again. Sex Lessons. Part deux."

The smile disappeared from David's face as he stood up. "We'll see." He walked over to the bathroom door and knocked. "Nina!" he shouted. "There's someone here to see you! An uninvited guest!"

"Give me a minute." Her muffled response could be heard through the door.

David returned to his seat and the two men waited in silence. When the bathroom door cracked open, Miss Jones—Nina—emerged wrapped in a cotton bathrobe and she was briskly drying her hair with a towel.

"You said somebody…" She looked up to see Paul, who had jumped to his feet when she came out the door, standing in front of her. "Paul," she said softly. A quick smile came across her face. "Paul!" She rushed over and caught him in a strong embrace. Paul was unsure about returning the greeting. She pulled back and took Paul by the chin and looked in his eyes, searching for that old spark that they once shared. When that undeniable lust flared in his eyes, she brought her lips down onto his.

Paul was lost, his tongue exploding as it danced with hers. He tightened his embrace, pulling her to him, willing her to feel his hardness pressed against her. That fire was still there. They broke apart and looked at each other. Paul battled between his pain and the pleasure that her body promised. Questions were raised and dismissed with each passing second that he watched her. *What happened? Why did you leave me? Why didn't you ever say goodbye?* He decided that this was not the time for such issues.

"Now that we've gotten that over with." They had forgotten that David was still in the room. "Let's get on with the business at hand."

"Well, it's easy to see that *Nina* is not your girl." She would never be Miss Jones to him again. Not anymore.

"Hold on here," Nina said. "I'm a woman, Paul. Nobody's girl. And definitely not his. Where did you get that idea?"

"It doesn't matter," David began. His words died in his throat as Paul and Nina stared at him.

"David wants me," Nina said. "But he can't have me. Not anymore. He had his chance and he blew it. But Paul, you're all grown up now. You're a man."

"Yes. That happened after you left me," Paul said. "So you meant to tell me that you're not giving him sex?"

"Ask him," Nina said.

"Are you?" Paul asked him.

"Nina, you need to stop playing with this guy's emotions. He's serious."

"Now is that a 'no' or what?" Nina pulled Paul down onto the couch next to her. "You know that you and I had great fun when you were my student. I bet you're even better now." She ran her fingers across his chest, her eyes sending signals that Paul couldn't ignore.

"She's not going to be yours," David said. "I know that's what you want. Won't happen, though."

Nina shot David a warning stare before she stood, positioning herself in front of Paul and opening her robe. She was wearing nothing more than a pair of black panties and a black bra. The fabric of the panties had taken on the outline of her sex, snaking up into the folds of her vagina until the outline was clearly visible. Paul was struck with the meaning of the lyrics of a song that he'd heard: *Black panties with an angel's face!* The sight of her near nakedness blurred his thoughts for an instant and she quickly wiggled her body between his legs and settled down on his lap with her arms around him.

"You're going to want it, Paul, but it won't be there. Not for you anyway." David hadn't moved from the couch, and his face was tight with controlled anger as he watched them. Paul thought that he looked like a man possessed. "You see, Paul. She started with me when I was young, too. I met her when I was seventeen, a freshman in college, still a little raw and naïve. Hell! I changed my major for her! I wanted to be a writer until…"

"David!" Nina interrupted him. "You are what is known as a cock blocker. Stop blocking. Leave."

"You've never been afraid of the truth before, Nina. Why stop now?" To Paul, he said, "This is the story of a woman who can't be satisfied."

Paul was doubtful. "You mean that you couldn't satisfy her."

"Ask her," David said. "Ask her if you will be enough for her."

"I'll make myself enough."

"Been there. Done that," David said. "You can't make yourself enough for anyone. I tried. There were times when I was deep inside of Nina and I knew in my mind that I was the only one that could get in there where I was. It made me stronger. Strengthened my manhood in a way that was nearly spiritual. Good pussy will do it to you every time!"

Nina laughed out loud.

"And she's right," David said. "I do want her. I love her. But here I am, years later, hating myself for being whipped. Still begging her for something I can't even name. I guess love is the only word that I can apply."

"Spoken like a true bitch," Nina said. "Aren't men supposed to be the conquerors? Emotionally hardened? Like bees, flitting from flower to flower, pollinating and then moving on to the next flower? How did you get so dick sensitive?" She turned to Paul. "I don't attach strings to my sex. If I want you, I get you. And then you please me and I please you. Can you handle that?"

David stood. "Yes, Paul. Can you handle that?" His anger had left him and he seemed resigned to accept the situation in front of him. Wordlessly, he turned and walked out the door.

Paul took Nina's hand. "The question is: Can you handle it?"

Bedtime. Wake up.

He spent the night with Nina. Once again, she became his teacher. Initially, she let him take charge, but her actions were a façade. She was simply giving him the opportunity to exhibit his skills, gauge what he had learned in the years since she had last schooled him. She measured how much he had discovered about the art of sex, testing his stamina and deciphering his desires, and she knew that she could take him further.

Nina rode him hard, began dictating the motion and building illusions which he would latch onto and pursue. She changed the pace and climbed on top of him, remembering how crazy he got when she was on top of him and wriggled her body like a porn star. She teased Paul to the edge but would never let him fall off the cliff. She would soothe his frustrated breathing with kisses, licking his body until his urgency subsided, and then she would push him again. She backed Paul up to the edge of the bed and ordered him to grab her ankles and ride her doggy style.

"I don't think this is a good idea," Paul said as he moved behind her.

"You're thinking?"

"It's just…" Paul entered her from behind. "This is my most vulnerable position."

"Mine too," Nina gyrated her firm flesh against him. "Now grab ahold and ride."

Paul lifted her ankles and felt her flesh shift. He felt her along every inch of his shaft as he began to move in and out.

"Harder!" Nina was moaning. Paul obliged. "Hit it harder! Harder than that!"

Paul didn't want to do that. He knew that he would lose control. And she had to know it, too. The visual was too much for him. Her ass bouncing back at him always ignited a spark that couldn't help but become a spewing fire. Nina was moving full speed now. Her cries of lust rang in his ears and he knew that she was near the point of orgasm. If only he could hold on until she got there. He looked down. Mistake. He saw her ass bounce against him. Their flesh slapped. Paul closed his eyes and called out. "Gawd!" Her sex clamped down on him. He really didn't like to make noise when he was having sex, so he tried to keep it to a minimum. "Sheeeetttt!" He felt her pressing her hot spot down against his hot spot while she clenched him. Trembling.

"Shit!" Nina yelled out and began her final ride. Paul knew, right then, that he was finished. He reached up, took a firm grip on each of her shoulders, and pulled her back toward him, thrusting with all the strength he could muster. For a moment, his world was nothing but pleasure as he exploded inside of her, firing off the first round. And the fire that didn't go with the first shot made him pump repeatedly until every round was exhausted.

They collapsed on the bed, spent, and lay there in silence for a while. Paul gently rubbed her back. *No one will be able to get inside of her like that. I know that.*

Nina lay back on a pillow and looked at Paul. "Are you glad that you stayed?"

Paul reached for her. Nina shrugged off his advance. Paul took a moment to look around the room. Nina's bed was soft with big, fluffy pillows and a mirror that served as a headboard. A television was pinned flat against the wall across from the bed above a dresser covered with bottles of perfume, lotions and other toiletries.

"Well," she asked again. "Are you?"

"I'm glad I found you." Paul put both his hands behind his head and looked up at the television.

"I wasn't lost, Paul. I simply moved."

"But you left without a word. You were always the great mystery to me." Paul looked at her. "That was cold."

"Paul, I hate to be the one to tell you this, but we weren't in a relationship. You weren't my boyfriend."

"I felt like I was, though."

Nina didn't respond. She picked up the remote control from the nightstand and turned on the television. A music video channel blared to life and Air Supply was singing. *Making love out of nothing at all. Out of nothing at all. Out of nothing at all.*

Nina giggled. Paul refused to meet her look.

"Let me ask you a question," Nina began. "Was I your first?"

Paul fidgeted. "Where did that come from?"

"I'd like to know. Was I your first?"

"No," Paul said. "You were my third. Couldn't you tell?"

"No. I was your first." She nodded her head. "That explains a lot."

"Like what?"

Nina turned the volume down on the television. "Your first time is supposed to be special, even though in real life it's usually terrible and quick, but you got the best you may ever get. I set the bar pretty high."

"That you did," Paul said, "but I got over it."

"Sure, you did. But you were still carrying my memory around with you. That's what got you here."

"You satisfied me, but I got over it." He pushed himself up on his elbow and gave her his full attention. "And I thought that I satisfied you, too. Now, let me ask you a question. Are you really insatiable? Is that even possible?" Paul tentatively reached over and traced a circle on her stomach. "Because I know that I filled you up. You were full. I could feel it."

"That is an ill-conceived notion of manhood."

"I don't have a notion," Paul said. "I have the manhood; something that no woman can define." Paul sat up. "Can you tell me you didn't feel me?"

She turned to him.

"At all?" Paul said. "Not even a hint of something different. Something…else?"

"Paul," Nina said. "It was great sex! But it wasn't love."

Her words hit him with more impact than he would have thought possible. He swung his feet over the edge of the bed so that his back was to her. He couldn't look at her. She would see the pain that she had caused. In his eyes.

"Oh," Nina said. "Did I touch a nerve?"

"No." He tried to make his voice sound normal. "There's no nerve to touch. It's just that you have no idea what it takes to be a man. Really. Maybe some idealized version, but you can't really define us."

"That's too bad. Because most men need some definition," Nina said.

Paul regained control. "Are we talking about in the bed or in everything else?"

"In everything, but especially in bed!" Nina had a hint of a smile on her lips. She swung her legs over the opposite side of the bed so that they were now back to back. "You want anything to drink?" she asked as she padded off into the kitchen before he could answer.

She can't be satisfied. David Valentine's words rang in his ears. *You're not going to be enough.* Self-doubt began picking at him. Nina was not the same Miss Jones that he had known in high school. She had been perfect then. Now, Paul could see all of her cracks and crannies. His father had once told him that the *wanting* is usually better than the *having*. And David Valentine was a wreck from the *having!*

"Nina!" Paul called out. "What if I was whooped like David? Would you treat me like that?"

She came back into the bedroom with a tall glass in her hand. "I'll treat you like the man you've become. David is like a lap dog. Sniffing around." She looked down at Paul with a piercing stare. "And what do you think that was all about? What do you think that he wants from me? Do you think his needs are anything more than physical?"

"Looks like much more than physical to me," Paul said. "You have a problem giving more than that to anyone. Don't you?"

Nina sipped her drink.

"I was in love with you," Paul said.

"No. You weren't."

"How can you say that? You can't dismiss my feelings."

"Paul, we were fucking! That's all! Can't you come to grips with that?"

He watched her for a second, taking her in, all of her. Those legs he wrapped around his back, those hips that he had held from every angle he could think of, those breasts that were still so very firm and sweet; and then he made a decision.

Without another word, Paul began to get dressed.

"So this is how you handle the situation, Paul," Nina said. "You mean, you really can't come to grips with the fact that I'm giving you this sweet-ass sex with no strings attached?"

"I just did." Paul got dressed and walked out the door.

Contemplate Life

Willmon was dead. He died with a gun in his hand and the thought caused a pain inside of Mugwump that refused to go away. He could have saved him if he had been paying attention, especially if he hadn't been getting high with him. Maybe with a clear head, Mugwump could have seen some sign of the pain that was inside his friend. Maybe he would have heard what Willmon was telling him. *I'm gonna kill the bitch!* The message could not have been any clearer.

Willmon died like a soldier! A soldier with a gun.

But how did Willmon get a gun? How could a *kid*, especially a kid like Willmon, get his hands on a gun?

Willmon's mother had been cold when Mugwump went over to visit. Truitt and Paul had gone with him to pay their respects and she seemed unaffected by her son's death.

"He had problems ever since he busted his head on the ground back there," she told them as they sat on her sofa, listening in disbelief as she talked about their friend. She was wearing an old, tattered housecoat, with pink rollers in her hair that were held in place with a hairnet that covered her head. A bottle of soda with peanuts floating in it sat at her feet next to her seat. "He was trouble at school—the teacher kept calling here about Willmon this, and Willmon that—I got tired of the whole thing. But then he started coming home and writing on my walls." She snatched the soda from the floor and took a long swallow. "One day he came home and wrote on my wall with the kind of ink that you can't wash off. That old, dark ink that won't move no matter how much I made him scrub it."

"It's still there?" Truitt said.

"I just said that," she said and looked at Truitt as if she were questioning his sanity.

"Can we see it?" Truitt asked. She took a drink of her soda and they waited until she was finished chewing on the peanuts before she answered.

"It's right over there." She pointed at a wall in the hallway at the bottom of the stairs. She directed them as they walked over. "Right there. By the foot of the steps."

Mother is God. And glory.
If God don't love you.
If words burn and smoke. In the air.
And glory can't do nothin' but cry.

"But I ain't never think he was gonna go and get a gun! And then shoot Leon! Lawd, mo' drama!" His mother sat in the chair looking straight ahead.

"Willmon was good. He was good people," Truitt said. He had taken the news of Willmon's death with the pain of losing a brother. He thought back to the many times he had been too busy with his own life to pay any attention to his childhood friend. Hadn't ever tried to find out what was really going on in his life. "I shouldn't need to tell you these things."

Her head snapped around to glare at Truitt. "Who you think you talking to? I just lost my son!"

"Well, act like it then!"

Mugwump glanced at Truitt and changed the subject before she got a chance to respond. "We didn't come here for this." To Willmon's mother. "Willmon was our friend and we came by to tell you that he was like our brother. We miss him already."

Her eyes were still glued to Truitt when she said, "Thank you. You need to teach your friend over there how to talk to grown folks before he get the shit slapped out of him."

"We used to play kickball with him over by my house," Truitt said. "He was always on my team." He closed his eyes, unable to continue, and Willmon's mother was touched by his concern. She visibly softened.

"Please pardon me for asking," Mugwump saw his opportunity. "But where in the world did Willmon get a gun? Who would give a kid a gun?"

Her coldness returned. "That nigga down the street," she said. "The thug. Peace."

"Peace?" Mugwump said.

"Sissy told me that she was coming out of Frances store when she saw Willmon. That was the only place he could have gotten it from." She took another swig of her soda. "Peace will sell to anybody. He don't care."

They sat in silence for a moment.

"So why would Willmon want to shoot Leon anyway," Truitt spoke in a harsh tone. "He didn't…he wasn't like that. Why he wanna go and do that?"

Willmon's mother was quiet as they watched her. "Leon is…I don't know," she finally said as she set the bottle of soda on the floor. "Willmon was going through a lot. His mind was all over the place."

"And you think that Peace gave him the gun?" Mugwump said. He knew Peace. Peace was a prematurely balding young hood that walked around scowling at everyone. He had done a long bid upstate and he came back with a jailhouse mentality that Mugwump was all too familiar with.

He left Willmon's house determined to find Peace.

He went down to the corner on Swan Street and waited while he contemplated what he would do next. Peace was a thug. The kind of guy who figured that the world was fucked up and he couldn't make it any worse. Selling a gun to a kid would be a good laugh for him.

A cop car pulled up to the curb next to Mugwump. When the window rolled down, the policeman called out to him. The cop had gray hair that peeked out from under the band of his hat and his forehead was creased with wrinkles across his weather-beaten skin.

"What you doing out here on this corner, boy?"

Mugwump experienced an eerie déjà vu. A fleeting sense of fear gripped him; memories of another corner long ago flashed across his mind. Shaking off the dread, he returned the cop's stare.

"Contemplating my next life choice."

"Well, you better contemplate somewhere else."

"Why?"

"Because this ain't a good corner; that's why. Nothing good happens here. In fact, this is my corner. You'd best find your way home." The window rolled up and the car pulled away. He watched until the police car rounded the corner on Swan Street before he turned his attention back to the house on the corner.

Mugwump eyed the door to Peace's house. It beckoned to him. Dared him.

Brother Black had once told him: "You don't owe me nothing, man. Nothing more than you owe the next man."

"But I never would have made it in here without you, Black," Mugwump said.

"That's because I am my brother's keeper. Just like you are. My life is only as good as yours. That's the only way that I can be counted. So you have to count, too. Be counted, my man. Be counted."

With a renewed determination, Mugwump crossed the street.

Peace opened the door wearing a wife beater T-shirt with his pants sagging off his hips. His newly shaved head glistened in the dim light and only added menace to the perpetual scowl that he wore.

"What you want?"

"I want to know why you gave Willmon a gun."

At the mention of a gun, Peace stuck his head out of the doorway and looked nervously up and down the street. A local crackhead was walking up the street and he stopped when he spied the trash bags sitting on the sidewalk. Mumbling to himself, he started digging through them.

"Larry!" Peace yelled. "What I tell you about going in my garbage? Get away from here before I come out there!"

Larry looked up with a puzzled expression on his face. "You ain't the one," he said in a faraway voice. "You ain't him." He scuttled up the street to the next house and started going through their garbage. Peace watched until Larry was at the next house before returning to Mugwump.

"You know better than to come to my door talking about guns and shit," he said. "I don't know shit about no guns."

"Yeah. You do. And normally, I don't care. But you cost my boy his life and you gonna tell me why. What would make you think that it was okay? Huh?"

Peace studied Mugwump a moment.

"That's all right, though, "Mugwump continued. "I don't need no light to see you. You one of them brothers that see the dollars and nothing else. Don't really care about anything else or anybody else. But I can make you care."

"Oh," Peace said. "So you that nigga now?"

"I ain't no nigga," Mugwump said. "And I'm ready to step to you."

"Come here then." Peace reached out and snatched Mugwump by the throat, yanking him off his feet and then flinging him inside of the house. Slamming the door, he turned on Mugwump, who was scrambling to his feet. He launched a kick that caught Mugwump in his side and sent him crashing against the wall. "So you that nigga now, huh?" Peace waited for Mugwump to make it to his hands and knees before kicking him again, this time knocking him flat on his back and causing him to struggle to breathe. "Yeah," Peace growled. Mugwump was helpless as Peace straddled him and rained blows down into his face. He tasted the blood in his mouth before his world flashed black and then came back in a fuzzy, out of focus picture. When his vision regained its sharpness, he was staring into the barrel of a gun.

"Now you gonna join your friend. Peace!"

Mugwump's body bucked once with the impact and then he felt nothing.

Laylow

Truitt and Paul scoured the neighborhood searching for Mugwump. His mother was frantic, not having seen or heard from him in over two days. That was something he had never done before and they were all in a state of panic. They went to everyone's house that they knew Mugwump had ever hung out with: DayDay, Bernie, Mike, and even Gordon; none of them had seen Mugwump within the last forty-eight hours.

"Man," Truitt said as they left Bernie's house. "This is getting crazy. Where could he possibly be?"

A frown of concern was etched into Paul's face. After Willmon's funeral, Truitt noticed that there had been a marked difference in Paul. His demeanor had become one of calm focus. The humor that he and Truitt shared had vanished and been replaced by solemn determination. "It's really getting to me, too. He hasn't been the same since Willmon's funeral service," Paul said. "I noticed that he sat there with his fists clenched throughout the entire ceremony. There was something much more intense going on there."

Truitt shot him a look. "People handle their sadness and pain in different ways. He was being quiet. He handled it."

The streets were bustling with people, and even though hazy sunshine beat down on them, their spirits were dampened as they made their way over to Laylow's house to find out if he could help them find Mugwump. If anything happened in that neighborhood, or anywhere in the city, Laylow would know about it.

Laylow lived on Western Avenue, which was a few blocks away, so they began walking, knowing they would cover the blocks quickly. A car pulled up to the curb ahead of them and they saw Norma get out of the driver's side and pause to reach back inside for her purse. Truitt remembered that she was a good friend of Mugwump's; Truitt often thought that they were more than friends, even though Mugwump always denied it. He knew that, if given the opportunity, he, himself, would have definitely tried to be more than friends. Norma was an older woman, but the thick hips she carried in the black skirt she wore told the story of someone much younger. She had sexy eyes too; they were the second thing that Truitt noticed about her when they met and he had even been turned on by her voice. It was smoky and throaty. Curly, black hair hung down past her shoulders, framing her dark, brown skin and soft, oval face when she turned and saw them approaching.

"Hi, Norma," Truitt said.

She came around the car and embraced each of them before stepping back and regarding them with a worried look on her face. "I heard about your friend." She looked from Paul to Truitt. "Are you both all right?"

When Mugwump spoke of Norma, he would only say that she had helped him in ways that were beyond words. She had "seasoned" him—that was the word he used, seasoned him—because she showed him a different kind of love. A love that would stay with him even when he was either stupid or wrong; especially when she knew that he was headed for trouble and was too hardheaded to listen to her. She cared enough to let him find out for himself.

"We're good," Paul said. "Have you seen Mugwump around?"

Norma was taken aback by the question.

"We haven't seen him in a few days," Truitt said.

Norma's eyes narrowed anxiously. "A few days?"

"A few. And that's not…"

"That's not like Julius. I know. He hasn't even called his mother?" Norma fidgeted with the car keys in her hand. "How was he after the funeral? Was he quiet? Mad? Did you notice anything about him?"

"He looked angry," Paul said. "Why?"

"Did he cry?"

Paul and Truitt exchanged a glance. They all had. "Yeah."

Norma's son had been killed by a bullet when he was

Willmon's age and she often spoke about the dark depression she had experienced. Her days had been spiraling darkness and her nights had been unbearable, haunted by images of blood and death. "Well, you better find him. Now!"

"You're making us nervous now, Norma," Paul said.

"I don't have time to explain and you don't have time to be scared. Two days is a long time."

"Yeah. You're right."

"Did his mother call the police?"

"And what are they gonna do?" Truitt said. "He's still got a lawsuit against them. They are not gonna do a thing."

"Did you check with Bernie? I know he used to hang out with him sometimes."

"He wasn't over there," Truitt said. "We're about to go over to Laylow's house. See what he's talking about."

Norma's features tightened. "I guess he could know something." Just as quickly, she seemed to relax. "That's a good idea."

"Is it?" Paul asked.

The frown reappeared on her face. Her voice was cold when she spoke. "Laylow is a bastard." The words tore out of her. "That son of a bitch knew something about when my son got shot but he wouldn't say anything."

Paul and Truitt looked at each other.

"He ain't shit!" Her eyes had narrowed to slits and her lips were twisted as if Laylow's name were bitter in her mouth. They waited quietly as Norma fought to bring her emotions under control. "But none of that matters now." She calmed herself. "You've got to find Julius."

"We're on the way over there now," Truitt said.

"Wait a minute," Norma said. The keys in her hand started jingling again. She raised the other hand to emphasize her point. "Joy told me that she saw Julius down on Swan Street, hanging out on the corner." She nodded her head. "You would have thought he would have learned about those corners by now."

"What corner?"

"By Frances Store down there. She said that the police had rolled up on him and they were talking to him."

"Shit!" Paul exclaimed.

"You remember what the police did to that basketball player—damn near beat him to death—and got away with it."

"And you know that Mugwump don't know how to talk to the police," Truitt said. "This is not looking good. Come on," he motioned to Paul and they started walking.

When they arrived at the house on Western Avenue, they knocked and Laylow snatched the door open.

"What you want?" Laylow was a huge man, towering over them and easily carrying over three hundred pounds. A wife beater tee shirt covered his massive frame and the hand that held the door open was the size of a ham.

Laylow had a small nose, petite lips and delicate features planted in the middle of his large head. Paul got right to the point.

"We want some information. That's all."

"Well, I don't do information."

"We're looking for Mugwump," Truitt said. "You seen him?"

Laylow looked at them for a moment as if he were contemplating whether to continue with the conversation.

"You know something, Laylow?" Truitt said.

"Mugwump?" Laylow said. Another moment passed, but then he stepped back and opened the door. "Come in," he said and ushered them inside. The house was dark, dimly lit by the bulb of a small lamp that sat on an end table next to a worn sofa. Truitt and Paul took a seat on the sofa, and Laylow sat in a chair facing them.

"Wump been gone for days," Truitt said. "You know if he been around here?"

"No."

"You haven't seen him?"

Laylow reached down and picked up a pack of cigarettes from the floor next to his chair and lit one while they waited for his answer. "Mugwump was my man back in the day. I always imagined him marching with protesters, on TV arguing with White people and shit, you know, using his brain. He was good like that; especially back then." He leaned forward, a slight smile playing on his face. "Boy, Mugwump sure knew how to talk shit to the police. He used to drop that scientific anger on they ass. They would get mad as hell at him, but they wouldn't mess with him because he talked an intelligent game and, on some level, I guess they had to respect that. Until that day that he got into some serious trouble."

Laylow leaned back in his chair and took a leisurely puff from his cigarette. Drumming his fingers on the arm of the chair, he sent a stream of smoke into the air. His face was masked in shadow when he spoke. "Remember when he got in that trouble? When po-po jumped him on the corner? He did over two years on that joint. Did his bid without a word." Another hit of the cigarette. "I was there that night…right there with him when we took Supercop out. Supercop was a brutha who needed to have somethin' beat out of him. He was the worst type of Black man. He didn't even like Black people…and he was a cop, so he got to take out his dislikes. We got him that night, though." Laylow paused a moment to savor that memory. "But Mugwump was a soldier. He never told the police nothing. Never gave us up."

Paul and Truitt waited.

"Wump was a dreamer too, though. He was too smart for his own good sometimes. He thought that he could use the law against the police. He thought that *right* mattered to them. It ain't just about what's right, it's about what is. And what is, is that we were a bunch of niggas hanging out on a corner and hustling. Mugwump decided to make a stand there, on a corner, of all places in the world." Another pull. Another stream of smoke. "But we got Supercop that night! He was the worst cop out of all of them. He had some type of evil inside of him." Laylow's next puff of cigarette was sudden and anxious. "Yeah. We got Supercop that night. I still got a scar on my skull from when that house nigga hit me with that nightstick one time. But not anymore. His ass-whooping days are over." His face emerged from the shadows when he leaned forward. "But Mugwump never sold us out. Never said nothing. A soldier!"

Truitt jumped to his feet. "Where is he, Laylow!"

Laylow looked at him with a touch of sadness. "Wump is dead."

Naked In The Air

A thunderstorm racked the air the day Mugwump's body was found. The grisly discovery
was made in the woods down by the city
dump; the body was partially decomposed and ravaged
by winged scavengers. The gunshot that killed him had
blown away a portion of his face and Teresa had collapsed from shock when they took her to the morgue to
identify the body. At his funeral service, more than half
of the city turned out for the young man who had taken
a stand and suffered the punishment for his beliefs.

The air of mystery surrounding his death served to
inflame emotions in the community. To some, he rep-
resented the ideal of standing tall for the belief in right;
still for others, he was the victim of police brutality and
the resultant corruption of the justice system.

Teresa sat in the front of Shiloh Baptist Church, rocking back and forth in agony as the mourners filed past
the open casket where her son lay. She refused to have
a closed casket for the service; she said that she wanted
the world to see, in shocking detail, what happened to

her son. Artis sat next to her with his arm draped over her shoulder, his eyes fixed on a spot on the wall while he fought back tears. Roman and Janese sat next to them. Janese's cries rang out as Roman held her, the pain of loss showing in the numb expression on his face. Paul and Truitt sat on the bench behind them, each struggling with the depth of their loss, not able to express their pain yet unable to mask it from each other. Truitt turned to his sister, Anna, willing her to understand and, finding acceptance there, leaned his head into her shoulder and cried quiet tears. Paul found that he couldn't lift his eyes from a spot on the floor. It was a dark spot that was the safest place for him at the moment. He didn't want to look up and see the casket again; didn't want to acknowledge the fact that his friend lay there, lifeless. He didn't want to do anything but look down and let the tears of grief roll off his face. Two friends gone so quickly. It was too much. When the thought occurred to him that only he and Truitt were left, he finally looked up. Truitt was watching him as if he realized it then, too.

In the days following the funeral, Paul and Truitt would often find themselves enveloped in silence; other times, they would sit around reminiscing about their friends, recalling what they had come to call the good old days and with each happy memory the pain gradually eased.

They met in the park one sunny day, sitting on the

bench overlooking the river. There was no wind, just warm sun and quiet, as if the world had taken a vow of silence and was listening to a cosmic heartbeat. This had always been one of their favorite places to hang out with Mugwump, and they knew how much he loved days like this one.

"Mugwump always knew what he wanted," Paul said. "I admired that about him."

"He was always true to himself," Truitt said. "True to his word."

"Paul. You remember that time when we built that big bonfire down by the river?"

Paul chuckled. "Yes, sir! It started out as a campfire but Mugwump kept running around by the pier, collecting any piece of wood he could find and throwing it on the fire. Next thing I know, flames are shooting fifteen feet in the air!"

"Now that's a fire!" Truitt joined in the laughter. "You know what cracked me up was when we heard the police sirens and Wump was like, 'I wonder where the police are going?'"

"They were coming for us!" Paul said.

"Yo! Remember that time we were racing our soap-box derby carts and went flying down the hill by the sewage plant? Me and Mugwump was flying! He was steering and I was in the back, holding onto the sides of the plank of wood that we sat on, hanging on while we flew down that hill."

"I remember," Paul said. "Me and Bruce were racing you guys. The White boys versus the Black boys. We raced downhill all the way down State Street to get there and you guys were killing us…"

"We left ya'll in the dust! But real talk! I was scared. We were going way too fast! And that was when I saw that turn coming up at the bottom of the hill and I had some doubts that we were going to make it without some consequences and repercussions!"

"But you should have been worried about the sharp turn into that construction site *before* the bottom of the hill! When Mugwump swung that turn and you fell off, next thing I heard was, ba-boomp, and he ran your head over with the back wheel." They both laughed at the memory.

"Ba-boomp! That's what your head sounded like."

"Ba-boomp!" Truitt said. "That shit hurt, too! Yeah, man."

The quiet of the park washed over them.

"You know what was something that I'll never forget." Truitt broke the silence. "That time when we went swimming at the quarry. Remember that?" The quarry was a reservoir of clear, blue water surrounded by monstrously high cliffs, a work of nature's beauty, both inviting and dangerous. On the west end of the quarry was a trail that plunged down to an outcropping of rock that stretched out only about ten feet above the water and people would often go to that vantage point to dive and swim in the pure water. "We got up there to the quarry, man, that place was like a picture: the bluest, cleanest water ever, and those cliffs that we would crawl out to the edge to look over because they were that high. But the water was so blue that sometimes we would be tempted to jump…but we never did."

"I would have had a heart attack before I hit the water," Paul said. "We did jump off the ledge of rock that was only a few feet above the water. That I could do."

"That's what I'm talking about," Truitt said. "That time when we climbed down there and that White dude was down there with his girlfriend and they were getting ready to go skinny-dipping when we got there. I know the White boy was mad, but there were three of us and one of him; what was he gonna do?"

"Only thing he could do," Paul said.

"Well, he wasn't going to let us stop him from skinny-dipping with his girl, so he held a towel up in front of her, so we couldn't see her when she got undressed."

"I remember he was looking at me for help," Paul said. "I was as anxious to see his naked girlfriend as everybody else."

"We wanted to see some nakedness. And when the girl got undressed, ran to the edge of the cliff and dove off. The next thing you know, you see Mugwump, diving through the air next to her—sideways! My boy was turned to the side, looking at her body. Naked in midair! Sideways!"

"Wump was unique," Paul said.

"Thing is…that was the way Wump was. Life tried to hide from him, but he always managed to see it. Even if it was naked…especially if it was naked in the air. Sideways!"

❊❊❊

Paul walked up to Nina Jones' door and knocked. He had come a long way from the days of sneaking through her back window with elaborate signals. The door swung open and he was once again struck by the pang of lust that she awakened within him. He supposed that he would never get over that attraction. She wore a light blue shirt and a pair of shorts. Her lips curved into a smile when she invited him inside.

"You don't seem too surprised to see me," he said.

"Paul, I'm glad to see you," she answered and led him into the front room. David Valentine was sitting on the sofa, leafing through a magazine while Nina went into the kitchen. He wore a plain, blue shirt and a pair of jeans. When he looked up, Paul was struck by how small David Valentine seemed, as if his penchant for Nina had robbed him of his vitality. Resolutely, he put the magazine on the seat next to him, leaned back with his legs crossed, and waited. Paul turned his attention to Miss Jones.

"Nina, I stopped by for one last look at you. And to thank you."

Miss Jones swayed into the room, her hips enticing in the short shorts as she stood in front of Paul, their bodies inches apart. "One last look? You going somewhere, Paul?" She took his hand and placed it on her breast. "Where are you going?"

"I came over to thank you." Paul slowly pulled his hand from her. "You helped me grow up…the long way, I must admit but you taught me a great deal."

"I can teach you more," she said. "Lessons not over." She moved in closer and rubbed her body against his.

"Maybe I graduated," Paul said.

"Maybe not."

"Yes, Nina." Paul stepped away from her. "You taught me about love. And what love is not. I don't even trust my own judgment anymore. But I also learned that it doesn't matter."

David Valentine stirred on the couch. Paul glanced at him but quickly turned back to Nina. "I've finally seen life naked in midair."

"What?"

Paul smiled. "I mean…good-bye, Nina." He leaned toward her and kissed her on the cheek before walking out the door.

❂❂❂

Paul was sitting on the park bench when his cell phone rang.

"Cara," he answered.

"You called me," her voice was cold.

"Yes. I wanted to talk to you."

"I assume that's what we're doing right now."

"I know I've been away a while…I've had a lot happen in my life."

"I know," she said. Paul thought he detected a slight thaw.

"But I'd really love to see you tonight."

He heard her take a big intake of breath. "Are you ready to give me what I want?" she said.

"Absolutely. I'll give you all that I can."

"Good." Suddenly the warmth returned to her voice.

"Since I'm confessing the truths of my heart," Paul said. "I want some truths, too."

"You want some?" Cara purred. "Come get some."

ABOUT THE AUTHOR

Nane Quartay is a native New Yorker whose novels include *Take Two and Pass* and *The Badness*. His work has also appeared in the anthology *Breaking the Cycle* edited by Zane, *Truth Be Told: Tales of Life, Love and Drama* and his most recent effort, *Negrodamus*. Nane currently resides in the Washington, D.C. area and is at work on his next novel.

He welcomes reader e-mail and visits to his websites at www.nanequartay.com or myspace.com/nanequartay

The BADNESS

by NANE QUARTAY

AVAILABLE FROM STREBOR BOOKS

CHAPTER 1
In The Flame

Doin watched as his life danced in the fire. Watched as the hot licks of flame's consequence and pain jumped higher with each kernel, fueled by deeds both hidden and exposed. The spectrum of heat ran the gamut—from demented to sinister, and, in the flame, there was a distorted reflection of the peaks and valleys of his soul's landscape. From lukewarm to hot, each episode carried the fiery brand of hell stamped indelibly on his psyche, imbedded forever. Dysfunctional tattoos.

He remembered the first feel of flame as it burned across his memory.

He was ten years old, huddled in fear next to his mother on the living room couch. They were still living in the projects, a five-bedroom of darkness. His drunken stepfather was embarking on one of his ranting, ghetto horror stories. Doin sat there listening but he never comprehended the full extent of the degrading insults that his drunken stepfather spat out.

"You and that bastard son of yours," he yelled at Doin's mother, through red eyes and spittle. "You know who your daddy is, boy? One of them slick-talkin' niggas! Talked her right into opening them legs and fucked her. Tha's right." His stepfather looked like Super-Bad-Nigga and Doin had learned the hard way that it didn't pay to fuck around with the SBN. The SBN lived inside of anger and menace and was more than willing to share his pain with all eight of his children; at any given time, in any given mood.

Doin looked to his mother with tears in his eyes—he knew that this was something bad just from the harsh tone of his stepfather's voice—but she simply looked straight ahead, eyes blank.

His stepfather railed on. "Then she gonna try to act like you mine! Skinny little, peanut-head nigga! You can't be from me. You too stupid for that! How? Shit." He shifted his gaze back to Doin's mother. "I betcha she just threw them legs up. It ain't never been that hard, though. Just like a slut. And then, here you come." Doin's stepfather was a big man, surly and violent...especially when spurred on by alcohol and anger. He towered over Doin and his mother with clenched fists; his body tense and poised in his drunken rant. His next sentence was a hiss. "I'll run this whore in the river down there...and she can take her bastard, too."

Ninth grade in high school.

Another memory and the flame licked higher. Doin's life was full of the abrupt feedback of combustion which lit the darkness of his youth.

A growth spurt had shot him up to five feet eleven inches in height, transforming him into a lanky one hundred and fifty pounds. The scar on his face was still fresh, and he carried it with a sense of sad novelty, an object of curiosity and wonder. When he returned to school after the bandages had been removed, his class-mates weren't exactly tactful with their questions.

"How did you get that?"

"Don't that shit hurt?"

"Damn! Man! How?"

Questions. Questions all. They stared at him like he was a rocky horror picture freak, some openly, some with disgust but Doin soon learned to file all of them in the "fuck 'em" category and leave them there for life. They didn't matter to him anyway. No one did.

Until he met Bonita.

She was a small, beautiful girl who had just moved to town and she had captured him with one gesture. He had first seen Bonita leaning against the wall outside of the school by the football field. Hudson High School had acres of land attached to it, including two football fields, a soccer field and a baseball diamond. Everybody played ball at lunchtime and the sounds of kids running, clashing and straining against each other manifested itself as the hum of laughter and joy. One of the football fields stretched out about thirty yards away from where Bonita stood and a bunch of jocks had a game going. Doin could hear the star quarterback, Rosand Babjack, yelling at his teammate for dropping a pass. "You are a fucking retard. A moron, too!" Rosand was a doo-doo hole. Doin spit in his direction.

When he saw Bonita standing by the wall, Doin slowly inched his way toward her until he was close enough to see her face clearly. She was staring out over the fields toward the perimeter of lush foliage in the distance. She looked just like someone who was lost and friendless on her first day at a new school. Her eyes were pretty, and her hair was pulled back in a ponytail and a thick, curly strand was hanging down over her eye. Doin watched her.

"Go deep! Go deep!"

On the football field, Rosand backpedaled into the pocket and set his body to throw the pass. He looked to his left, then to his right, reset his body and threw a bomb, straight up into the air in a high graceful arc, perfectly leading the receiver. The tall, gangly kid was flying full speed down the sidelines with the defender a players all looked up to watch the flight of the ball, open-mouthed, as it sailed up into the air and came down in the kicker's hands. All heads turned to Doin.

Doin turned to Bonita.

"Hi," he said, smiling. Bonita darkened a bit and shyly looked at the ground. When she raised her eyes to meet his, there was a worldly silence, because his world had stopped turning, and it seemed to last an eternity. Doin pinned his hopes on her smile.

"Hi," she said.

A hand clapped onto Doin's shoulder and spun him around.

"Hey!" The wide receiver stood before him with the ball in his hand. "You play football?"

Doin became the new starting quarterback of the football team and Bonita became his girlfriend. If there had ever been a period in his life that Doin could call blissful, it was at that perfect moment. He was a natural at football and after his first game he became the starting quarterback, mostly due to the strength of his arm and his elusive quickness. Bonita was his dream come true. She was his joyful escape from the madness at home that he lived with every day. He never talked about that. They went to movies, played pinball games and darts and sometimes they went on long walks together. She even let Doin put his arm around her when they were alone in the park.

That peaceful respite was short-lived. It ended that fateful day when the flame blazed to life...

half-step behind him. The football came down to earth and landed thirty yards down the field…a full five yards short of its target, bounced over the head of the defender and into the arms of the exasperated receiver.

"You got a rag arm, man," he screamed before he angrily reared back and dropkicked the ball. It slanted off the side of his foot and sailed toward the wall where Doin stood watching Bonita. The football rolled to a stop at his feet.

"We ain't got a chance tonight," the kid screamed. "You ain't shit!"

"Fuck you, man!" Rosand yelled back. "Your mother!"

"Throw the ball," the receiver yelled at Doin from the far side of the field. Doin never took his eyes off Bonita, who was still lost in the woods, oblivious to the football game. "Throw the ball back, dickhead!" Doin turned sharply to see who had said that word; it was Rosand Babjack. Then he quickly turned to see if Bonita had heard. She turned toward him and Doin half-smiled at her. She smiled back.

"Hey," screamed the kicker. "Throw it back, punk!"

The smile faded from Doin's face. He bent down and picked up the ball, slowly turning it over in his hands. He turned to face the guy who had yelled him punk. He stood about fifty yards away.

"Throw it to me, superstar," the kicker jeered. Doin stepped up and heaved the football down the field as far as he could. A hush fell over the entire field. The